An Imp of Aether

W. H. PUGMIRE

An Imp of Aether

Edited, with an Introduction, by S. T. Joshi

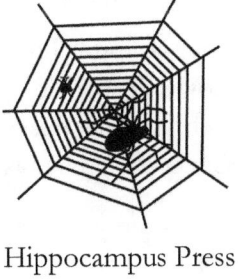

Hippocampus Press

New York

Published by Hippocampus Press
P.O. Box 641, New York, NY 10156.

www.hippocampuspress.com

Hippocampus Press logo by Anastasia Damianakos.
Cover artwork by gracious permission of the artist, Andrea Bonazzi,
web.tiscalinet.it/sculptus/
Cover design by Daniel V. Sauer, dansauerdesign.com

First Edition
1 3 5 7 9 8 6 4 2

ISBN 978-1-61498-276-0

Contents

Introduction

ew writers in the field of weird fiction were as beloved as Wilum Hopfrog Pugmire (1951–2019). A kind, gentle soul, he melded a number of seemingly disparate characteristics: he was unabashedly gay, he was a fixture in Seattle's punk rock scene, and he was one who remained faithful to the Mormon faith in which he had been born in spite of his church's decades-long banishment of him because of his sexual orientation.

Pugmire had come upon the works of H. P. Lovecraft while on missionary work in Ireland in the early 1970s. There, at the height of Ireland's "troubles," he somehow managed to dodge bullets and bombs and found solace and inspiration in the tales of Lovecraft, Robert Bloch, and other weird writers. But his literary tastes extended far beyond the weird, and he counted Shakespeare, Oscar Wilde, and Henry James among his literary favorites. He was profoundly interested in the theory and practice of poetry, from Dante to Gerard Manley Hopkins, and he also made a profound study of Judaism.

All these diverse qualities are reflected, in one form or another, in Pugmire's weird fiction—but chiefly his devotion to Lovecraft. Even though he frequently referred to himself self-deprecatingly as nothing but a "Lovecraft fanboy," his work is as far from mechanical pastiche as could be imagined. His study of Lovecraft was profound: he absorbed not only his weird tales, but his essays, poetry, and letters, as well as the smallest particulars of his life.

Pugmire's greatest tribute to Lovecraft was in fashioning a parallel landscape of terror and strangeness. Lovecraft had vivified his native

New England with a constellation of imaginary towns—Arkham, Kingsport, Dunwich, Innsmouth—in which he infused a lifetime's interest in New England history, culture, and architecture. Pugmire similarly brought to life the primeval forests and imposing mountains of the Pacific Northwest in the creation of his mythical Sesqua Valley, enlivened by such redoubtable figures as the "beast," Simon Gregory Williams, and the poet William Davis Manly.

But Pugmire wasn't content with merely adapting Lovecraft's topography to his own native realm. He may not have been as attuned to "the cosmic quality" as Lovecraft was, but he had a sure sense of the weirdness that arises out of human beings' encounters with the bizarre. He shattered the stereotype of the woman-scorning gay man by featuring a number of vividly realized female characters in his tales, ranging from "The Hands That Reek and Smoke" to "Pickman's Lazarus." This book also features several collaborations with two notable female writers, Maryanne K. Snyder and Jessica Amanda Salmonson.

One of the transcendent events of Pugmire's life was his trip to Providence in 2007. After decades of admiring his literary mentor, he was now walking in Lovecraft's footsteps in the city of his birth. The visit led to a rejuvenation of Pugmire's imagination—at the exact time when a new cadre of writers, editors, and publishers were transforming the realm of Lovecraft-inspired fiction by probing more searchingly into the essence of Lovecraft's philosophy of the weird. Pugmire happily contributed to many of the magazines and anthologies that featured Lovecraftian fiction, and his appearance in these venues carried the assurance of at least one contribution that was certain to reflect the core of Lovecraft's aesthetic rather than the mere externals of his literary creation.

In his later years Pugmire teamed up with David Barker and Jeffrey Thomas on novels and tales that continued to expand on his fusion of Lovecraftian elements with those drawn from his own life and temperament. He had earlier faced some criticism that his tales were largely mood-pieces with minimal narrative drive, even though this attention to mood was Lovecraft's own chief desideratum as a weird writer ("Atmosphere is the all-important thing, for the final criterion of authenticity is not the dovetailing of a plot but the creation of a given sensation"), and even though he evolved a prose idiom whose fluidity, musicality, and evocativeness was rivalled by few contemporary writers. Indeed, it could be said that Pugmire's vignettes and prose poems (some of which are included here) are among the most powerful of his works. But with the aid of Barker he produced two short novels (*The Revenant of Rebecca Pascal,* 2014; *Witches in Dreamland,* 2018), while with both Barker (*In the Gulfs of Dream and Other Lovecraftian Tales,* 2015) and Thomas (*Encounters with Enoch Coffin,* 2013) he produced scintillating tales, both solo and in collaboration, that added to his standing as one of the leading lights of contemporary Lovecraftian and weird fiction.

But Pugmire didn't need to rely on others to achieve his goals. In his hundreds of tales, long and short, he fashioned a legacy of accomplishment that will be difficult to surpass. And, belatedly, his work is reaching a worldwide audience. A German edition of his tales (*Der dunkle Fremde,* 2018) appeared less than a year before his passing, and Spanish and Russian editions are forthcoming. There will also be further efforts to gather his fugitive tales, as well as his poetry, essays, and literary commentary.

Shy and humble as he may have been; unwilling as he was to engage in self-promotion or (to his eternal credit) to engage in the bitter feuding that has created so much needless antagonism in recent years, Wilum Pugmire stands as a man devoted to the essential act of writing as "self-expression," in the exact spirit that H. P. Lovecraft intended when he coined that expression. It is this, along with his undoubted and multifaceted talents, that will allow his work to remain a literary treasure for the foreseeable future.

—S. T. JOSHI

The Hands That Reek and Smoke

for Robert Bloch

I.

Lisa came to me on that fateful night of revelation, her purple hair as wild as her intoxicated eyes. Her pixy face had lost is usual mirth. She was dead serious. "You must see Nyarlathotep," she panted, refusing the chair that I had offered her, preferring to pace the wooden floor instead. One hand clutched a canvas that was covered with a sheet of cloth.

"It amazes me," I answered, "that hair as short as yours can look so disarrayed."

"Screw the hair," she shot back, at the same time running a gloved hand through the unruly mess. "You've been moaning for months about your inability to write. I tell you, go see Nyarlathotep, and he will *drench* your dreams with wondrous vision."

I blew air. "I doubt that the parlor tricks of some cult figure will inspire new work from my dead pen. No new Lord of Disillusion can save me. Stephen was here, too, yakking about this bloke of yours. Seems he's arrived three months ago to set up in some building downtown. No, I have no need of tricks."

"You know, it's really stupid the way you allow your cynicism to keep you cooped up in this depressing little apartment. Things are happening, can't you feel it?"

"I feel only this intolerable heat wave. Such appalling weather for mid-October. Autumn is my favorite time of year; it heralds absolutely the death of torturous summer, that wretched period when ugly human apes strip off their gaudy attire and shriek to cancerous sun. How you can wear such thick gloves when it's so hot quite bewilders me."

How oddly she smiled as she placed one hand before her face and gazed at it as if in rapture. As she did so I noticed two curious things. First, the gloves that encased her hands were not composed of cloth but rather of some fine mesh of metal. Second, with the movement of her hand there came a wave of smell, a scent not unlike the festering of dead lilies. I watched as she silently stared at her gloved hand, and something in her expression unnerved me. I jabbered on. "I've not been able to sleep because of this diabolic heat. When I am able to catch a few winks I have monstrous dreams, horrid visions that soak my sheets and shake me out of slumber."

She looked at me with her serious face. "*He* will make you dream," she sang. "You would find your muse again if you knelt before him."

"Oh, please. You speak of this freak as if he were a god."

"By god, he could be! He looks supernal, with his golden eyes and scarlet robes. I worship him."

"Great Jesu, you're worse than little Stephen. But, no. I fear I'm far too old and faded for such radical wonder as you hint of."

She looked as if she would spit at me. "You see, you do that all the time. Using your age as an excuse to be a boring little shut-in. You could be the poet you once were! *He* will show you the way!"

"Enough!" I shouted. "You've gone on long enough about bold new vision and great creative guts. Stop your mouth and *show* me this new that you've done, if that's what you think will induce me to rush in fevered pitch to kiss this Narlywhosit's hand. *Show me,*" I told her, indicating her canvas.

Lisa set the canvas onto the floor and let it lean against a chair. Deeply inhaling, she placed her hands together in a semblance of prayer. With the movement of her hands there came again the peculiar odor, one that did not inspire my lips to smile. Expecting her to remove the gloves, I frowned in perplexity when she did not. Pulling my desk chair out, she placed the covered canvas on it so that the sheeted work sat upright. Irritated with her theatrical manner, I yawned in feigned *ennui*. She took no notice of me, choosing rather to place her face into her gloved hands and rock to and fro as her mouth hummed an odd melody.

"First," she whispered, "tell me what you know of Nyarlathotep."

I spat air, annoyed. "Very well. What did little Stephen tell me? Let me rack my brain." Delicately, I touched hand to brow. I, too, can be dramatic. "This Messiah with the preposterous name came to our city in middle or late June. He has rented the old lecture hall where the J. Duds used to hold meetings. It is claimed that this Nyarlathotep has crawled through the blackness of several centuries to our modern age, and thus we see proven that the more outlandish a cult leader's claims the more anxious are fools to follow him. I'm told they do follow—in droves."

I watched as Lisa stopped her swaying as she listened to my reply. She continued to clasp her face with those gloved hands, and I looked at their strange material, which queerly caught the light of my little room. "I'm told," I continued, "that he won't allow his image to be photographed or his voice to be recorded. Early on some friend of Stephen's smuggled a recording device into a lecture, but when the tape was played back all they could hear was a weird variety of buzzing sounds. You remember Stephen's pal, the boy who recently disappeared?"

"I remember," her low voice answered.

Really, her odd attitude was too much. I spoke with more frivolity, in a voice that mocked. "It seems this darkie is a splendid showman and works a multiplicity of mechanical geegaws with which he spellbinds the rabble. Funny, how little Stevie shuddered when he mentioned these devices. Like you, he urged me to go and witness this fantastic creature. I declined then, as I do now. The only beast I chose to worship is myself."

Lisa's hands fell from her face. "What a lonely veneration yours must be. You're so full of empty talk. But I remember a dim and distant time when you spoke beautifully, when you penned exquisite verse."

I sighed sadly. "Dim and distant indeed."

"Look, Hyrum, I know what it's like to lose energy and vision—it sucks. But you can regain yours. As I have recovered and cultivated mine. Look at how Nyarlathotep has inspired me!"

Summarily, she pulled the sheet from the canvas. I shouted in shock and outrage. Lisa's wonderful work had always been delightfully inventive and filled with color, in the tradition of Gorky. I was thus expecting a work of multi-hued genius. Instead, I was confronted with a vile composition of filthy soot and fuzzy ink and wash, with here and there a bruise of blue and purple. The scene was a gargantuan ruins set deep within a riotous growth of jungle. Standing among the debris of antiquity was a shrouded figure that wore no face, yet by its stance seemed haughty and implacable. The entire scene unnerved me. I knew not the origin of the ruins, for they were nothing I had known in history or art. Oh, yes, it was original, this vision, but not one that I could embrace or applaud. I hated it absolutely, and yet I could not turn my eyes away. The image beguiled as much as it appalled. My senses were stunned by the aspect of *age* that Lisa had been able to evoke. But what a horrid medium for her who had once been so clever with color! Quavering with emotion, I turned to the witch.

"*This* is your new achievement?" Oh, how I wailed. "This *sorry* depiction of a dead and haunted past?"

How oddly she smiled. "My dear Hyrum, this is a vision of the dead and haunted *future*."

I gagged with choked fury. My emotions seethed. "Really, this is too utterly nauseating. Please, *do* cover the wretched thing. I'm sorry to be so blunt, but you have shocked me." She made no movement, and although I turned my face away, my eyes slid inexorably to the painted surface. "And what in the blessed name of all the gods is *that* supposed to be? You've not given the silly creature a face!"

"The faceless god wears no visage."

I could not refrain from shuddering. Muttering profanely, I reached for the sheet of cloth and tossed it over the canvas; yet even as I did so my eyes ached to look again upon the painted surface. My companion smiled in eerie triumph. I rose and paced the wooded floor. "I simply do not understand why you should surrender your wonderful sense of vibrant color and sensuous line to replace them with ink and wash and whatever the hell else this new medium is. The thing lacks life. It is naught but a concoction of blur and blotch. What did you use, an old bath sponge?"

Ye gods, her peculiar smile! "I used my fingers." She grabbed hold of me and stopped my movement. One gloved hand stroked my cheek. Great Saturn, what was that monstrous stench? It was a stink of decay, yet tainted with some fragrance the likes of which I had never inhaled. It revolted and enthralled, like her painting. "I used these fingers that he had kissed." One metallic finger smoothed my eye. I watched as she slowly removed the glove that touched my face. Horrified at the nefarious sight, I cried and fell into the nearest chair. I cowered from her hand. But, oh, I longed to feel its touch upon my brow. The pale mists of smoke that spilled from the tiny wounds and bruises were the origin of the unholy stench. She bent to me, and I pretended to cover my eyes. What could have caused such mutation in hands that had once been so lovely? How could fingers become so disfigured? What could cause them to become so flattened, their tips so *erased?*

She removed the other glove. "These hands that he has sanctified."

"No . . . no . . ." Yet even as I whimpered I reached for one of her smoky hands and brought it to my lips. It tasted of nightmare. The nauseating smoke plunged into my nostrils and found my brain, which it teased ruthlessly with esoteric shape and shadow. I curled my nails into her transformed flesh. Lisa hissed with pain and drew her hands away. With cloudy sight I saw her indistinctly. I beheld the fuming appendages that bled from where I had clutched them, saw them slide into their outré gloves. I watched as they reached for the sheeted painting.

"New vision requires radical treatment. This is the sacrosanct gift with which I have been blessed. Perhaps you lack backbone and prefer to sit here and quiver in your impotent existence. So be it. But, oh, I remember a time when your world was filled with magnificent language and stunning vision. You could find that world anew." Her words were like needles in my brain. Weakly, I tried to rise from the chair, only to slip from it to the floor. Blinking streaming liquid from my eyes, I crawled to where she stood. My fingers found her shoes. I reached for but could not find her hands, the palsied flesh of which I ached to kiss.

Cool breath bathed my ear. "You must see Nyarlathotep. He is wonderful, and dreadful. He will show you prophecies of the cold bleak abysses between the stars, where dead gods fumble in dream-infested slumber. The great ones were. They are. They shall be."

A hot tongue licked my lobe. I listened as she sucked in breath, then jolted as she uttered unearthly howling. Instantly afterward, I was alone.

II.

Thus it was in that hot October that I ventured forth one night in pursuit of Nyarlathotep. As I crept along the silent sidewalks, I passed certain individuals who looked at me queerly and askance. I sensed that they had been to see this foreigner from an alien land. How anxious they seemed to speak to me, and yet how timid and hesitant they looked, peering at me in silence as I passed them by. I came at last to the lecture hall and gaped at the throngs of lingering rabble. They leaned against the building and sat on the curbing; they congregated near the threshold that led to a narrow stairway. One man was especially fidgety. I watched as he snatched at his hair and muttered lowly. I watched as he rushed into an alley and disappeared from view, and I shivered at the sound of anguished howling that issued from that alley. The noise sent a quiver of emotion through the crowd.

Pushing through the horde at the threshold I climbed the silent stairway. From somewhere above I could hear low fluted music. I walked down a dimly lit hallway that led to the double doors of a lecture room wherein I would confront the alien. The piping of discordant music came from behind the closed doors, and my old flesh prickled at its sound. Shutting my eyes, I leaned my forehead against one of the doors, pushing it open. With eyes still shut, I stumbled into the room. I could smell the candlelight. My eyelids opened.

He stood on a slightly raised platform, the shrouded one. Swarthy, slender, sinister, he was robed in scarlet silk. On a table beside him was a device similar to a child's magic lantern. Its diseased illumination cast obscene shapes that moved along the walls. My attention was caught by the nebulous form that squatted at the feet of Nyarlathotep, the thing that held in clumsy paw an apparatus of tinted ivory or pale gold. It was from this instrument that the fluted music emerged. Yet the more I tried to scrutinize the gadget, the more it seemed to fluctuate subtly in form, reshaping with a sensual movement that ached my skull. I listened to what sounded like whipping wings, as the music melted into silence. My heavy eyes demanded closure, and shutting them I saw upon their lids a multitude of spinning shapes that caused a vertigo that weakened my knees. I crashed onto the floor.

Weakly, I raised my agonizing head. He stood before me—grim, austere, merciless. My hungry mouth kissed his chilly feet. The room was still and silent, and I looked about but could not see the thing that had played the music of the spheres. Boldly, I clung to Nyarlathotep's garment and pulled myself to my feet. Swirling light and blackness played upon his regal visage. Fantastically, he smiled; and as he did so his face slipped, as though he wore some tight-fitting mask that had momentarily lost its hold. He lifted a hand, and I saw upon his palm a living symbol. Tilting to it, I licked the pulsing insignia. It was sharp and ripped the tongue that touched it. As I swallowed blood, the daemon moved his hand away, then thrashed that hand against my forehead. Splinters of bubbling ice pierced my brain.

I was inside Lisa's painting. The awful heat that had so plagued our autumn season weighed heavily in dead air. To breathe was to burn. He stood before me still, the black alien, in shapes that did and undid his being. I looked beyond him at the mammoth buildings, the ruins of distant time. It was a time over which Nyarlathotep was Lord Supreme. But how could he exist in future epoch? How had he escaped the nip of Death?

"That cannot die which stands outside time."

Behind him I detected throngs of writhing black gargoyles that mindlessly pranced beneath a dying sun. Why did I ache to join in their frolic? Oh, how his liquid mark burned upon my brow. Scorching wind arose and pushed into my eyes, burning wind that blinded.

A large rough hand poked at my face. Rubbing torment from my eyes, I beheld the young man who gaped at me in desperation. I watched his mouth twitch in an effort to talk, but which was unable to function. I saw him pound with fists at his head, as if to knock some profane vision from his brain. I saw the blackness that crept into his eyes as he raised his head and wailed in lunacy.

I escaped, fleeing the place and running until I came to the street where Lisa lived with her epileptic mother. My brain buzzed with semi-vision, with a prophecy of disaster that I ached to share with she who understood. And I overflowed with lust to see again her painting. Not pausing to knock, I boldly entered the quiet house. A lamp burned with pallid light next to a sofa on which I saw the twitching form. The elderly woman did not look at me as she spoke.

"She's quiet now, perhaps we don't want to disturb her. Yes, quiet, quiet. No more howling now. What a funny sound. But she's quiet now. You don't need to stay."

I left the creature to her confusion and walked the cluttered hallway to Lisa's studio. I could smell incense, could smell that other fragrance of my friend's altered state. Stopping before the studio door, I leaned my head upon it, pushing it open. Her lifeless form lay on the floor, its arms sprawled over a canvas. An overwhelming stench emanated from the stubs that had once been hands, those nubs that stank and smoked. I knelt beside her and saw that her terrible eyes wore a wild expression. I looked at the image on canvas, that image composed of a filament of transfigured flesh. I saw the hooded thing composed of soot. From deep within the folds of its hood I could discern the shifting features of his many forms. Yet even as I watched his image faded and was gone.

I raised my shivering face. I closed my liquid eyes. I stretched my mouth with noise.

The Zanies of Sorrow

From childhood's hour I have not been
As others were—
—EDGAR ALLAN POE

It was music that brought me into the twilit world of wonder and terror. I had lived in my new quarters for a few days, delighted in my escape from a wretched former existence. My frugal savings were such that I could live in comfort for six months without employment, enough time to complete my novel. Quietly, without spectacle, I left my dreary job, my boring friends, my unsympathetic family, and found a lonely apartment in a forgotten and desolate section of the city. My escape was complete. I had my cat, my laptop, and my library, and no one knew of my department, my destination. For half a year I would live what I had yearned for—a life of reading and writing, undisturbed by humanity, in complete solitude. I realized, of course, that getting one's wish is not always the happy situation one imagines it might be. As Oscar Wilde once wrote, when the Gods wish to punish us, they answer our prayers. Still, the first few days were a time of joy absolute. My rooms were spacious, the furniture was good, the neighborhood free of racket. I had informed my new landlord, Mr. Bullon, that *quiet* was essential if I were to be able to work on my book. He gave me a room with windows facing a back garden, so that I wouldn't hear any possible traffic on the road in front of the building.

All went well until late one evening when, as I sat in my cozy armchair with pen in hand and cat on lap, there came from across the hallway a faint sound of someone at their pianoforte. At first I was an-

19

noyed at this intrusion of sound, subdued though it was; yet the longer I listened, the more I was beguiled. The music contained a quality of sorrow such as I had never experienced in art. I strained with listening, astounded as tears welled within my eyes. And when, abruptly, the music ceased, I found myself longing for its continuation.

The next morning I encountered my landlord in the laundry room. "Things are going well, Mr. Stone?" he said. "Your writing?"

"Yes, very well, thank you."

"Your rooms are very quiet, yes?"

"They are. I did hear, last night, the piano playing from across the hall, but that is all."

"*At night?* That cannot be allowed. I will inform Miss Greive to 'keep it down,' as is the saying here."

"Oh, it's not a nuisance," I replied hurriedly.

"I will mention it to her, no worry." He rushed off before I could protest further. I spent the afternoon feeling agitated and could not concentrate on work. Finally, I made bold enough to step into the hallway and rap on my neighbor's door. It opened, and my nostrils took in a very pleasant scent. The woman who stood before me was alluring, so much so that for a moment I could not find my tongue. She raised her brows in query.

"Do forgive me, miss. I live across the hallway and . . ."

"Ah, Mr. Stone. I had meant to knock on your door this evening. Mr. Bullon—"

"Has misunderstood me. I was in no way complaining. Your playing is very faint, not at all disturbing."

Disarmingly, she smiled. "You are very kind." By her accent I took her to be European. Her green eyes were kind but seemed guarded. It surprised me when she stepped back and opened the door widely. "I was just preparing my evening coffee. Will you join me?"

"Certainly," I said. Crossing the threshold, I entered into another world—an older realm. I could not believe that this apartment was identical to my own. Soft lamplight illuminated many fine pieces of old furniture, and one entire wall was taken up with sturdy oak bookcases crammed with hardcover editions. The shades of many beautiful lamps were covered with squares of silk or lace, and scented candles perfumed the room with fragrance.

"Be seated, Mr. Stone," she told me, motioning to a chair beside a wooden stand.

"Please call me Albert."

She smiled and bowed her head. "And I am Lucretia. Pardon me one moment."

Rather than sitting, I crossed to the bookcases and examined titles. She returned after a short while, holding a tray of coffee cups and scones. "You are an author, I'm told."

"Yes; mostly of short stories, although I'm now working on a first novel." My attention had been caught by a row of titles by Henry James, one of which looked like his unfinished novel, *The Sense of the Past*, in its original New York Edition. My rule was never to handle books belonging to another's library unless invited to do so. Setting down her tray, and perhaps sensing my bibliophilic ache, Lucretia reached for the James volume and offered it to me.

"Oh, thank you!" I said. "He was such a skilled writer—such discipline."

Her low, musical voice replied, "Discipline is a lesson one cultivates with years. You are very young."

"I'm twenty-seven!"

"As old as that?" Her smile was playful. "What is it you write of—your genre?"

"Human relations, social curiosities, with a touch of the uncanny. Maupassant and James have been my chief influences in shorter fiction. I've had one short story collection published by a specialty press, but it sold poorly. Most modern readers find my style a bit antiquated and affected. My novel is actually an attempt to write something like James's book here, a semi-ghost story that overflows with ambiguity and implication. I want to conjure up a thing that may or may not exist, with the novel's focus being the perplexing state of a mind that is haunted."

"I am very fond of Henry James. There is poetry in his prose. Much digging into strange human psyche. His tales of innocent Americans lured by the debaucheries of European 'decadence' so amuse me."

"You're from Europe?"

She tilted her head a little and then nodded slightly. "I was raised in a small village, a very simple town; but I have been in your glorious country a long time and have absolutely adapted."

I studied her and tried to deduce her age. Although she looked in her early thirties, there was an air about her of someone much older; but perhaps that was merely her European manner, to which I was unaccustomed. Returning her book to its shelf, I sat in the chair she had indicated and reached for the coffee cup she offered me. The brew was perfection. Miss Greive sat on a small sofa and placed her tray on the low table before her. We sipped, and munched, and talked of literature. Now and then I glanced at the piano that stood in one corner of the room. She seemed at last to notice. "Do you play, Albert?"

"No, I'm not at all musical; but I enjoy listening to others perform."

The woman hesitated, sucking at her lips. "Pardon me if I do not play for you. It is a very personal expression for me, my music, perhaps as your writing is for you. I can play in privacy, but I cannot perform." She shrugged her shoulders and attempted an apologetic smile.

"I understand completely. I need total silence and solitude when I write." I hoped my grin concealed my disappointment. "Well, I've kept you long enough, and I have work to do." Setting my coffee cup on the stand beside my chair, I rose and walked to the door. When I stopped to look at her again, I saw that she had not risen from the sofa.

"Will you visit me again, Albert?" I was suddenly overwhelmed with a sense of isolation in the room. She seemed, in that moment, small and foreign and very much alone.

"I'd like to, yes." I turned from her, crossed through the threshold, and shut the door.

For the next fortnight I was consumed with creativity. Something about that encounter with my mysterious neighbor had set my imagination on fire, and I modeled a main character in my novel on my fantasy of what her life might have been before coming to the States. Lucretia became a kind of vision for me, more a personality I had created than an individual I had actually encountered. Finally, I ached to see her again, to judge if my memory of her character was anything like the persona I had depicted on my pages. Our second visit was pleasant enough, and it interested me that the woman kept her aura of mystery, a thing I found I had no wish to penetrate because I liked the quality of unreality that was my fantasy of her. Thus I was a little disconcerted when, preparing to return to my room after this second visit, she stopped me at the door.

"I know that you are busy with your book and that you are not a social person; but I was wondering if you would care to join me next Wednesday afternoon to visit . . . an old relation. He is a lonely creature who loves literature as we do." She stopped speaking and gazed at me quizzically, perhaps thinking that her sudden invitation had been an impulsive error.

"I'd love to. Is he your grandfather?"

"No. An uncle, from the old country. Quite advanced in years and but recently arrived from our homeland. Really? You will come?"

"Of course I will."

She took hold of my hands, and for one moment I thought she was going to kiss me. When she didn't, I lifted one of her hands to my mouth and touched my lips to it. She gazed at me with the queerest expression on her face, and then we both burst into laughter and I returned to my quarters. Now, I had always been a bit of an introvert, socially awkward and shy. I believed with Wilde that the only possible society is oneself. Yet I had been touched in a strange new way. It wasn't a romantic sensation, for I had no sexual interest in women. I think it was simply that I had never met anyone like Miss Greive before, and she intrigued me in ways that were original.

Wednesday arrived, and I felt a kind of enchantment as I walked beside her on the sidewalk. Nonchalantly, I studied her face for the first time in daylight and tried once more to determine her age. Her complexion was smooth, void of spots or wrinkles, and her happy eyes looked youthful. She had insisted that we walk rather than take a taxi: the distance was not too great, and the weather was pleasant. At one point we passed a high granite wall, to which she gestured.

"Have you been in there? It is a calm and pleasing place. You're not morbid about graveyards, are you?"

"Not at all," I reassured her. Coming to its entrance, we strolled into the cemetery. There was a slight breeze, and I watched the subtle sway of the laburnum, with their poisonous yellow flowers. I took in the plumes of white and pale pink lilac. At one corner of the old stone wall stood a gigantic willow tree, its long pale vines drooping to the ground. With a burst of boyish glee, I rushed to the willow and wrapped some vines around my hands as I frolicked on the sod. "I dance with the dead and evoke their shades from their immemorial pits of blackness. Rise, neglected souls, and join in my gambol!"

Lucretia laughed and clapped in time to the movement of my feet. I watched as she lifted her hands above her head and formed her fingers queerly. A cloud must have swallowed sunlight, for the place darkened and the air grew cool. I noticed some few peculiar spots of shadow that formed on the ground just beyond her, and I ceased my movement as those patches of gloom seemed to writhe and swirl and rise. It was a phenomenon I had seen before, little whirlwinds of dust and debris that formulate at times—dust devils, I think they're called. These were very small, and yet something in the way they *formed* themselves unnerved me. I watched, and a kind of worry engulfed me as one of the minute whirlwinds took on a quasi-human form. Lucretia turned to smile at me; but when she noticed the expression on my face she lowered her hands and stomped one foot onto the ground. Swiftly, the tiny whirlwinds broke apart and faded as the sun regained its splendor.

"That was a merry little performance," she told me as she walked to where I stood.

I shrugged. "I sometimes play the fool. But I do love graveyards, to dwell among the happy dead."

"The dead are happy?"

"Of course they are—they're dead, you see." We laughed together.

"But what of the spirit?"

"I never think about that," I answered, releasing my hands from the willow vines. "I rather hate the idea of eternity. You and I are material matter, chemical components. We live our story and end as dust and ash. That, at least, is my fervent prayer. To go on, eternally, as spirit or any other entity—god, what could be more damnable than eternal life?"

She stiffened momentarily, and her eyes clouded as if she had been seized with weird emotion. The brightening sunlight played upon her eyes, and I thought those eyes were wet with pearls of tears. Then she smiled and brushed the tears away with one lovely hand. "We've dawdled long enough. Let us go."

Departing the cemetery, we continued our walk, arriving at last at a neighborhood that seemed deserted. Many houses were vacant, their doorways and windows boarded. I detected a smell of decay in the air and was nonplussed by the neighborhood's sense of abandonment. We encountered no one. Lucretia led me to a stone house that was tall and tilted and black with age. I turned to look at her and noticed a kind of nervousness in her expression—as if she regretted having brought me and wished there was some way to lead me away. Reaching for her hand, I squeezed it reassuringly as we climbed the porch steps and she rapped on the wide wooden door, which was opened by a lean elderly gentleman. They exchanged words in a strange tongue, and then he allowed us entrance.

"My uncle is in his courtyard, resting. He's been ill—his heart, I think. We mustn't tire him." I nodded as she led me to a back door through which we passed onto an expanse of yard surrounded by a sturdy growth of tall shrubbery. Beneath a fig tree, fanning himself as he lounged on a large divan, was a creature so grotesque that it shook my fortitude to look upon him. If the caterpillar in *Alice in Wonderland* had risen from its grave as a bloated, lichenous thing, it might resemble the being at which I gawked. I sensed that he was fantastically ancient, the oldest person I had ever encountered. Not an uncle, but a triple-great ancestor! Lucretia motioned for me to wait and went to the divan, conversing with the horror in an alien language. Then, turning to me and holding out one hand, she said in English, "This is Mr. Albert Stone. Albert, my uncle, Nicodemus Greive."

Screwing my courage to the sticking place, I stalked toward the figure on the divan, took his proffered hand in mine—and shuddered at the heavy press of moist and flabby fingers. He held me tightly, and too long. It proved impossible not to stare at his face, with its bumps and rolls, its growths and moles. He smiled horribly, and his visage seemed a mask of false mirth from which a pair of sapient orbs observed me. Why would he not let go of my hand? His touch, the fabric of his flesh, contained a kind of force, an unsuspected energy. I fancied that I could detect something—some component of his corporality—weave into the texture of my skin. His dewy lips stretched wider still, and a voice that dripped with pleasure spoke.

"You are very welcome to my home, Mr. Stone. Lucretia has spoken of you with enthusiasm, and I am happy at last to make acquaintance." His accent was far more pronounced than that of his niece.

He at last released my hand. "Thank you, you're very kind," I murmured.

"Please to sit, that lawn chair is most comfortable. Lucretia is not one to form so fast a friendship. Where we come from, we keep mostly to ourselves."

I turned to look at her as Lucretia and I sat in chairs. "You've never actually told me where you're from."

The old man answered for her. "A little village that no one has heard of." He shrugged and smiled at his niece, and I sensed a cryptic exchange implicated in their furtive glances. I noticed him peering at me again, with a kind of longing in his eyes, for conversation, perhaps; and as I tried to smile at him I intuited his profound loneliness, his need for social connection. Why, then, he had settled in such a derelict part of town was beyond comprehension. He looked a sad old fellow, his dainty fan held limply in one hand. His grotesque frame was encased in what looked like pajamas of yellow silk. I saw that his malformed feet were bare.

Feeling awkward, I fished for something to say. "I've never been abroad. Lack of time and money. Too, I'm very stupid when it comes to learning languages. Now and then I've borrowed recordings from the library that teach French and Italian, but my lazy brain revolts at such exertion."

"I am familiar with both languages," he informed me, "from the old books of my ancestral library. My poor English I learned from a fellow with whom I spent time in prison." A pregnant pause. "I was for many years incarcerated—is that the word?" This last was spoken to his niece, who replied in a scolding tone in their native idiom. He answered shortly in the same tongue, and then smiled at me and nodded. "With little to do except read from inadequate libraries and sing to the dust, I passed the time learning your so peculiar language. One new delight, since coming to your country, is to read the books of America. None of the books in my former library were in English. I miss those books—they were scattered while I was locked away— except for some few of the very oldest books, the books of my ancestors. They were hidden from village thieves and returned to me."

"Your English is quite good," I assured him.

"My companion behind bars was poet; he taught me language by reciting verse from memory. In Europe our prisoners are mostly poets and madmen—Misters Wilde and Villon and de Sade. Is not an easy life, incarcerated by ignorant village idiots who lack imagination." His voice had risen with emotion, and his eyes flashed with subdued fury. One hand went to his chest.

His kinswoman frowned. "Do not excite yourself, Nicodemus."

Ignoring her, he kept his eyes on me. "I was so long locked up in my little cell my captors could no longer remember my great offense. But they *never* lost their fear and hatred of our kind. No, that does not become forgotten!"

"Enough," she told him.

"Pah! Our guest is author, student of life. I give him glimpse of life such as he cannot imagine. He should know that in this modern world, in small neglected places, souls are still imprisoned for necromancy. Pah!" The ancient face had become flushed, and moisture formed on the bottom lip.

Miss Greive smiled apologetically. *This is my eccentric uncle,* her expression seemed to say. Yet her eyes revealed that he was also someone whom she loved.

"I'm not much versed in the black arts," I offered lamely.

The creature laughed. "Black—no, no. The *old* arts, the very old religion. The secret ways taught on scrolls, in ancient tomes. Spilled from ancient tongues. We learn the simple things—the calling to the wind, the summoning of storm. In time, we learn the oldest arts—to call down dwellers among the stars, to raise up jesters from beneath the earth."

"You raised the dead? That's what necromancy is, isn't it?"

"Enough of this silly talk," the woman suddenly injected. Her uncle held up one hand to silence her. I found myself unusually interested, and it suddenly occurred to me that I was no longer concerned with the fellow's wretched ugliness. I had read accounts of persons who, when first encountering Oscar Wilde, were repulsed by his physical appearance; yet the longer they sat with him and listened to the music of his voice, the more enchanted they became. I found myself in a similar circumstance.

"Nigromancy is more art of speaking with dead, and in our circle we learn ways to speak with the dreaming dead, although we make no sacrifice to them, as I had been accused. It was usual that we were arrested for crimes of others, because we are hated." He scanned the sky, which was now brilliant with sunset. "Of course, I had been in prison before, as child—for stealing and begging, you know, what a hungry child must do. Once," and he smiled at the memory, "I was imprisoned for raising storm that frightened the governor's horse. Do you remember, Lucretia?" I glanced at her and saw her smiling. She, too, had evidently been caught by the weaving of his vocal spell. "But it was for my great 'crime' that I was put away for so long time. My parents and an uncle had been falsely accused of murder, and executed. It was *injustice!*"

His emotional state increased, and he put his hand to his heart once more. "Do not work yourself so," Lucretia chided him, and then she looked at me. "His health is delicate, but he will not see a doctor. Now I am going for refreshments, and this nonsense talk will cease." We watched her rise and walk into the house. When he began with his narrative, he almost whispered the words, as if to conceal their sound from other potential listeners.

"We had ancient scroll that teach the summoning of Iog-Sotot, the Outer One who, through dreaming, instructs in raising of dead matter. It is terrible alchemy, and the use of it was mostly forbidden to our clan. I did not care! I was young! But in the frenzy of my emotional state I must have misspoke the spell. My art was flawed. I had risen my departed loved ones, for which I was placed in prison. I watched from my little window as the authorities tried once more to execute my parents. They could not. I do not know how I erred when I spoke the arcane language and threw the runes. Perhaps I was not myself, overwhelmed as I was with emotion." He shrugged and peered ominously. "Perhaps I was not entirely sane. But such was result of my sorcery, Mr. Stone, that they whom I had raised could never again depart in death. They would exist forever. Is that not *unspeakable*, Mr. Stone?"

We sat in silence and observed the rising moon, an orange medallion that glowed in the *demi-jour* of dusk. I watched as Lucretia and the elderly servant fellow exited the house so as to join us. She carried a jug of liquid and three glasses, and he a tray on which an assortment of snack items had been arranged. She set the items on a small round table near us and then took the tray from her servant. "Fritz, perhaps we may have some music."

The fellow bowed to her and returned to the house as she poured golden liqueur into the glasses, which she offered to us before returning to her chair. We sat in silence and listened to the night, and then Lucretia began to hum softly to herself. I was inwardly alert, for the melody was the one that she had played on her piano, the eerie melancholy tune that had so beguiled me. The woman's old relation began to hum as well, in a voice that was sweetly melodic. I studied them in silence, noting the sadness that dwelt within their moonlit eyes. A sudden wave of profound despondency took hold of me, and tears gathered in my eyes.

Distant music sounded, and I turned to watch the servant as he drifted toward us playing a violin. The sound of his performance pierced my heart with grief, and I trembled in my chair as the old man in his silk pajamas struggled out of his chair and began to move in dance across the grass. His caper was uncouth, and moonlight revealed the peculiar expression on his face, which somehow reminded me of Emmitt Kelly, the circus performer who had created the clown called "Weary Willie."

Mr. Greive jerked his limbs as he moved, as if he were some awful marionette that had escaped its strings. I watched as he raised one hand above his dome and moved its fingers in a curious manner; and this reminded me of the incident in the cemetery, where his niece had performed a similar gesture. The subdued sound of the old man's humming increased in volume as wordless song, and the mourning on his expressive face augmented. I became aware of circles of churning shadow in the grass not far from where we stood. One of these swirling disks convulsed, and elements of it lifted into the air as obsidian froth that shaped itself into a phantasm. Protruding branches that imitated limbs formed spasmodically from the specter as it began to jerk in imitation of Mr. Greive's unnatural contortion. It raised a kind of countenance to the moon, a visage that mimicked the old man's sorrowfulness and deepened it. The pathos expressed in the eerie violin music seemed to wring my heart, and I wept freely as I stood and stepped to where the woman sat.

Another circle of gloom, the one nearest us, began to rise as a shifting eidolon. I imagined that a current of frigid air wafted from it, and I shivered. With staccato sound issuing from the place where it wore a kind of mouth, the being jerked toward us in an almost comical manner. Its face, now near my own, took on solidity, and I was again reminded of Emmitt Kelly and his world-weary tramp. God—that ghastly face!—like the visage of a clown whose heart had broken. Its expression seemed to sum up all that was sick and wretched in the world.

The thing jerked away, nearer to the ancient man, and opened its mouth in moaning the elderly fellow's haunting tune. They both began to judder spasmodically in a way that, under different circumstances, would have been uproarious. I imagined that the earth trembled beneath me in response to the heavy footfalls of the mammoth old man whose movements increased with wildness. Turning to gape at Lucretia, I saw that she had risen to her feet. Her eyes were shut, and she swayed as if enchanted with the sound surrounding us. I watched as she raised her hands and saw, some distance from her, the new circle of churning darkness that began to form.

And then there was a strangled cry, of pain, and the music stopped. I heard the thud as some weighty object fell to earth. Turning, I saw that Nicodemus Greive lay prostrate on the ground, his hand clutching at his chest just above his heart. The macabre buffoons of shadow stretched their spectral mouth with wailing and then began to break apart. I watched as their essence dropped to the ground and vanished beneath the overgrown lawn. Fretfully, I turned to Lucretia and yelped in horror when I saw that she, too, had collapsed upon the earth, where she twitched convulsively. I rushed to her and lifted her torso in an embrace. She clasped her arms around me forcefully for some few moments, and then pushed herself away from me and crawled to her relation. Gently, she lifted his head and set it onto her lap. One of his awful hands reached to her tear-stained face, and they exchanged words in a language I did not understand.

I crawled to them as the fellow's heavy hand fell to the grass, and I reached for his hand that once had so repulsed me. His grasp was weak, and the former power that I had experienced in his hold had grown diminished. I squeezed the hand, and he looked at me and managed a feeble smile. Then he turned his eyes to his kinswoman and whispered, "Forgive me. Perhaps, once I have faded, you too will be released." His eyes closed, and the faint force that once generated in his hand departed.

"*In pace requiescat,*" I whispered, as Lucretia graced me with a smile of gratitude. "Why did he beg your forgiveness?" I was bold enough to ask her. "What was your uncle's awful woe?"

Her voice was raspy and choked as she answered. "He was not my uncle. He was my son."

Dust to Dust

Then turning to my love I said,
"The dead are dancing with the dead,
The dust is whirling with the dust."
— Oscar Wilde, "The Harlot's House"

He entered the dark and lonesome chamber and squinted at the smoke of incense. Before him stood the shrouded figure, the thing that smiled down at him and nodded its lean head.

"You have brought your father's ashes?"

"I have."

"Excellent." It held out a skeletal hand, to which the boy surrendered a leather pouch. The Old One brought the pouch to where its nose should have been. The youth saw merely a blur of almost-features, and gazing hard in an attempt to discern the shifting images made him so dizzy that he nearly lost his footing and had to close his eyes.

"About payment . . ." the boy stammered.

The other raised a long and leathery hand. "If we are successful we shall discuss requital. The spell is difficult. It requires the crushed bones on a murdered infant." Pausing, the Old One lowered its lean head; the boy then noticed the box of black marble. "I have obtained such an item, and so we may proceed."

A scroll was unfolded, and a lean talon traced faint symbols. The creature closed its eyes and spoke in a hushed tone. "The rite evokes the name of an Antient Power that is a Key to Thresholds. The gateways between light and dark, life and death, are difficult to conjure. Caution is in order. Now—tell me of your father."

The boy sucked in the perfumed air, and then he sighed. "My sire was a wise yet strange man, who spent his life in quiet study. His lifestyle mystified the folk around him, and odd rumors circulated. Two summers ago a wealthy man's son vanished, and my father was blamed and charged with sorcery and murder. But warning came to us in time, and I was sent to stay with an aunt. My father promised to use all his wisdom to prove his innocence, and said that he would join me in time. After months of silence, I returned to our cabin and found what remained of my father's corpse hanging from a tree." Blinking tears, he paused in his retelling. The creature before him touched a lean and leathery hand to its breast. "My aunt and I cremated my father's remains, which I left with her as I contemplated vengeance. But my hatred has cooled, replaced with sorrow and loneliness. I have lost my finest friend, my constant companion. I want him returned, so that we may study and grow old together."

The shrouded one shifted and gazed at the boy with cloudy eyes. In the smoky darkness the lad could almost discern those spherelike orbs, and thin nostrils, the black flaps that were lips. "I know all this," the creature whispered, "but wanted to hear it expressed. I have personal knowledge of the kind of loss that you have expressed so eloquently. I lack your human emotion, but your words have oddly touched me. I need you to be still and silent as I work my craft. I will inform you when assistance is required. Prepare yourself now, and together we will arouse the name of Yog-Sothoth."

A tall yellow candle was lit, its dim glow throwing silver shadows into dusky corners. The boy stared at the thing that towered before him, once more trying to discern the necromancer's visage. He saw shadows from which globes that were eyes gleamed momentarily— that was all. And then the arcane words were uttered, and the aether thickened and pulsed around the lad. Air grew heavy, illumination darkened, vision distorted. Sound and scent overwhelmed his senses, and a mordant chill cut into his flesh. He shuddered.

The Old One opened the marble box as a banshee wind rushed to it and stirred its contents. The thick powder of crushed bones rose as whorl before the spectators. The sorcerer held high the leather pouch and let its human ash fall into the whirlwind. Dust mingled with dust and danced in heavy air; they blended and began to form an outline that contains tiny arms, diminutive dome. The boy watched, spellbound.

"Prepare to be joined with thy sire," the shrouded thing whispered, and then he spoke the name of Threshold. The lad seemed not to notice as the creature stooped toward him and pushed a talon through the whirlwind, reaching so as to thrust a sleek claw into the boy's throat. The youth did not cry out as his blood spilled from him and followed the stained talon into the wind and dust and ash.

It was done. The threshold dissolved. The whirlwind became a thing of fury and the candlelight extinguished. The chamber grew still and silent. The Old One glanced at the youthful corpse, the soul of which was now joined with that of its sire in the realm beyond mortality. Next to the corpse, struggling as it attempted to lift its lean body onto trembling limbs, was a skeletal creature that mewed as it moved. It raised its spherical eyes to the creature that towered before it. The necromancer reached down and tenderly touched the trembling thing. "My child," it whispered.

The House of Idiot Children

with Maryanne K. Snyder

I.

Samuel Shammua watched the tree coming toward him just in time to avoid collision. True, the moist fog had been thick, limiting visibility; and true, the road curved endlessly, making navigation treacherous. Yet truest of all was that Samuel had been dreaming, that he had not been paying attention to the little road that wound before his bicycle. So of course that bicycle ran off the road, onto an area of grass where, despite his putting on the brakes, the vehicle slid for a while before coming to a stop just before the great old oak.

"Oy," Samuel muttered, hearing again the scolding inner voice that was always so condemning and condescending. "Always with your head in the clouds, as if you were already in the next world." He never understood whose voice it was—his father's, some old teacher? His own? No matter; he ignored the scolding and hopped off the bike. The cheder was just around the bend, better he should stroll than pedal if inclined to dream. So walk he did, until he entered the lush woodland property that surrounded the ancient wooden edifice that had, almost a century before, served as secluded temple for a fledging Jewish community, until most of its congregates had moved to settle in a section of town that was more suitable to an increase in prosperity. Thus the old building served as Hebrew school, until even that proved unfeasible. Still, the community loved the building and wished not to sell it,

37

and so it became a school for children who were autistic, a place that instituted a radical program of learning by facilitation.

Parking his bike, the young man wiped moisture from his face, and then he looked to an upper window where he saw a figure waving at him. The pane of glass was thick with a residue of mist, yet the figure of his student, Moshe, was clearly identifiable. Shocked and delighted at the sight, Samuel raised his hand in greeting; but then it became clear that the boy was not waving but rather pressing fingers against the fogged window and writing a Hebrew letter. Samuel watched, astonished and then confused, for the letter written was oddly formed, resembling a mishmash combination of different characters of the alphabet. The misty image of the autistic child took its hand from the pane of glass and began to bow to the letter, as if in prayer. A chill crept Samuel's spine as the malformed letter began to glow subtly, as if struck with ethereal illumination. Turning, the teacher scanned the skies, yet saw no speck of sunlight filtering through the density of fog. When again he looked at the window, Moshe and his shimmering letter were no longer to be seen.

Samuel climbed the steps that led to an expansive porch, kissed fingers that touched the slightly ornate mezuzah, his fingertips lingering just beneath the opening wherein the name of God, Shaddai, was written on the back of the klaf, the rolled parchment on which the Shema prayer from Deuteronomy 6 had been handwritten. Softly, he spoke the prayer, elongating the pronunciation of "echad." Then he pushed open the door and entered the building, smiling greeting as Rebbe Paloy approached him.

"Ah, Rav Samuel," the old man enthused, holding out one hand in greeting as his other hand grasped a sheet of paper. Beaming excitedly, he held the paper before Samuel's face. "This is remarkable."

Samuel waited until the paper had been placed within his hands. He saw on it a poem that his student had written in English two days previously. The English of the lines was awkward, but the composition of the poem had been an exciting milestone in Moshe's progress. "Yes, Rebbe, it is wonderful."

The elder gentleman's eyes twinkled magically. He held a finger before Samuel's nose. "Aha," the Rebbe said, almost laughing the word,
then reached into a pocket and produced another sheet of paper. "This
is my Hebrew translation of the poem. What do you make of it?"
Samuel studied the Hebrew letters and said he found it a fine translation. Before him, the elder man fidgeted with anticipation. "A fine
translation? You notice nothing?" The Rebbe watched impatiently as
Samuel frowned in concentration, and then he shrugged. "You were
never so good with numbers, eh, Rav Samuel? You see? Every line re-
duces to nine."

Samuel scanned the sheet before him and then looked again at the
poem on the page he held. He frowned again. "Rebbe, the poem was
written in English."

Again the Rebbe's significant finger poked the air before Samuel's
nose. "Aha!"

"But—that would mean that Moshe mentally composed the poem
in Hebrew and then wrote it out in his awkward English translation."

"Aha!"

Samuel shook his dazed head. "I don't know what to say."

The Rebbe shrugged. "Say nothing. What's to say? Your student
awaits you." And with a triumphal air, the old man strode away, humming to himself.

Thoughtfully, Samuel climbed the stairs that took him to one of
the upper facilitation rooms. The door to his room of destination was
open, and looking in he saw two tables where students and teachers
worked together. His heart filled with sudden tenderness at the sight,
at how lovingly the teachers held their students' hands, at how gently
the children nodded their heads as they spoke by way of assisted writing. There was something sacred in the sight; Samuel felt this deeply.
In one corner, at a table near to a window, sat his student, with feath-
ery fair hair escaping beneath a yarmulke. Samuel walked to the still
and silent child.

"Hello, Moshe."

"Hello, Rav Samuel," came the boy's thick voice, from a face that
did not acknowledge him. Samuel sat next to the boy and felt, as he

always did, that he was in the presence of a special creature, one of the
elect. And then he felt a twinge of guilt, for it was important in this
school not to treat students as if they were anything but normal. Gently, Samuel took a sheet of paper from a small stack and placed it before his student, then placed a pencil in Moshe's hand. Tenderly, he
took hold of his student's hands, and then he closed his eyes and offered up a silent prayer. The hands began to move, from right to left,
and when Samuel opened his eyes he saw the verse from Isaiah that
they had been studying being written in Hebrew. Samuel nodded and
smiled; but then he frowned as the boy's hands ceased their movement, except to tremble slightly. When he raised his eyes to regard the
student, he saw the boy's nodding head turned to the nearby window,
through which a misty light filtered into the room.

Light altered, transformed in hue, became a lustrous entity. A par-
ticle of it detached and drifted to them, floated to Moshe's mouth, and
touched his slightly moving lips. The boy sighed a sound that was almost audible to his teacher—a sound that Samuel *felt* in the core of his
being. The patch of light drifted to and rested on the sheet of paper,
paper that became a brilliant whiteness. Uneasiness filled Samuel's psyche as he watched his hands, still joined to Moshe's, move into the
light. The pencil in Moshe's grasp moved swiftly and formed what at
first seemed to be a Hebrew letter, although one that was unfamiliar.
Samuel stared at the alien glyph, which seemed more symbol than alphabet, and realized that it was an ambigram, a symbol that is exactly
the same read backward, forward, or upside-down. The Star of David
was such a symbol, as was the yin yang or the runic swastika. Trembling, Samuel bent to study the symbol and carefully released Moshe's
hand so as to touch the diagram that shimmered with pale illumination
on its sheet of white paper. Eyesight blurred, and ice water surged
through Samuel's veins. Soft lips touched his ear and breathed into
him a fantastic whispered sound, one that his brain could not perceive
or his mouth replicate, much as he ached to repeat what had been
pronounced into him. He tried once more to utter the sacred sound,
and then his brain became a cloud as Rav Samuel tilted from the table
and fell heavily to the floor.

II.

Rebecca Shammua bent over her garden, tending to a cluster of daffodils that fought for space among the pale petals of the poet's narcissus and the gorgeous red and white flowers of the few amaryllis that had been added for a contrast of color. The woman's long free-flowing hair touched the blossoms, and lines from Dante Gabriel Rossetti came to mind:

> *She had three lilies in her hand,*
> *And the stars in her hair were seven.*

How wonderful, she thought, for a poet to have as part of his byline the name of an archangel—an angel of fire! Rebecca had seen several Christian representations of Gabriel, in which he held a lily rather than a sword. As she knelt, lost in thought, a cloud moved away from the sun, and celestial fire crowned her head. Lifting her eyes to the sun, she squinted momentarily at its glory; and then her eyes took in the figure that shambled toward her, the human outline that was blurred by the glare of bright light that had been caught inside her eyes. Dimly, she made him out, the young man with the boyish beginning of a beard, whose dark haunted eyes peered from a face of extremely pale flesh.

Her brother knelt next to her, smiling at her petulant frown. "Why are you out of bed?" she scolded. "Are you hungry?"

Samuel laughed. "Food is your answer to all the ills of life."

"Food is a gift from Hashem and a blessing for our bellies."

Samuel paused in thought, trying to remember if this was a Rabbinical saying or merely his younger sister being womanly wise. "I've yet to eat," he confessed, "but I'm getting hungry." Abstractedly, he smoothed fingers to the small bump on his head.

"How are you feeling, really? Yes, I'm worried—of course I am, having you brought home in such a state. A fainting spell! Why would you faint, unless you're forgetting to eat?"

"I didn't faint from not eating, Rebecca, I eat plenty. No, I . . ." He stopped to think back on the events of the previous day, absentmindedly playing in the dirt with his small finger. He tried to remember his fainting spell but could not—everything was like a memory of a dream: his teaching Moshe, his weird accident, those who helped him home. Turning to smile at his sister, he was struck by the odd expression on her face. She was watching intently the movement of his hand. Looking down at the dirt in which his finger dallied, he saw that he had been forming letters in the dirt.

Rebecca's hand covered his. "What are you doing?"

"I ... I ..." And suddenly the sod turned cold, and he moved their joined hands way so as to study the queer semi-letter he had scrawled, letters that looked like a child's first attempt at forming members of the Hebrew alphabet, letters that looked almost correct yet contained odd mistakes, strange additions. Swiftly, he reached with his free hand and wiped away the letters, and then he struggled to his feet and momentarily wobbled as his sister, rising, cried in alarm and tightened her arms around his waist. Her brother trembled in her embrace, unable to understand the element of wonder and fear that filled his soul.

"I'm ... fine," he tried to reassure her, in a voice that belied his protestation. Slowly, they returned to the house, and he sat at the kitchen table and watched as she prepared a meal. "How is Mother?" he asked as a plate was placed before him.

"Still sleeping, probably. I'll check on her later. Eat, eat!" And she sat next to him with a plate of her own until a knocking at the front door took her from the kitchen. When she returned, Rebbe Paloy accompanied her, smiling his calm smile. Thanking Rebecca as she placed a cup of hot tea before him, the Rebbe reached into a small bowl and took from it a sugar cube, which he placed in his mouth. Thoughtfully, he sipped from the teacup.

"You are feeling better, Rav Samuel?"

"Yes, Rebbe, I feel fine. Just a bit perplexed. I'm not prone to fainting spells."

"It wasn't nice. Little Moshe was very upset."

"I'm very sorry that it happened. I can't explain it."

Shrugging, the old man reached into a coat pocket and brought forth a folded sheet of paper. He set it on the table before them and slowly opened it, watching closely the strange expression on the younger fellow's face. Samuel watched the Rebbe's fingers trace the Hebrew verse of Isaiah that had been clumsily written. The finger stopped at the place in the paper that was faintly discolored, as if it had been slightly scorched. The Rebbe watched, fascinated, as Samuel touched the spot of discolored paper, watched as Samuel's dark eyes seemed almost to grow pale with memory and emotion. "Can you explain this mystery?" asked the Rebbe, his finger just touching Samuel's.

"I . . . it . . ." the young man stammered. "It defies explanation. It appeared out of a cloud of fire."

The Rebbe's friendly finger tapped Samuel's. "Like Ezekiel and his cherubim? Of the nine classes of angels, they are most associated with fire and lightning. Are you becoming a prophet, Samuel?" He laughed and winked at Rebecca's worried face, who had been preparing another plate of food for the Rebbe.

"I must go check on Mother, Samuel. Excuse me, Rebbe."

"Go, go," he pleasantly replied, nodding at the plate of sandwiches that she set before him. The old man ignored the food and looked again at Samuel. "Nu?"

"No, it wasn't an angel I saw. It was . . . a letter, or a queer combination of portions of different letters, and it contained a quality of light." He tried to laugh. "It seemed so real, and it seemed—this is so strange—it seemed to *beckon,* as if it longed for adoration."

Rebbe Paloy picked up a sandwich and ate in silence for some thoughtful minutes. "And was this a Hebrew letter that was illuminated?"

"Moshe wrote it—there." Samuel tapped the discolored spot.

"A twenty-third Hebrew letter, a letter of fire." The elder man raised his hand to thoughtfully stroked his beard. "An angelic letter, out of which nothing is formed."

Samuel's face felt odd, and he ran his hands over it, trying not to shudder. "You know of this, Rebbe?" His voice was laced with fear, for never had he experienced such a conversation. The mysteries of kabalistic lore were something with which he had never trafficked. He had known certain friends become utterly obsessed with studying the Zohar and other such books, to the detriment of everything else. It was a lure in which he had no wish to find himself. He was a teacher and he had a duty to his students—to Moshe. Whatever this thing was, it had nothing whatsoever to do with him.

"The Creator used the alphabet to form the worlds, this one and the world to come. When we study Torah, when we speak the holy language, we help to recreate the world. There are worlds of substance, of which we are eternally a part. And there are other realms, of naught, formed of nothing, of an alphabet of nothingness."

"Forgive me, but I've never heard of such a thing."

"Well," the Rebbe laughed, eyes twinkling, "it's not something one learns about in cheder. And I do not think it is something we need to dwell on. This sandwich is very good. You will return to work tomorrow?"

Silently, Rebecca returned into the room and took the empty plate from the Rebbe's hand. Samuel didn't watch as they left the room together, his mind too preoccupied with uncanny thought. Thus he did not notice as his sister anxiously whispered to the Rebbe as she escorted him from the room.

III.

Samuel parked his bike and anxiously looked up at the window where he had seen Moshe the previous day. No one stood there, watching. He walked into the building, greeted by anxious smiles, and sensed that he had been a topic of conversion during absence. He knew that the Rebbe would never relate their topic of conversation, and so he tried not to appear nervous as he walked into the classroom and saw some students who, sitting at various tables awaiting instructors, watched his entrance, some very still, some moving slightly to and fro. Samuel shocked himself with feelings of sudden jealousy. What did they see with their autistic senses, what could they hear with an inner ear? The world saw these children as idiots who would always have difficulty functioning in the "normal" world; and yet these children each contained a singular degree of genius. One excelled in mathematics, another had memorized weighty portions of Torah and Talmudic lore, in both English and Hebrew. And Moshe, who sat awaiting him, had excelled in the art of gematria, which art had so excited the Rebbe, but which would have little importance in everyday experience.

Samuel walked to the table and sat next to the child. He was almost afraid to utter a sound, or to place a sheet of paper before the boy. A pencil was placed in the boy's hand, and the ritual of facilitation commenced. He watched his student's face as Moshe's hand moved the pencil over paper. The boy's face was bland, but Samuel noticed a slight twitching of the mouth. The eyes looked dull, as though they lacked even the idea of thought or communication. Once again, Samuel wondered at the world wherein this child's mind was encased. How wonderful, he thought, if *he* could spill into that skull and, with intellect and sophistication, experience the realm of idiocy. He blinked his eyes and then looked down at the words that had been written onto paper, startled to see a poem in awkward English. He whispered the words to his student.

> Do you hear singing in your head?
> Pound like ocean in ears?
> Scream pain, on fire with color?
> The color on fire, cold light,
> Cold pain behind my eyes
> And burning in the normal place,
> Where learn to be
> Like mother father teacher who holds your hand.

Moshe, silent still, swayed slightly. "What is it, Moshe?"

"Poem."

"It's a fine poem. But—where do you see the cold fire?"

The boy trembled, and Samuel feared that he was entering a dangerous realm, a place that was forbidden. "Eyes. It burns. And then I see."

"You see?" he asked, hunching lower like some conspirator.

The child began to shiver, and then he leaned so that his forehead touched Samuel's. His breathing fanned Samuel's eyes, moved to his ears; cool air pushed into that cavity of sound, a whispered word, just below the sound of breathing. It was an unintelligent sound, phrased as only autistic lips could speak it. Samuel's adult brain refused to take it in, to comprehend it. The uttered sound was too *unearthly*. Chilly air pushed into his ear, air that seemed almost to freeze his brain. Once more a sound was breathed into him, and it echoed in his skull like a vibration he could almost taste. His tingling lips parted, whispering. But something in the sound frightened him, and he covered his mouth with moist palms as he forced himself to his feet, away from the boy who wore no expression. Moshe swayed as if in time to a song that only he could hear. One hand still held a pencil, the point of which tapped fitfully on paper. Samuel looked around him and saw other facilitators glancing at him with worried faces. Smiling, he calmed his nerves and returned to his chair. With fingers that he made an effort to control, he took hold of Moshe's hands and began to work.

More than ever, it felt like holy ritual. The child beside him was a vessel, a ferry to a spiritual plane that Samuel could not comprehend. Tender bones moved beneath Moshe's thin fabric of flesh as delicate muscles pushed the pencil across bright paper. "Concentrate on your pupil," Samuel silently chided himself. "Step out of dreaming and do your job." Thus the work progressed, until the end of day when the students returned to the rooms that were their temporary homes. Samuel stepped outside and watched late afternoon sky throw its misty light through spreading branches and leaves, and then he sensed that someone watched him. He turned and waved at Avram, who seemed to hesitate before walking so as to join Samuel, who watched the play of light and shadow on the face of the man who moved beneath the trees.

"How are you feeling, Samuel? No more fainting spells?"

"I'm fine, Avram. A little tired maybe."

"Exhausted by your genius, no doubt. He's a handful, your Moshe. Excelling in gematria now, whoo! I didn't know you dabbled in Kabbalah."

Samuel laughed. "I never have. When I was a kid our Rabbi warned us against the enticing of esoteric lore. The mysteries were not for us, but for the elect. Or the slightly loony. I had a friend who became obsessed with the Zohar, who eventually had to be institutionalized. He was a genius—although a raving one. Such brilliance can be terrifying." A sense of sudden caution stopped his tongue, and so he shrugged and changed the topic. "How goes it with your Joshua?"

"Very slowly. I sometimes get impatient and want to coax, as we are reputed to do."

"Feh," Samuel spat. "I was paired with Moshe because of my standing as an amateur poet. Moshe showed poetic ability, nu, we became a team. This other stuff is far beyond me. It's for Hashem to comprehend and direct. Our critics, who say that we influence our pupils (consciously or not), should mind their own business."

"They don't want parents to become overly encouraged when these kids begin to seem—more like others."

"They're *not* like others, that's the point!" Samuel suddenly shouted, his face flushed with anger. "They are special creatures for whom we especially care. And what the hell is normal, Avram, answer me that! Were we normal kids? Our religious and ethnic heritage makes us outsiders in the 'normal' world, and that's why we're hated, why madmen seek to destroy us."

"I'm sorry, Samuel. Please, settle down."

Samuel shuts his eyes and fought to control his breathing. He smiled and tried to laugh. "It's been a long day, yes? Forgive me, I'm tired. Listen, come eat with us. Halibut, as only my sister can bake it. Talk about esoteric know-how! Come, Avram, it's been weeks since you've visited Rebecca." He smiled and winked at his friend, then linked his arm with Avram's and guided him away, looking one last time as light died in heaven.

IV.

The woman in white exited the metro bus that stopped near the cheder and walked in semi-darkness to the old building. The few lights that still burned behind windows did not dispel the sense of isolation that subtly troubled Rebecca as she slowly made her way up the steps and through the door. Three young students quickly passed by her, and the young woman felt as though they were observing her without directly looking at her. She realized that a woman was a rare thing in this place, especially a young woman whose luxurious hair was worn to her shoulders. She was unmarried, sans ring and wig. Sudden panic seized her brain with dread—for she felt like a creature that had wandered into a domain in which she was unwanted. But then Avram entered the hallway and his puzzled smile calmed her a little.

"I was looking for Samuel. Is he still here, do you know?"

"I saw him in the library earlier. Is something wrong?"

Rebecca shrugged, and then looked around to make certain no one was within hearing. Still, she spoke softly. "I'm a little worried. He didn't come home last night, and now it's getting late again and . . ." A teardrop spilled from her eye, and she tried to smile as she brushed it from her face. "I'm being foolish, of course."

"No," the man assured her. "Samuel's been acting a little—funny. I saw that you were worried that night he unexpectedly brought me to your home for that amazing dinner. Come, let's find your thoughtless brother." She followed him as he led the way up the stairs to the library, where they found the reclining form of Samuel sleeping with his head rested in folded arms that were surrounded by books and sheets of paper. Avram smiled at her and rolled his eyes, and then he left the room. Timidly, she approached the table and picked up one of the books, a slight volume on Jewish mysticism. Scanning the other titles, she saw they were of like matter. She reached for a sheet of paper near her brother's hand and frowned in bewilderment at the characters that had been scribbled on it. When her brother began to stir, she softly called his name. He raised a very pale face and gazed at her with eyes that were dark and confused.

"What are you doing here?"

"No, what are *you* doing here? I've been worried sick."

"Just like a woman . . ."

"No," she firmly responded. "Like a loving sister. What, I shouldn't worry when you're acting all crazy? This is not like you, Samuel. And what is all of this? You're suddenly obsessed with Kabbalah? Since when? You know the warnings of the Rabbis, how this stuff gets into you and takes hold of your brain. What, suddenly you're Isaac the Blind?"

Her brother's fist slammed onto the table. "Zol zein shah! I don't need to be lectured. Who's with Mother?"

"Sadie Kline. Samuel . . ."

"No. I have studying to do. This is my profession. I'm a teacher, it requires studying. Stop acting crazy and go home."

"Oh, I'm the crazy one? When have you eaten last?"

"Always with the food!" He noticed two figures hovering in the hallway near the library door. "Avram, are you driving Rav Sheldon home? May Rebecca accompany you? It's not a problem?"

"It's not a problem," Avram replied. "What about you?"

"*What* about me? I'll be here a little longer. I've got my bike." He turned to his sister, and something in her expression softened his heart. He smiled. "We have a kitchen full of food. I've had a sandwich, I'm okay. Go home." He turned to the gentlemen. "Have you two eaten? There is some excellent soup left over from last night. Such good healthy soup my sister makes. Rebecca, feed these hungry young teachers. I'll be home in a few hours. I'm solving a Torah puzzle that won't let go of my brain. It's what we do, okay? Goodbye. Drive carefully, Avram, I have only one sister." He reached for her hand and gently kissed it.

"Very well," she answered. "And if you're not home in a few hours, I'll be back." Turning, she walked to the others. "Come," she commanded.

Samuel waited a little while, and then he sighed and stretched. Looking at a sheet of paper, he frowned at the symbols he had scribbled on it. Not one of them was correct. Shutting eyes, he tried to conjure a mental image of Moshe's letter. Perhaps it was something he could see only in dream. Perhaps he could enter into a half-dreaming state and therein see the esoteric thing that so beguiled. One other sense alerted him that he was not alone. Half opening his eyes, he saw the small form studying titles on a shelf. The Rebbe selected a volume and turned to study the younger man.

"Rav Samuel, you are still here. So, still with this mystery?" he asked, motioning to the sheets of paper that littered the table. "I hope that you are not neglecting your duties while pondering this thing. Remember why you are here."

"Yes, Rebbe. I'm just playing with a little thing, my little mystery. It's fascinating, you'll agree."

"Fascinating, yes; important, no. And what will you do with your answer? Write a book, perhaps? Express it in a volume of poems?"

"I like finding answers to questions, Rebbe. That's one of the reasons I became a teacher. By teachers others I teach myself."

"An excellent thing, education." The Rebbe reached under Samuel's arm and tugged free the sheet of paper that had been concealed beneath it. "Mysteries, of course, do not always edify. For some things, there is no illumination. This thing that has you so perplexed, what do you think it is?"

"I can't say—that's part of the beguilement."

The Rebbe studied the diagrams that Samuel had sketched with pencil. "We know that Hashem has created all things with His holy alphabet, all things in all the worlds of matter and spirit. There is a legend of a secret name of G-d that is spoken only among the angels. This symbol that you image to have seen may be that awful name, not to be uttered."

"Moshe spoke it."

Did you actually hear him speak it, or are you remembering a daydream? You're a dreamer, Rav Samuel, always with your poet's head in a cloud of language. To dream does little to advance the work of this facility. We must be wide awake if our program is to succeed. Don't be led astray by secrets of the Torah. Leave that to the tzaddik, who wears with wisdom the heavy ordeal of ultimate righteousness."

Samuel smiled and nodded his head. "I'll do that, Rebbe. I promise not to let all this interfere with my duties."

"Good. Now, tidy up all of this and go home. You aren't looking so well, and I am weary of worrying about you. Do me a favor, please. Go home and eat a good meal. If I had such a sister, so talented a cook!" The Rebbe nodded, and then he squinted his eyes as if trying to decide if he could trust the young teacher. Nodding again, he turned and vacated the room. Watching him, Samuel yawned and glanced at a window and the darkness beyond it. Yes, he should go home. There was just one last book that he wanted to delve into, and then he was gone. Opening the volume, he tried to read a passage, but the words began to blur. His heavy eyes lost their focus, and then they shut.

V.

The small figure entered the room, walked to the slumbering man, touched with a small hand one of the sheets of paper on which symbols had been scribbled. He turned over one sheet of paper, picked up a pencil, and placed it in his teacher's hand. Samuel stirred, uncertain where he was. He saw the delicate hand next to his own, the hand that gently took hold of his and began to guide it over the sheet of paper. Samuel watched with eyes that wakened and saw the joined hands that clasped a pencil create a symbol with the pencil's point. He started as that point suddenly snapped and broke. The symbol had not been completed. With trembling lips, he whispered the child's name, and the boy leaned over him and patted his face with friendly fingers. A small white hand was placed on the table, palm upward. Samuel breathed deeply as his hand that held the pencil was guided to Moshe's up-turned palm. The splintered wood of the broken pencil was pressed into the innocent flesh. The facilitation continued, as a symbol was etched into flesh that parted and grew wet with blood.

The symbol was completed. Moshe touched his mouth to Samuel's ear and breathed a forbidden sound, a sound that froze Samuel's blood and shook him from his chair. He fell to his knees, still clasping the boy's wounded hand, and he gasped as that hand was pressed against his forehead. He wept, with tears that mingled with the tiny streams of crimson that slid softly from the hand pressed against him. Through blood and tears he saw the others who had entered the room, Moshe's autistic kindred, those souls who had never looked directly at him. They did not look at him now as they silently surrounded him, as they bowed as one in a circle of davening. The room must have become unnaturally chilly, for streams of mist issued from the prayer mouths, those slack mouths. Samuel remembered and spoke a favorite Psalm. "With the Word of G-D, the heavens were made, and with the Breath of His mouth, all their hosts." He marveled at the sight before him, this circle of frail creatures that now appeared more angelic than human.

He turned to Moshe, to the eyes that, for the first and last time, peered directly into his own. There was a light behind those awesome eyes, and also a light behind the moving mouth—the mouth that sighed the magical letter's name. Samuel kissed his fingers and touched them to Moshe's mouth. He felt the lips move beneath his hand as they uttered still the sacred sound. He felt that angelic name gather in his flesh, and he shivered as it found his mouth. Swaying in time to those who encircled him, Rav Samuel spoke the sacred name.

Beyond the Realm of Dream

She held tightly to my hand as we passed beneath stars and gaslight. Trying to look up at her anxious face, I stumbled and fell upon the pavement. Her huge face loomed before me, and the expression in her dark eyes so frightened me that I began to weep.

"No, my child," she cooed, her soft hands brushing away my tears. Her lips stretched widely in curious mirth, on the face that was not the countenance I had hitherto known. Sitting next to me in the dim pool of gaslight, she pressed those thick lips against my ear. The faraway sound of horse and carriage echoed hauntingly from some distant place. "Tell me your dream," she whispered.

Leaning heavily into her maternal warmth, I shut my eyes and forgot my strange fear. "There were angels," I spoke to twilight. "They were singing. And you were singing. I wanted to sing, but I was afraid." The memory of that fear crept to me once again, and I shivered in her black arms.

"It's a beautiful dream, child, one of music and vision. Oh, beautiful." Her tremulous mouth began to vibrate with sound that was perhaps a moan, perhaps a tuneless song. Her breath was hot as it pushed into my little ear and sank into my soul. I could feel it fumble inside me, her demented noise, churning near my heart. That tiny organ began to pulse to the rhythm of her weird groan, and my own wee voice began to accompany her, soft and low. Sensations that were new to my childhood pricked my flesh. Her mouth was on my scalp. Her black arms wound around me. We swayed beneath starlight. I opened my aching lips as mists of recollection seethed inside my skull. (I can feel them now, so many years afterward.) Together, we sang the esoteric words of an ancient song, and from some distant place a chorus of tender voices accompanied our own. Her rough fingers rubbed against my eyelids, then fell away, and I saw the crowd of orphans that surrounded us. They swayed beneath dimming starlight, with secret song issuing from filth-encrusted mouths. The mist that flowed from those dirty mouths combined into a cloud that rolled toward us, a cloud that hovered just before her dark face.

"Arise, child," she commanded, staggering to her feet, gathering me again in her midnight arms and offering me to the cloud of swirling vapor. Fearfully, I covered my mouth with shaky hands, trying to stop my song. The children raised their voices in louder melody, countering my attempt at silence. They were soon accompanied by a deep unearthly voice that filtered through night's sky, a sound that escorted the flapping of awesome wings. I gazed beyond the cloud of mist and saw the cluster of crimson stars. I saw those stars transform, become a multitude of incandescent eyes. I beheld an angel that was many angels, a creature that waved countless undulating arms beneath black wings. Those magnificent wings stretched toward the clutch of children, touching them. Those lost abandoned faces shuddered in ecstasy, and the creature turned to study me. Innumerable fingers flowed toward my eyes and sank into my unblinking jelly. Then *her* black fingers wound into my hair as I floated impossibly into dark aether. Her hot rough flesh turned as chill as mordent nightmare.

In dream I beheld an angel with numerous faces, all of which wore aspects of the Negress who had found me. Innumerable eyes sparkled with her awful love. "I'm homeward bound," she uttered. "No, don't be afraid. One day you will be mine own again. Until then these kindred will watch over you. Together you will wander among the dull numb mortals who inhabit this globe of dust. But you are selected, a child of fancy and fate. Your song is of this mirthless pack, and it outlives all mortal utterance. Your flesh will shift and change, your brain will blossom; yet you will always be my child. And at the end of time, I will come for you again."

She sighed, and I felt her forceful breath upon my face. I was kissed by many mouths, as a multitude of hands investigated my flesh. Her features began to flow like unto the roiling cloud. She was gone. I knelt on solid ground. The hands of many orphans clutched me, kindly. Gazing toward dark heaven, I saw the cloud that moved away to the roaring of its mighty wings.

An Implement of Ice

I awakened in a chilly room and shuddered beneath bedclothes. At first I was uncertain concerning my whereabouts, but then I remembered the room from the few times I had visited it in childhood. I had come to Canada to handle my great-uncle's estate, part of which was this old café that he had transformed into living quarters. The smallish room in which I had awakened had once been the café's pool room, and my uncle had turned it into his bedchamber. Shifting in the antique mahogany bed, I became aware of the sounds and smells of cooking. I moved my legs from underneath the bedspread, stood and pulled on my trousers and socks, and then hobbled into the kitchen at the back of the establishment. Karla Ambrose smiled at me from the stove where she was creating breakfast. I watched the elderly woman for some few moments, until she signaled for me to sit at a low table.

"It feels weird being here again," I told her. "Mom always spoke so ill about Uncle Silas, but we were always nice to him because of his rumored wealth. Then he journeyed to Burma and lived there for a year, and when he came back—well, the family kept its distance. I'm glad he left you so much of his money: I think you took good care of him."

The old woman shrugged her petite shoulders. "I did what I could. He was as generous as he was difficult. No one else would have much to do with him, mostly on account of Chodon."

"That was the Tibetan dwarf he brought back with him from Burma, right? Yeah, that's when the family began to get weird about him."

"We all kept our distance. I limited my time considerably after he returned from his year away. Things had been so different before he left. We would spend many evenings together before the fire, and I would read to him. But when he came back—I don't know, he was changed in ways I can't explain. He'd become secretive, particularly about the odd books he began to study, those books in other languages. And he had that disgusting runt staying with him."

"The dark dwarf, yes. Mom encountered him once, and that was the last time she visited Uncle Silas. Racial prejudice, I suppose—although her revulsion seemed excessive."

She brought me a plate of food and then went to pour a cup of coffee. Her face, when I studied it, was very serious. "Chodon was extremely ugly, but in an almost inhuman way. His face was . . . twisted, and it gave me the creeps to look upon it. His teeth were gray and bent inward, and he had lost an eye. This ugliness seemed to have an unnatural aura about it—as if it were a trait of an evil nature, melodramatic as that sounds. I never understood their relationship, and I stopped working for your uncle shortly after his time away. There were rumors of odd goings-on, but no one knew anything as fact. I thought perhaps Silas was tutoring the creature, for I would sometimes find them studying together and pronouncing passages from the foreign books. The freak had been seen by more than one, out there in the woods, dancing naked during snowfall and gesturing to the sky. Well, there's your breakfast." She looked about the place and scowled. "Can't say I'll miss this place. Silas was a strange one, sure enough, but he was good to me, and I'll always be grateful. But after his—*change*—all I could think about was how to escape his employment, much as I needed the income."

"I never took Uncle Silas for a drinking man."

"Nor was he."

"And yet he was found frozen to death in the woods, sitting against a tree in the dead of winter. He must have been on a bender and wandered out there and nodded off. My cousin had an alcoholic friend who died in similar fashion three years ago, in Montana."

"Well, Silas is gone now, rest his soul, and he's been very generous to both of us. Shall I return in the morning? We can do laundry if you like."

I nodded in the affirmative and waved at her as she exited through the back door. The kitchen area was fairly spacious and had been the workplace when the café had been in business. Rising, I took my plate and set it in the sink next to the dishwashing machine, and then I went to look inside the larger of the two walk-ins. It had, in earlier years, been the place where café foodstuffs had been kept, but there was little inside it now, and most of what remained would have to be thrown out. I exited and walked around to the smaller walk-in, but the door refused, at first, to open as I yanked on it, and I thought it might be locked. Summoning vigor, I pulled on the handle and nearly fell on my backside when the door opened through the force of my exertion. The walk-in was very narrow, not much bigger than a large closet, and its glacial air testified that it was a freezer. Stepping gingerly into the icy rectangle, I saw that there was no bulb inside the space, and the pale kitchen light did little to illuminate the icy surfaces of walls and floor and ceiling. The air seemed abnormally chilly, and I imagined that my liquid eyes were beginning to freeze. I stepped out into the kitchen but left the door open, rubbed my eyes with frigid fingers, and squinted again into the dark enclosure. As I stood there, I seemed to detect a subtle yet unpleasant stench, as if something inside the walk-in had rotted. Grimacing, I searched the area just inside the doorway and found an upper switch, and when I pushed it the hum of the freezer's motor ceased. Turning on the oven, I left its door slightly ajar. The freezer would drink in the kitchen's warmth, and then I would then return to investigate it.

Walking through the main room of the building, I frowned at its dilapidated state. My great-uncle was a man of means, and yet he had chosen to dwell in this dim and dreary place. I suppose it was comfortable enough, this large room with its three sofas, antique lamps, and sturdy bookcases. There were a couple of faded photos on the wall, depicting the place when it had been a café; it certainly couldn't have had room for many tables, especially since one wall had been reserved for the bar. This was probably its main attraction for the locals, who would come here to drink and trade talk after a long day of labor. Going to the front door, I stepped outside and gazed to where the road curved. It was an isolated spot, although the main section of the small town was just beyond this point. Forested hills surrounded the area where I stood. I heard an approaching rumbling, and soon a large truck passed by.

Returning indoors, I went to make the bed, then sat on the bed and took up my great-uncle's journal. Perhaps the jottings in it would make more sense when read in the light of day, as they didn't when I had glanced over them before going to sleep the previous night.

"It is true that I've become nervous—dreadfully so; indeed, I suffer what I may call an *ecstasy* of foreboding. The damn howling haunted my dreams again. I awakened to find the Little One was playing on his pan pipe. Pah!—his smile as I approached him, the curling black lips in the jaundiced face! I tried not to look at the ugly slit that is his eyeless socket. His remaining eye, of course, captivated me again, and this time he allowed me to kiss it. An infinitesimal remnant of eye-jam clung to my lip as I backed away from him, and he was quick as he shot toward me and chewed the stuff away. His stiletto teeth sliced into my mouth, and my tongue tasted blood. I think he is especially happy because of the early snowfall. His orb—it shimmers when he's merry, like some green gem of rare beauty. But then he begins to laugh, and my eyes return to the cruel black slash that is his diabolic smile. I hate him then."

I set the journal aside and wiped my hands on the bedclothes. The room had retained its earlier chill, and I decided to return to the kitchen and its warmth. I had forgotten about the freezer, and when I again approached it its space was not so frosty. Small rivulets of water seeped from the doorway onto the floor's tile. I entered the walk-in and found it to be empty except for one curious thing that rested on a tall block of wood. Touching the object, I found it frightfully cold, and so I got a large towel from a drawer by the sink and used it to carry the object to the kitchen worktop. Never had I encountered anything so bizarre. I had, of course, seen ice sculptures in some of the fancier restaurants in which I had dined, and I supposed that the object before me could have been some such decoration. What is mostly reminded me of was a large frozen *Amoeba proteus* composed of sparkling ice, a solid mass from which weird tentacular protuberances extended near its top. Queerest of all was the yellow face encased within the ice, a small countenance that might have belonged to a malformed child. The disturbing stench that I had detected earlier in the walk-in oozed from the object, a smell so hateful that I wrapped the object in the towel again and took it out back, where I set it and the towel on the ground. The October air was crisp, and a breeze carried the fragrant scents of autumn. I studied the wooded area that spread behind my great-uncle's abode, the woods that rose before me for some distance. A sense of intense isolation came over me, and I suffered a sudden yearning for the lights and noise of America. I would soon bring the business of my relation's estate to a close and return home.

Re-entering the large living space, which had originally been the customer dining area of the café, I considered it a place in which a man of means had meant to spend his life; and this added to my already perplexed picture of my great-uncle, because I could not imagine anyone deliberately choosing to dwell in such a dim place, so far from real human activity. Why had my relative decided so to distance himself from the world? Was it because of something that he feared, or something he wanted to conceal about his life? I sat on one of the large soft sofas and reached for the decorative wooden box that sat on a small nearby table. Undoing the latch, I opened the box and drank in the aroma of the item that nestled within—the crudely constructed pan pipe. Taking up the instrument, I pressed its reddish wood to my nostrils and absorbed the thing's ligneous fragrance. Bringing the flute's tubes to my mouth, I breathed into it and made music; and as I played my impromptu tune I was subconsciously aware of the wind outside the walls rising in force and sound, as if in accompaniment to my mindless melody. I played for a little while, but soon the music began to sound uncomfortably forlorn, and I was struck by the solitude of my surroundings, the loneliness in my life. Removing the instrument from my lips, I gazed for some moments at the moisture from my mouth that lingered on its tubes; and then I returned the implement to its box, rose to walk to the bedroom, and reclined on the bed, determined to nap.

The rising gale shook the window panes, and the bedroom air was cold. I rose and put on a sweater, and then I noticed my great-uncle's odd journal and, sitting again on the bed, glanced through its leaves. As I read, I seemed to comprehend that my relative had not been merely over-imaginative—he had been a little crazy. I knew no explanation for an entry as bizarre as this:

"His eye stays open as he slumbers—wide, wide open—but wears a glaze that shimmers like ice in firelight. The Little One likes the frozen snow that falls after he has called to the Wind-Walker with that accursed flute. He has taught me the phrase we studied from the ancient text, but I have trouble mouthing it precisely. I have seen the Old One through the blizzard, that ill-formed Behemoth of Storm, with its eyes of burning embers. Flaming eyes—and the eye of jade that glints in parchment of yellow flesh. Awakened by a moan of wind, I find the horror on my chest, like something out of Fuseli—a nightmare indeed! I pushed the squat fiend from me, forcefully, and he did not rise from the floor. His pallid mask—so deadly still. How easily it is removed with the aid of a smooth cool blade. And though the pygmy husk is buried deep within the woodland, there are reports of a Little One dancing between trees during snowfall. Well, let it frolic as it will. That butchered face can no longer mutter the words of calling to the Old One, encased as it is in dark frigidity."

Setting the journal aside, I listened to the wind; and coaxed by its song, I walked to the kitchen and out the back door, into the biting storm. The snowflakes were large and lovely, and I giggled as I caught some on my protruded tongue. Pursing my lips, I whistled the odd tune that I had played on the pan pipe, raised my hands to whiteness, and did a little dance, until I slipped and fell against the sculpture that I had removed from the walk-in. The thing still stank atrociously, and it looked more weird than ever, half-melted yet still frozen, with some few of its protruding spears still intact while others had broken off due to my crashing onto it. The hideous mask was soft and easily removed from its cavity of ice. I could not ascertain the fabric from which it had been fashioned—pigskin, perhaps. One eye socket had been damaged. Getting on my knees, I pressed the mask against my face, to which it clung; and I fought the urge to gag, the smell was so revolting. I could feel the gash that was its mouth tighten against my own, its lips curling and opening as if it wished to speak. One of the tentacular spears of the ice-sculpture lay near me, and I picked it up and admired it. Some distant thing moaned above me in the storm, as if it begged to be summoned. My face felt as if it was shrinking beneath the fleshy mask. I listened to the thing that pulsed beyond the wind and allowed the mask's mouth to utter phrases in a language I could not comprehend. I raised the implement of ice to the storm, and then I stabbed its sharpest point into my eye. Oh, exquisite pain! Ah, how vision blurred and turned crimson! I laughed as my scarlet liquid became icy, as the world became a kaleidoscope of blood and slime and snow.

Although my eyesight was blurred, I could make out the thing that pranced about me, the faceless imp that moved before me in the snow. Together, it and I made sigils with our fingers to the sky, and I pressed our twin lips together as we whistled a weird tune to the curtain of storm, behind which, subtly, I could almost see the monumental promise of doom that had been summoned.

Garden of Shattered Faces

I found the place of which my master had spoken.

"It is an exotic garden of rich blossom, and you will find therein the peace of mind for which you long. However, you will confront your secret fear."

I entered, trembling with anticipation. I could hear no birdsong, but a cool wind whispered at my ear. I looked about cautiously yet found nothing of which to be afraid. The flowers beguiled with gorgeous beauty. Bending before a group of tall lilies, I drank their musky bouquet, an overpowering scent that made me dizzy. Shutting my eyes, I beheld an image from childhood. The walls of some dusky chamber surrounded me, and in each corner were the pots in which Mother had placed heaps of lilies. Among the plants I saw the dolls that Mother made so as to earn a living. I had feared and hated these dolls. They were my rag-and-ivory siblings, whom Mother loved more than she loved me. Oh, how she had tended to them, with what tender care, cooing the love that she never sang to me. My eyes blurred with weeping.

I wiped away my anguished woe and looked about. Turning from those petals of painful memory, I saw the distant pond. Ponds had been a favorite childhood delight. With what happiness I had watched the carefree goldfish move nonchalantly through the water. Joyfully, I approached the pond and knelt, removing my hat so that my long hair fell around my head. Leaning over the encircling stone ridge, I gazed at my liquid reflection.

And I shuddered.

At the bottom of the pond I beheld the horde of handmade dolls. The face of each had been violently shattered, and the cracked faces leered at me with dark accusing eyes. I reached into the water and took up the nearest toy. Windsong sighed as drops of water wept from the sodden figure held in trembling hands. Its shattered visage seemed familiar. When again I caught sight of my rippling reflection, I understood why. I held the ruined face before my own. I pressed the dark wet hair to my nostrils. Overwhelmed with sorrow, I fell upon the grass and clutched the ragged creature to my chest. Weeping, I sank into a void of dream. I saw the dolls approach, holding their sad crushed faces in their mangled hands. Each face was presented to me. Glass eyes gleamed, and crooked mouths bend to my mouth, whereon I tasted dusty kisses. As they took their lips from my own, I saw that each shattered visage had been restored to smooth unblemished wholeness. At last the doll that wore my face approached. I could not read the expression on his tattered countenance, but his eyes seemed moist with emotion.

His kiss tasted of sacrifice.

I awoke to chill wind that sighed through my face. The tender doll lay beside me. Its face was smooth and whole. Tears of perplexity dropped from my eyes, slipping smoothly through the cracks that lined my shattered visage. As I staggered to my feet the world seemed strangely huge. Like some drunken clumsy fool I hobbled toward the beckoning pond. How very large it looked, how high its stone perimeter. Overcome by crippling numbness, I fell lightly on the lawn. Gentle hands wound their fingers around my waist. With tender grace they placed me into the pool of water. As I sank to the depths I saw the rippling wavering face that sadly watched me. But why be mournful? For here I lie in this cool and comfortable pond, surrounded by my rag-and-ivory companions. We watch the world reflected on our water, as happy goldfish nibble playfully at our floating hair. We watch the leaves that fall upon our water as the sky transforms in shade, and we sigh to silver moonlight as it plays along the surface and coaxes us toward slumber. All is peace and happiness, just as my Master said it would be.

Pickman's Lazarus

I. The Past

She was sitting in a North End café when the gentleman first approached her. Introducing himself as Mr. Richard Peters, he expressed keen admiration for the young woman's two collections of decadent poetry. She smiled and invited him to join her at the table.

"It's a novelty to actually meet someone who's read my books. No publisher would touch them, so I published them myself and lost a heap of money. Thankfully, I have lots of Bohemian pals who wanted copies, so I got rid of a bunch of them at Christmas, that dreary holiday."

She watched as the fellow reached into the satchel that he had set on the floor and bring out a small sketchpad. "Would you mind if I sketch you as we speak? Your face fascinates me."

No one had ever drawn her portrait, and the woman found the idea ridiculously appealing. Leaning back in her chair, she pouted prettily as his pencil raced across the paper. "Are you native to Boston, Mr. Peters?"

"I'm from Salem; but Boston is my adopted home, and I feel a close affinity with its soil, with its history. You were born here, were you not, Miss Eliot?"

"I was—and please call me Tara. I like what you said, about feeling a kinship with the city's soil and past. That's a recurring theme in my work." The woman stopped talking and observed him as he sketched. He possessed the strangest face she had ever seen; and although he was not handsome, something, some kind of weird vitality, made him alluring. She shivered slightly when his jade eyes shifted from looking at his sketchpad and peered into her own; for she imagined that he could see the depths of her being, all the things that twisted her soul and tainted her wild imagination.

Tara's fingers itched for her own pad and pen; for the presence of this peculiar fellow so agitated her mind's eye that she wanted to try expressing the sensation in lines of verse. Without realizing that she was speaking aloud, the poet began to improvise a poem.

> "Then from some realm of dream and darkness came
> The stranger with his quite peculiar eyes,
> Those orbs of jade that seemed to paralyze
> My soul, as if my senses he might maim.
> I knew that I would follow his commands,
> Would ache to know the secrets of his soul,
> Would bend to his implacable control,
> Would relish any peril by his hands."

Holding up one large dark hand, he stopped her speech. "You weave a fantasy I have no intention of realizing. If I desire to capture your 'soul,' it's on paper only. *Voilà.*" Tara gazed at her portrait on his pad. He was good—very good, if a trifle macabre; for he had some-how managed to suggest, subtly, the formation of the skull beneath her face, and he had infused her eyes with an expression that suggested the secrets that may be burning in her brain.

"I'm impressed. Where may one see more of your work?"

He lowered the pad and studied the ceiling light for a moment, and then without looking at her he said, "I have a studio down an alley nearby. It's a crumbling place, but it suits me. I paint in the cellar, by amber candlelight, as I listen to whatever scuttles behind the walls in search of food—that never-ending hunt." He smiled at her in a way that made her feel slightly hunted herself, and the way Tara returned his smile suggested that she would not mind any chase. She stood and, bending, reached for his carpetbag, which was surprisingly weighty. Tara then offered the artist her free hand; and, after a moment's hesitation, he stood, took the young woman's hand in his, and led her to his secret haunt.

Tara breathed in cool autumn air as the tall hulking figure beside her led the way through forgotten alleyways, past crumbling buildings with gabled roofs and weathered chimneys from which dislodged bricks had tumbled to the ground. She watched, slyly, the tread of Peters and wondered why he seemed so clumsy; and she noticed the way the moonlight shimmered on the dusky surface of his face and within the depths of his green eyes. They entered a darker, narrower alley, and then the artist stopped before a worm-eaten wall where planks covered windows. Reaching into his pocket, the fellow produced a small flashlight, and in its glow there was revealed an ancient ten-paneled door, which the artist unlocked. But before he pushed open the door, he turned to face her and frowned as she laughed.

"What?" he asked her.

Tara pointed to the antique door. "They've put it on crookedly. Look at how it slants."

Peters offered her an oblique smile and leaned his shoulder against the door. Tara gazed beyond him, into an aperture of gloom. "The world, you'll find, is just a bit aslant here. Set my bag on that wooden chair near you." The artist shut his eyes and breathed deeply of the alley air; and as Tara observed his behavior, she fancied that his nostrils seemed far wider than she remembered them being. But perhaps this was merely the result of how the shadows of the place played upon his visage. "It's like being in another world, isn't it—an elder realm? There's some heaviness in the darkness that one feels pressing against one's soul, and the smell seems a fragrance from another age." Holding the flashlight at his waist, he raised its head so that the beam of light illuminated his face from beneath; and the effect of his partial countenance thus irradiated had a sinister quality that thrilled Tara's imagination with a sense of subtle fear. The man chuckled lowly, turned from her and pushed open the door, then led her into a bleak hallway where the walls wore a remnant of dark-oak paneling.

Tara watched him close and lock the door behind them. "I can't imagine you need to do that in so desolate a place. I've never felt so—

far away from life." Reaching to a table, Peters picked up a box of wooden matches, struck one match, and used it to light a candle. The small flame appeared impossibly bright, and in its glow Tara noticed the look of superiority that danced in the fellow's eyes—and perhaps a touch of lunacy as well.

Peters walked a little from her and raised his candle's flame to the nearest wall; and the silence in the hallway seemed to change into a different kind of quiet, an almost supernatural hush. Without speaking, Tara went to the artist, took the candle from his hand, and held it to the canvas nearest her. "This is blasphemous," she told him. "The bestial priest who holds up the Eucharist, with the tangled strands of filthy hair that conceal so much of his face, cannot be wholly human. There's something wickedly canine in the way he slouches, and an evil glint twinkles in the eye that is not concealed by matted hair. His crooked mouth is cruel, and you can just make out the bit of— something— hanging from one corner of it. The host itself, held in two dirty paws, is larger than usual and jagged in its shape; and then one notices how it resembles the hole in the hanging eidolon of Christ, that hole where a portion of skin is missing." Tara raised one hand and touched it to the canvas, and then shuddered as she took her hand away quickly. "Can you sense how the painting is as aged as it is immoral—old in an almost impious way? And that hoary frame is from another century."

"The frame is indeed antique," the artist acquiesced. "But the work is modern—for I painted it last year. But how charming that you fancy it so old. It exhibits my one great artistic aim—to catch an aura of the past, an evocation of ancient things." He smiled at her and winked. "I had a hunch you'd like it, decadent artist that you are." Tara backed away, turned her face from the wall, and handed the candle back to Peters. He watched her for a while as he held the candle near her face. "You turn from its image, and yet you quiver to gaze on it again. Of what are you afraid?"

"That it will consume me," was her instant answer, and then she frowned at her improbable words.

"What ecstasy—to be consumed by Art!" was his reply. "But

come—my studio is in the cellar, and I think you'll appreciate my newest work, which is close to completion."

Tara's host guided her through a candlelit movement that took them down damp stone steps to a large open space crowded with easels on which unfinished works were propped. Peters walked to an acetylene gas fixture on one wall and turned a valve until the room was dimly lit, and then he walked to another wall and repeated the action, so that faint but steady lamplight fell upon a queer display. Tara saw the low rectangular slab composed of mortar-held bricks and with a smooth cement top on which a figure reclined. Peters moved to place the candleholder on a tall stand that stood beside an easel that held a large quadrangular canvas. Approaching the canvas, the young woman studied the almost-ethereal being there depicted. The creature's flesh was of a pale sepia hue and silky in texture, without wrinkle or blemish. Long strands of flat amber hair extended from its wide dome, and one lean arm was raised above the body, stretching toward a spherical blur that might have been a weird representation of the moon, or perhaps a primordial face.

"Like the other work you saw above, this is religious in nature, my inspiration being the rising of the biblical Lazarus of Bethany. Have you read the Gospel of John, Tara? It's the one gospel that completely captures my imagination—there is so much strangeness in it. Now the Christ raised the corpse after it had lain in its tomb for four days, and I can't help thinking it should have rested only three days, to align with the myth of the Messiah's resurrection. This restoration to life was the seventh of Christ's 'miracles.' Numbers can have an uncanny significance, one finds; they can bend the barrier betwixt reality and dream, between existence and extinction. I rather like the idea of such a dimension—indeed, it's a bit of a fixation for me! Thus I've tried to express it in this work. I obtained a model that was but newly deceased, and etched between her thighs the sigils that signify the potency of exhalation." He stepped toward her through the shadows, until his face was very near her own, and she felt his hot breath on her face. "Oh, the *power* of the pant! How is it described in Genesis? 'And the Lord God formed man of the dust of the ground, and breathed into his nostrils the breath of life; and man became a living soul.' The nostrils, mind you, not the mouth." He bent to Tara then, and for a moment she fancied that he would kiss her. Instead, he lifted his mouth to her nostrils and inhaled.

A hollow noise sounded in the spacious room. Tara pushed away from Peters and looked at one obscure portion of the cellar's earthen floor where she espied a circular brick promontory that rose six inches above the ground. "Is that a well? I've heard about the hidden wells that exist in some of the oldest dwellings of the city. There are supposedly networks of underground tunnels that were used by smugglers and pirates in the early era."

Peters watched as she drifted to the brick curb, knelt before it, and placed her hands on the heavy discoidal cover of cool wood that concealed an aperture. A dull echo sounded deep beneath the disc, and Tara moved with outré motion as she crawled onto the thick wooden surface and pressed her nostrils to it. The fetor that infiltrated the cellar issued from whatever place existed beneath the well.

The woman turned her head and glanced at Peters; and then, noticing the large camera on a long table, she pointed to it. "Take my photograph, Richard. I'll pose with your creation on its slab. Then, when you bring the photo to life on canvas, you can call it a macabre marriage of life and death." Pushing off the disc, Tara walked crookedly to the display that was depicted on the painter's canvas. Sitting next to the reclining, motionless model, she touched her hand to the texture of its faux flesh. "It's warm, this thing. Whatever did you construct it with? It's so silky, like some kind of polished bone." Scooting up the slab, Tara ran her fingers against the model's strands of hair. "The head has a rather monstrous shape—and yet, there seems to be a hint of nobility in the width of brow. How clever of you, to combine beauty with grotesquerie. Yes, it does look like something that hasn't been dead for long, that hasn't yet been completely corrupted by extermination. Lord, as I smooth its sensuous mouth with my fingers I can almost sense an overwhelming hunger on its lips."

Shadows moved around her as Tara bent low and pressed her lips to the model's mouth. Shutting her eyes, the woman moaned as a silky hand wound its talons through her hair and began to combs the strands. She lifted her head a little and saw the colorless eyes that gazed into her own; and then the model on the slab raised its head to the poet's and began to suck the breath that issued from Tara's nostrils.

II. The Narrative of Grevel Zhukovsky

I moved among the crowd, in the small gallery, with a plastic cup of peach champagne in hand, when I espied the youthful figure of Miles Kogos working his way toward me, his bright eyes aimed at mine. He stopped a few feet from me, hesitant and awkward; and so I held to him my hand and smiled. Stepping forward, his hand clasped my own.

"Mr. Kogos. I'm an admirer of your 'Midnight' series; and in those canvases, if I may be bold, I see the influence of Pickman, especially in choice of color. Is this your first glance at the exhibition?"

"It is, Mr. Zhukovsky."

"Please, call me Grevel. Come, let us examine these prints together." He looked at me strangely, and I knew that my sudden friendliness surprised him. I cultivate an antisocial reputation, and the only time I make myself available publicly is where there is a new opening that interests me. I rarely exhibit my own canvases, and I never 'entertain' at home.

We pushed through the throng, to the wall on which the framed photographs had been arranged. "It's rather incredible, these photos being found." Kogos spoke in a high-pitched voice, the nasal quality of which many found annoying. "Weird things keep cropping up in the cellars and attics of old Boston. Do we know how Tara Eliot came to possess these originals?"

"It's rumored that she knew the artist personally, but that has never been confirmed. She got to know his elderly father quite well, and Mr. Pickman presented these stills to Miss Eliot in his final years, after his failure to place his son's paintings with some of the Boston galleries and institutions. Amusing, isn't it, how institutions are still cautious about obtaining Pickman works, despite the ridiculous sums some of them now command."

A low breathy chuckle escaped his mouth. "They're still intimidated by the power of his revelations, and confused by the emotions his canvases can evoke. Look at that largest of the photographs, the one people call his 'Lazarus.' That image contains everything that made Pickman a genius—and everything that made people call him monstrous. I've never known an artist whose personal character was so tied to his art, in a defaming manner. Because he captured so completely what has been labeled 'inhuman,' the myth imparts, his heart and soul must have been those of a cruel and satanic monster. When Rupert Coil's brief biography of Pickman came out, and he quoted from the correspondence of people who knew the artist, he published only those excerpts that painted Pickman as some unearthly beast who began to grow more hideous as he aged—mentally, spiritually, and physically."

I stood nearer the photograph of Pickman's 'Lazarus' and fogged its plate of glass with my breath. "It's so peculiar, what some of you observers say and see. I find nothing 'monstrous' in this image; unless you mean the reclining figure—and that merely looks alien, in an eerie yet beguiling kind of way. As with so many of Pickman's 'models,' this figure seems almost an eidolon of a thing perhaps less than human— or other than human. How different it is from the artist's dark-hued ghouls. It's so pale one fancies that a special source of illumination had been rigged near or over it, so as to enhance its pallidity. The scene itself, the dirt of the alley and the hoary brick of the leaning warehouses or whatever they may be, are Pickman staples and illustrate his love of olden things, of hidden spots, those pockets of the past that may be found in New England. These 'abandoned' lanes or alleys reappear again and again on his canvases. So many of the places he portrayed have now been lost, destroyed as the city became restructured and modernized; and now so many of his scenes seem, to me, places of fable, and it's difficult to believe that some of them actually existed in mundane reality—despite such photographic proof as we have here."

"Well," my companion said, "his creatures are certainly mythical. I mean, look at the figure reclining on its slab! That is a creation of pure imagination that has nothing to do with reality. God, I wish he had painted this photograph!"

I smiled secretly. Looking around, I saw that the gallery was becoming more crowded, and the sight of so many people annoyed me; so, making my excuses to the fellow beside me, I made my way through the crowd and stepped outside. Some few stars twinkled above, but the moon was concealed behind a sheath of dark clouds. I was about to hail a cab when I sensed someone near me. I turned and encountered again the smiling, anxious face of young Miles Kogos. "Would you care to share a cab?" I asked, sensing his desire to speak with me a little longer.

"I have a car, actually. Let me drive you home. There are so few people that understand and appreciate Pickman as I do, and it would please me to share some ideas and such with you—if you wouldn't find it boring."

"It wouldn't bore me at all. It's early yet. I had to get out of that crowd, I couldn't breathe; but it would charm me to sit with you in my library and discuss art, or whatever else you like. We could look at my work and you could explain the similarities you see between my canvases and Pickman's."

"Great! My car's just over there."

He was in a state of heightened excitement and chattered nonstop during our drive to my house in the Hyde Park area. We stepped out of the car and I led him along the gravel path that took us to a side entrance leading into my kitchen.

"Why don't I brew some coffee, and then we can retire to my library and discuss art."

"Could that wait until after I've looked at some of your work?" He was trying to act adult and restrained, but I could see a kind of juvenile stimulation shimmering in his eyes. "It's so seldom that I get to speak to others who appreciate Pickman as I do. And you are more than just an admirer—you're an actual student of his style, an artist who pays homage to his genius with works of your own. I don't understand why you don't exhibit your work more vigorously, and then spread the word about Boston's most notorious painter."

"The world would not welcome such advocacy," I explained; and then I walked to a long hallway and switched on the special lighting I had had installed there. I turned to Kogos, but he looked past me, at the frames on the hallway walls. When he took a few steps forward, I held up my hand to halt him. "Pickman was universally reviled when he lived, when he wasn't being utterly ignored. His canvases unnerved communities, as did his character; and this dislike heightened as he aged, causing several former associates to split with him. When Coil interviewed some few survivors of that company when he was working on his book, the message was always the same: Pickman became diseased as he aged— mentally, spiritually, and physically. It was as if traits of the fiends he painted were being applied, in subtle yet unspeakable measures, to his persona. It's really an extremely unusual phenomenon, if it contains any validity. What could possibly cause Pickman's art to breed alterations to his form, his core being? The more he changed, the more . . . *powerful* . . . his art became. He painted darkness as if he understood every aspect of it intimately. He revealed aspects of shadow, and what lurks within it, that no one had ever perceived before; and to witness such things while gazing on his canvases is to feel a kind of psychic threat. His art was the work of madness, many claimed, and to look on it was to be threatened with implacable lunacy oneself."

I moved down the hallway and stopped before one of my paintings, a canvas that I had labeled "Old Brick Row." It was a work of almost vague darkness, oppressed by formless shadows and blurred lines. Yet the more one looked at it, the more one discerned, and the lines became the walls of brick structures that had reached a state of great decrepitude. In the middle of the painting was a street or alley composed of packed dirt, and the road seemed, in some strange way, as shabby and decayed as the buildings on either side of it. Within the midst of unrelenting darkness, however, one could almost detect a faint mist or cloud of meager illumination that might have been a reflection of moonlight; but then one sensed that the thing was in fact a questing wraith that roamed down the lane in search of something lost and unattainable.

"This painting is clearly in the Pickman tradition," I explained to my guest. "But it lacks his *power;* it doesn't pull the viewer in. We stand and study it, but we do not become a part of it. That's where my work fails, you see, no matter how near I get to his manner. This is merely a representation, an echo—not a thing that *lives*. On a Pickman canvas, the fabulous darkness throbs with a kind of uncanny promise, and as we stare at that darkness we feel as if we might become lost within it. We feel his murkiness creep beyond the framed canvas and imagine that it might nestle in the chamber with us." I turned to Kogos and smiled whimsically. "I can never compete with his genius, much as I want to pay tribute to it in these paintings."

He nodded as if he understood. "And so you don't exhibit them, feeling yourself a failure." He got closer to the painting as if trying to see things in it that had eluded him. "But still—you've captured *something* . . ." We walked slowly past two other canvases. "But, yes, I see what you mean. Your trees are very different from his—they lack the sensuousness of the limbs he painted, and their peculiarity of color. And all your works are merely scenic, vacant of beings. It was Pickman's ghouls and daemons that gave his paintings a lot of their potency. The faces he portrayed— *God!*"

We came to the end of the hallway, and he studied the large painting on the wall that faced us. I could almost feel his sudden confusion as he peered at the image on the wall.

"It is with this canvas that I have gotten nearest to my Maître," I whispered. "And, as you see, there *is* a figure on the slab. You'll recognize the source of inspiration, of course."

Kogos nodded. "It's a fine imitation of the 'Lazarus' photo," he agreed. "And here you really *have* captured the voluptuous character of Pickman's trees, with those two creatures that spread their branches over the mortuary slab. Damn, I almost want to wind myself inside those supple limbs and feed on leaves." He laughed feebly; and then his voice grew strange. "This isn't at all like your other work. Why, it could be by Pickman himself. Even the color tone is far closer to his than anything in your other stuff," and he waved to the canvases behind us. "And that model—holy hell! It's even weirder than what he used in the photograph! It—it *lives!*"

I tilted my head and nodded. "But in what an odd way it exists— almost as if it represents the ultimate symbol of everything a Pickman model should express, ideally realized. Because a part of Richard's fantastic ability was to capture a kind of dimension between what is and what should never be, a dimension between reality and dream, darkness and light, existence and extinction. That was one of the reasons he was shunned in life, you know—because in his ghouls people could see their own potential fiendishness, an unspeakable part of themselves that was morbidly less than human."

"But the figure painted here is unlike his dark ghouls and decayed humans. It's completely alien. The texture of its flesh might be composed of corporeal moonlight, ridiculous as such an idea seems. And, damn, it has a kind of hunger, doesn't it? Similar to the sensuousness of Pickman's trees, the limbs that are so diabolically inviting." Kogos backed away a little and looked at the painting as a frown began to form on his youthful face. "You didn't paint this. You couldn't have captured Pickman's essence so completely. It's by him, isn't it? *By god,* a lost Pickman! It's priceless! No wonder you never invite anyone into your home. If word got out about this . . . !"

My chuckle was low and soft. I sighed, turned from him, and walked out of the hallway, to a door that opened onto the back yard and its high stone walls. Stars twinkled in the sky, but a dark cloud still concealed the moon. Eventually Kogos came out of the house, and when he saw the slab at the farthest end, between two trees, he nearly yelped. He began to babble questions, but I ignored him as I removed my shirt and hairpiece and let them fall onto the ground. Walking to the slab, I reclined upon its cool surface and raised one hand to the cloud that obscured the moon. That cloud began to drift from the lunar disc, and my flesh drank moonlight. I could feel the astral chill on the texture of that which was my semblance of flesh, and I moaned in pleasure as my upraised arm began to glow with a kind of shimmering luminosity. The air around me became frigid, as was attested when Kogos stood above me, his breath issuing as fine mist from mouth and nostrils as he witnessed my transition and its revelation. My upheld hand motioned to him, and he sat beside me on the antique slab. I wound my fingers into his hair and pulled his face to mine; and then I lifted my lips to the breath that wafted from his nostrils, pressed my mouth against the fabric of his face, and inhaled rapaciously.

Totem Pole

Hatred is a curious thing, an odd instinct. Some aspect of someone's personality can trigger it, ushering one into a mood of madness. When first I was spawned from Sesqua Valley's supernatural shadow, I came upon an edition of Poe and fell under the spell of his genius. I read "The Tell-Tale Heart" and smiled at the idea that some bloke would murder another because of the shape or hue of an eyeball. Then I met Fanny Menton, and Poe's story took on especial significance. But *my* wary hatred had a very real *raison d'être*. I had to protect my homeland.

I met Fanny at one of those literary gatherings that I had enjoyed attending in the city. It proved a nice break from the rustic charm of Sesqua Valley, and it sometimes introduced me to poetic young men with whom I enjoyed intimate pleasure. Women were a source of great intellectual delectation, and Fanny initially captivated me with her profound knowledge of Romantic and Victorian verse; but as we became more familiar, I saw more clearly her pride and egoism, her nasty self-righteousness. I had foolishly let her look at a sampling of my verse, and she shocked me after reading one of my sonnets.

"Did you write that about the mountain in Sesqua Valley? I found an identical reference in a book of poems by William Davis Manly. Do you know him?"

I grew uneasy and silently cursed Manly for his book, which was issued after his disappearance. His book had brought unwanted visitors to the valley, and I feared it would do so again. Forcing a smile, I nonchalantly answered, "Yes, Manly and I share a common background. I'm surprised you found a copy of his book, it's such a rare item."

"I inherited it after my uncle's . . . demise. He became fascinated with this valley of yours. Took me there once, but I have trouble remembering anything about it. I try to recall it, but all I see is mental fog. I usually forget that the place exists. Something about you brings back wisps of memory, something in your eyes. What strange uncanny beauty they possess, your eyes." I did not care for her sloppy smile. "I think I'd like to visit Sesqua Valley again, to see if anything will jog memories of my uncle. Would you serve as guide, should I return to your demesne?"

"I would be delighted. And if you bring your edition of Manly's verse we can use it as a guidepost to the sites described therein."

Thus, within a fortnight, Fanny Menton arrived in Sesqua Valley by train, to meet her curious doom. I ascertained her alternative motive as she playfully linked her arm with mine. As the day wore on and my patience wore out I began to feel hostile and invaded. She sat in my easy chair, perusing a manuscript copy of my poetry.

"Why do you write such—stuff?"

"Because it gives me pleasure to do so."

"You have talent, certainly; but all this babbling about hungry shadow and—where is it?—'dark throbbing doom.'" She sniggered. "So silly and morbid." I knew then that I hated her.

"An author doesn't always choose their genre. We happen upon it, because of influence or inclination. I cannot agree that it's 'silly' to disregard one's nature or one's muse."

"My work deals with reality," she replied smugly. "To take the common things of life and give them new meaning in poetry, now that's a wonderful and meaningful thing. But you seem to want to escape reality."

"I cannot imagine how one escapes reality, it so constantly surrounds us. And death, my dear woman, is our inescapable reality."

She sniffed and tossed my manuscript upon the sofa. "I find it a bit pretentious, is all. I don't wish to hurt your feelings, Adam. I always express my mind."

"Have no fear, my feelings are tough. All my work is based on the fundamentals truths of my homeland, this especial vale."

"I dare say. Now that I'm here again, I begin to recall some of the odd legends my uncle told me of this valley. Of frogs with human faces, of trees that dance in moonlight. It's all coming back, of how he took me across a dismal plot of land, to a wooded area near the white mountain. He wanted to follow a pebbled pathway that led up the mountain, but I was too afraid to follow. Yes, I'm remembering it all. When I look into your eyes, I seem to see others with such eyes. They hold a kind of mystery, your silver eyes."

"This valley overflows with mystery, my dear Fanny. The frogs with human faces are perhaps inspired by our Sesquan physiognomy. You can see it in my own visage. If you like, I'll warble you a croaking lullaby."

"Adam Webster, how you tease." Yet how oddly she studied my countenance.

"Come to my attic, my beauty. I have a wee collection of items linked to Sesqua Valley that you'll find fascinating, as consuming as I find you."

Great Yuggoth, how she simpered. Linking arms, we climbed the narrow steps that took us to my attic. I smiled as she gazed around the spacious room, as her gazing became gaping.

"This is where I pen my silly poems. I find the atmosphere conducive to eerie moods and morbid imagination. You'll notice, perhaps, that many of the items are mentioned in my verse. That rather large bestial skull on the table near you, for example. What on earth explains the three hollow eye sockets? Ah, the world is a place of riddles."

She reached so as to touch the skull. "It's ghastly!"

"It was discovered by one of the first white men to settle in the valley, those invaders that awakened us children of the shadow from our deep repose. This particular gentleman did not stay long, but he left a written record of impressions, of how local Native Americans tried to persuade those early settlers not to linger in this uncanny valley. Those redskins were afraid of an ancient force they knew of vaguely but could not comprehend. There was one Native woman who defied her tribe and came to settle with the white folk. She was a woman of many talents, and created some marvelous things. This is one of my favorites." I held up the curious item. "It's very old. You'll notice that it resembles a miniature totem. If you look carefully at the carven faces, you'll see how their expressions seem to alter, to shift and distort. Rather wonderful, I think. And observe the wings. One would first imagine that they were eagle wings; but then one notices their curious, their reptilian design. And when one touches the thing . . ." Here I tossed the object to her, and she quickly caught it. How delightful, the way in which her face contorted with revulsion. "Feels almost alive, doesn't it? Like a snake, perhaps, with dryness that hints of life. And it leaves such a nasty feeling on your fingers, an electric oscillation, an invisible slime."

"What the hell is it?" she violently interrupted.

"It's a flute. I've grown quite fond of it. I sometimes sleep with it beneath my pillow, and, oh, the dreams with which I am blessed! I hear within those dreams a cosmic song that is known as the Winds of Yith, that tempest that shocks the cosmos beyond the rim. If I shut my eyes and listen attentively, I can hear the song within my pulsing brain. Shall I play it for you?" Taking the flute from her grasp, I placed it at my mouth, watching as the room grew dim with eerie shadow. I played my ghastly paean. I awoke an elder thing. The cloud began to form above her, near the low ceiling. The stupid woman gawked at its bubbling essence and opened her mouth in screaming. The thing of boiling aether spilled hungrily into her mortal mouth. I watched, fascinated, as her transformation took place. I saw the skin darken and splinter, and smiled as she tore at her blouse, ripping it open so as to expose her ponderous breasts, thus revealing the face that formed beneath her heaving bosom, the visage that malformed her flesh. I closed my eyes and continued to play my eldritch tune.

That was many years ago. The mystery of her disappearance was never solved. She had made precautions and written to a friend of her impending visit to Sesqua Valley. City officers came to call, and I answered their dull questioning. I allowed them to examine my abode. They checked the attic room, of course. I went with them and ignored the thing that tilted in one dusky corner, the thing they failed to notice. It was a small totem pole reaching almost to the attic's ceiling. Had they examined it they might have noted the *outré* faces carved thereon; had they touched it they would have felt a sinister dryness that pulsed with subtle sentience. Had they examined the topmost visage, they might have noted that the twisted and terrified countenance resembled the photograph they carried with them. For there, chiseled with lifelike precision, was the stupid face of Fanny Menton.

Visions of William Davis Manly

to ye memory of J. Vernon Shea

I.

Desmond Peters stared at the old gentleman for a long while, amazed at the man's reluctance in agreeing to Desmond's request. Determined not to lose patience, he breathed deeply and addressed the man once more.

"Mr. Vreeland, my request is a valid one. As I mentioned in my letter, I have a solid reputation for bringing out quality small-press books of poetry and prose in the supernatural genre. The books I sent you are an excellent representation of my skill—and my tastes. My titles sell extremely well, and so whoever holds the copyright to Manly's work will get a bit of money. William Davis Manly is a wonderful poet, and I wish to shine a light on his work."

"His obscurity was his choice," Nathan Vreeland replied. "That slim volume of his work was never meant for wide circulation, and it is unfortunate that copies have been scattered hither and yon. We published the book after his disappearance, as you have read in the brief preface that I wrote for the thing. I fear that I was foolish in taking it to an outside press—for obviously additional copies were made and sold 'on the sly'. That is probably where your copy originated, for it is not one of the numbered copies. You see? The autograph page is missing."

"Autograph page? But I thought that the poet vanished before the book came out."

"He did indeed. But I had him sign a stack of numbered sheets that were sewn separately into the finished product. The book required many years before coming to fruition. There were those who did not want it to exist. They would certainly not allow *your* reproduction of it now."

The young man laughed. "Surely most of them aren't around anymore. I mean, the book was published way back in the early 1950s, wasn't it?" He turned to the title page of the book in his lap and nodded. "Yep, and your address is on the opposite page, as the publisher. You've lived here a long time. You knew the poet well, I'd say." Vreeland said nothing, but he watched the book in the young man's lap with keen attention. "Look, his poems are fascinating. They get to you and have this strange affect. Everyone that I've sent xeroxes of the poems to really admired them. He wrote like a man obsessed with this valley, this town that nobody has ever heard of. To read his poems gave me the oddest dreams about this place—dreams that were so compelling that I knew I had to come and check it out for myself. What I want to do is illustrate the volume with my own photographs of Sesqua Valley . . ."

"No!" Nathan Vreeland wore an odd expression on his alarmed face. "No. I'm sorry, but it's quite impossible."

Peters bit his lower lip and, trying to think of something to say, looked about the room in which they sat. It was a chamber of curiosities. In one corner stood a small totem pole, its carved faces resembling no beasts that could exist in the real world. In another corner stood a somber life-size statue of what appeared to be some African fetish deity, a faceless figure that wore a kind of triple-crown. Near to where he sat was a small stand on which there was a lamp and a framed photograph. "Is that you?"

The old man grinned. "Many years ago."

"And the guy standing next to you—it's Manly, isn't it?" Peters opened his copy of Manly's poetry and turned to one of its few illustrations, which had been executed by the artist in a simple yet elegant style. He found the last illustration—a self-portrait of the poet. "Yeah—it's him. He looks kind of weird in the photograph. Look at his eyes, some kind of light must have shone in them just as the picture was snapped—some kind of silver light. It's not reflected in your eyes. Maybe we could use that photo in the new book."

"Mr. Peters," said a low voice. Desmond turned to face the old man. Vreeland had been staring at him intently, but now the old gentleman's eyes softened, as did the harsh line of his mouth. The old man rose to his feet. "Let's get out of this stuffy room." Rising, he motioned his visitor to follow him out the front door and into Sesqua Valley's brilliant sunlight. The large old house stood on an inclined road, on which there was a row of similar stately homes. The silence was absolute. "This is a quiet town, Mr. Peters. Most of us inhabitants are of a reclusive nature—we like our solitary ways. Outsiders are few. I came to the valley as a very young man, fifty years ago in 1928. Now, you've mentioned feeling—distance, if not hostility, from some of the inhabitants that you've encountered when you first arrived and sought directions to my home. I'll be blunt and tell you straight that we don't like strangers here, especially you modern gents with your new-fashioned ways. Now"—and he raised a finger to the younger fellow—"if your book proved popular, it would disrupt our little town with visitors, curious tourists who would hound us for information on William Davis Manly, wanting to see the curious cabin in the woodland where he lived his secret life . . ."

"His secret life—yes, I wanted to ask you about that, and I'd like to see the cabin."

"I doubt that its current occupant would allow such a visit."

Desmond frowned. "Shucks. I find it all really fascinating. There's something about the way he wrote about this valley in his poetry—it fills you with a kind of weird intrigue, makes you want to know more."

"Exactly. That is why you will not publish his work in some new edition. He's a rather romantic character, our William. His life, his poetry and drawings, the way he mysteriously vanished—all this instills a keen fascination to those who hear the tale. You are not the first to have stumbled upon that volume of his verse and come here looking for him. It was stupid of me to print so many copies. In a moment of playfulness I decided to name my non-existent press Sesqua Valley Press." The old man scanned the sky with a faraway gaze. "I was very young. I did not understand the repercussions that would follow," he whispered, more to himself than to his visitor.

Desmond turned to look around and noticed for the first time the twin-peaked white mountain. "That's Mount Selta, isn't it?"

"Hmm?" asked Vreeland, awakened from reverie.

"The mountain. Manly wrote of it in some of his sonnets, where he describes a titanic mountain of white stone that had a weird influence on his dreaming. In his dreams he knew the mountain by another name, 'Khroyd'hon,' and the poem is a mental search for the meaning of that weird name. Seeking the mountain, the speaker of the poem comes to a place near it, where the ground is mutated by what seems to be a kind of daemonic force."

"Yes, I recall the poem. 'Khroyd'hon' is Manly's dream-name for Selta."

"And that's the mountain, obviously. A white mountain with twin peaks that resemble wings folded on a monster's shoulders. Funny, I didn't really notice it when I drove into town—but how could I miss it? It's overwhelming!"

Vreeland smiled. "Our poet had quite an imagination."

Desmond's eyes squinted. "But it does look—I don't know—weird." He gazed at the mountain, and his eyes began to play tricks on him. The aether directly around the mountain began to darken subtly, and the mountain itself seemed to tilt slightly toward the house and the porch on which he stood. Desmond was vaguely aware of the voice that spoke to him.

"This is a 'weird' place, young man, quite peculiar indeed. To enter its confines is to have some strange element lay siege on one's imagination. Outsiders such as you begin to feel a queer disquiet—city folk seem especially susceptible." A hand touched Desmond's arm, and he turned to face the old man's kindly smile. "It's not wise to gaze at the white mountain for too long a time." Playfully, the old man winked. "Have you been considering all that I have told you?"

"Yes. I can sort of understand. I do find the place enchanting—it's so alien from city life. Just the silence—it's almost eerie! I guess I've grown used to noise. But even the silence here has some kind of special element, just as Manly mentioned in one of his longer poems." He smiled and held up his copy of *Visions of Khroyd'hon.* "Yep, I know them all real well, many of them by heart. How did he phrase it, in 'An Elemental Quiet'? Something like,

> *'Beneath the hush of quiet one can sense*
> *The presence of an ancient audient thing*
> *That knows the passions beating in thy breast*
> *And all the secrets seething in thy brain;*
> *The joy reflected in thy twinkling eye,*
> *The fear that lingers in thy haunted dream,*
> *The words of power spoken to the air,*
> *The revelations whispered back to thee.'*

I can feel everything he described in that poem. It's weird, the way his poetry has affected me. I've had dreams about this valley, and especially that mountain, ever since I first discovered Manly's work. Ah—there's a breeze. Damn, the air here—it's almost sweet, like misty syrup." The young man turned to regard his companion. "I think you exaggerate the effect a small-press book with a limited production can have on this place. And if the people are drawn to Sesqua Valley by poetry—well, I'd think they'd be a little less crass than your typical tourist. I really want to publish the book. If there aren't any living relatives of Manly's around anymore, then who do I ask for permission?"

"Oh, his—people—are still here. Indeed, one still occupies Manly's hidden cabin in the woods. But they won't help you. No one will. You're an obstinate young fellow."

"Yep. Well, thanks for the information, such as it is. I'll think about it as I walk around and get more of a feel of this place. Nice talking to you, Mr. Vreeland."

The old man nodded and watched the young man hop down the porch steps and walk toward town. He watched the fellow for a few moments, and then he turned to gaze at the sun-drenched peaks of Mount Selta. He shivered when from somewhere among those peaks there soared the sound of distant baying.

II.

Desmond Peters drove his jeep toward the mountain, until he came to a kind of desolate plateau, its flat land inclined slightly as it swept toward Selta. The ground looked gray, like sand, with here and there sickly growths of yellow grass. He gazed at the few scattered piles of large black rocks that, to his imagination, looked like menacing altars in diabolic formation. One of the weird black trees looked very strange, and then he realized that there was a figure standing before it. He opened the door to his jeep and stepped out onto the road, curling his nose at the stench that had entered into the air, a smell of decay. Cautiously, he stepped onto the ugly soil and walked toward the girl who was cutting a symbol into the diseased tree with a small dagger.

"Hello."

There was a long moment of silence before she turned to acknowledge him. "Hi," he said, trying to smile even though he was feeling slightly nauseated at the rancid smell of the place.

"You lost?" She was a black girl, very young. He thought that her long dark dress must have been a cast-off, perhaps an older sister's or a mother's dress. It was too old-fashioned for someone so young.

"Well—sort of. I'm trying to find a road that will take me nearer to the mountain." He pointed to the titanic twin-peaked thing that towered above them and blocked the sun. For some reason, Desmond did not want to look at it in this sickened place.

"No, not a good idea. And you don't want to be wandering around in this particular place."

"Because of snakes?"

At this the girl laughed. "You afraid of snakes? A big man like you?" But then she glanced at the ground surrounding them and lost her smile. "There's venom here, sure enough. This place is infected, you see—it feels too deeply the shadow of Selta, and a portion of the valley's devil heart lies planted beneath this ground, pounding out its poison. Can't you taste it? Yes, you need to clear off. What's that book?"

Ignoring her question, he stepped nearer to the tree and examined the glyph that she had carved into its dark bark. Leaning to the tree, he placed his hand upon the symbol and felt his flesh grow cold. Some queer sensation entered his teeming eyes, which befogged with nasty vision that he felt would spill as tears among the awful sod and patches of sickly grass. Trying to steady his stance, he spread out his arms, and Manly's book was plucked from his grasp.

"It's a book of poems," he informed the girl as his vision strained to regain normalcy.

"Ah," she replied. "You're offering it to the tower, I suppose. Simon will be glad to have it." She looked at him and laughed. "Damn, you look sick. What are you doing here?"

"I'm—trying—to reach the mountain. I want to speak some of his poetry from among its heights."

"Then you must be crazy, or ignorant. You mustn't speak this poetry aloud while in the valley. It would bend the aura and disrupt our dreams if you did that." He shook his head, as if in an attempt to clear it of unwanted vision, and reached out for the book. "You're a city boy, I take it. Don't know what you've stumbled on. Come on, give me a ride back to town and get out of this place. No, forget the mountain. You look like you need a drink. Let's go and I'll buy you a beer." Touching the sickly tree, she mumbled some strange words, then turned and walked to the jeep. Unwillingly, he turned toward his vehicle and watched the girl get into it. His limbs felt heavy as he walked the small distance to where he had parked.

Desmond entered his jeep, and his stomach lost some of its sour taste once he no longer stood on the tainted ground. A beer suddenly seemed like a very good idea. "What's this tower you spoke of? I want to look around before I get back to city life."

"It's a kind of library."

"And who is Simon?"

She smiled uneasily. "He's the beast who tends the books."

He glanced at her as they rode back toward the small downtown area of the old town. "How old are you, by the way? Way too young to be drinking in a bar."

"I'm seventeen. Hi, I'm Miriam Snyde."

"You live here with your folks."

The girl was silent for a long while. "No—they're gone." Glancing at her again, he could not read the strange expression on her pretty face. "But don't worry about the drinking. We do things different here than you city folk."

Once in town, the girl indicated where to park, and then she led him along the wooden sidewalk to a large building that proved to be a saloon. Guiding Desmond to a table in one corner of the room, Miriam told him to sit, then went to the bar and got two schooners of golden brew as she chatted with a young fellow who stood next to her. Desmond watched the two youths approach him and smiled at the pitcher of beer in the lad's hand, suddenly very thirsty.

"Good afternoon," said the young man as Miriam placed a glass of beer before Desmond. "Miriam tells me you're an admirer of William Davis Manly. That's a rare book." The young man reached for where the book sat on the table and pretended to glance through it, and then he handed it to Miriam. "Where did you find it?"

Desmond watched as the two young people, sitting, joined him at the table. "In Boston. A friend of mine has a bookshop there, and I was delivering some copies of a new volume I had recently published, kind of combining business with a very pleasurable vacation. I operate a small press that specializes in supernatural poetry—there's a growing audience for the weird stuff. My friend knew my tastes and had found the book in a collection he had purchased from the children of some dead professor. He gave it to me as a gift." As he spoke, Desmond studied the face of the young man who had joined them. There was something distinctly odd about that youthful countenance, with its almost wolfish aspect and pale silver eyes. Of what did those eyes remind him, Desmond pondered. "I've become rather obsessed with Manly's poetry, so I've come to ask permission to reprint it in a new illustrated edition."

"What?" the two young people cried simultaneously.

"With photographs of this place, I mean. It'd make a great little book. There's something compelling about his poetry, it conjures up pictures of Sesqua Valley in one's brain—one's dreams. Why are you both looking at me like that?"

The young man leaned back and smiled. "Sorry, I find the idea rather unimaginative is all. I mean, if the poems create such wonderful visions with the power of their imagery and language, then it seems wrong to fill the book with mundane *photos,* which never can compete with the mind's eye."

Desmond considered this and thought, as Miriam picked up the thread of conversation. "I agree with Cyrus. How could boring photographs compete with—how did Wordsworth phrase it?—'that inward eye that is the bliss of solitude'—something like that."

Desmond thought some more, then shook his head. "But they wouldn't be boring. Perhaps living here has dulled you to the rich weirdness of the place. I promise you, Sesqua Valley has an atmosphere that can, I think, be caught by a clever photographer. Just that mountain alone—my god! I've never seen anything like it. That would make for a wonderful image on the front of the jacket, especially since the book seems to be named after the mountain. How did that old guy, Vreeland, phrase it, something about 'Khroyd'hon' being Selta's dream name?" He was gazing forward as he spoke, and thus he watched as a tall figure entered the establishment. The youngsters saw the outsider's face grow pale.

"What is it?" asked Miriam, but then she felt the eyes upon them, and knew who it was that had entered the building. She could feel his shadow chill her flesh as he drew near to them.

"It's him," Desmond whispered. "William Davis Manly!"

The tall strange man stopped before the table. "Good afternoon, children," said a deep voice. "Who is your friend?" Without saying a word, Cyrus stood and offered the stranger his chair, and then he walked slowly out of the saloon. Desmond stared at the freakish face with its cruel mouth and slanted alabaster eyes. He saw the bestial nostrils flair as the newcomer sat. "You reek of the detested realm. What have you been about, hag? Trying to heal the sickness of that nauseating sod?"

"Nothing that concerns you, beast," the girl haughtily replied. Desmond studied the fellow and smiled. Of course it couldn't be the vanished poet that was sitting with them—this man was far too young.

But his resemblance to the photo of Manly that Desmond had seen at Vreeland's was remarkable and unmistakable.

"Hi, I'm Desmond Peters." Simon gazed at the proffered hand without moving; but then he smiled and, tilting toward the outsider, wrapped his paw around Desmond's fingers. As Simon leaned closer so as to stare into the young man's eyes, Desmond felt bewildering fear and tried to release his hand. Simon's grip was unyielding.

"And what brings thee to our demesne?" Miriam, who had been hiding Manly's book of verse under the table, produced it and set it before the beast. Simon's slanted eyes grew dark with anger.

"Bah. Another one. I should have known."

"Yes, I wanted to ask your permission to reprint your relative's poetry, in a new edition illustrated with photographs of the mountain and its environs."

Simon's sudden smile was not a pleasant sight, nor was the soft chortling that issued from the misshapen mouth. He let go of Desmond's hand. "But that's a magnificent idea! I am Simon Gregory Williams, your servant. Please, expand on this fascinating conception."

"It would only be a small run of five hundred. You would, of course, receive a portion of royalties."

"*I,* my dear fellow? What does this have to do with me?"

"Well, you're obviously one of the family. I saw Manly's photograph at Nathan Vreeland's home—your resemblance to the poet is remarkable."

Simon Gregory Williams tapped a talon onto the book before him. "I never could understand his penchant for being photographed. I abhor the modern lens and will not surrender my image unto it. Click, click, click. Pah!"

"You knew him? Was he your uncle or something? I was wondering if you could show me his cabin in the woods. Mr. Vreeland told me that one of Manly's people was living there. Is that you?"

The beast gazed at the outsider with an incomprehensible expression in his strange eyes. "How freely Vreeland wags his tongue. Your kind brings it out in him."

"My kind?"

Simon ignored him and reached for the girl's glass of beer, brought it to his nostrils, and sniffed its contents. He sipped a portion of the brew, then returned the glass to the girl, who stared at Simon with dislike. "Manly's cabin in the woods. What say you, hag? Shall I shew it him? Ah, I see that you are moody, my little Ariel. Why don't you flutter away and leave me to tend to our new friend?"

"Simon—" Desmond noticed a sadness enter into her eyes as Miriam turned to look at him. She reached out and placed her hand over his, tenderly. "Goodbye, Desmond."

III.

They entered the woodland wild—the outsider and the beast—and as they walked deeper into the woods, Desmond's senses became acute. Everything that touched him, sight, smell, the feel of valley ground beneath his feet, seemed subtly transfigured and made into something he had never before experienced. The color of the trees and shrubs felt cool upon his eyes; and the air, breathed in, tasted strange as it wound inside his throat and investigated his flesh and bone and blood.

"You are very silent, sirrah," Simon said as he strolled beside the lad.

"Yeah. It's weird. I've never really felt—enchanted. I could easily believe in fairies here."

"There are no pixies in the valley, I assure you. Goblins, perhaps— but sprites, no." He chuckled softly as he led Desmond down the slim path.

"Yes, Manly wrote those three interconnected sonnets about the goblins of these woods, something about the shapeless gnomes who dance around a sacred red tree."

The beast sighed. "He wrote intimately about the valley. That was why I demanded that the book not be published. I knew that it would lure disruptive outsiders to the valley if it had a wide circulation. Manly was no longer within our confines to control the situation, as he should have been. Oh, Vreeland was sly. He pretended that the book would have a small output, and he had Manly sign thirty 'autograph sheets,' as they were called. We were placated for a while, as most of those thirty copies were given as gifts to locals. What we did not know was that Vreeland had three or four hundred other copies printed and bound, which he sold on the sly during his book-hunting jaunts to various cities. He's a sad and dishonest man, is Vreeland. Happily, I found where he was hiding the boxes of books and destroyed most of them—but some have eluded me, such as the copy in your hand."

"But why on earth would you want to destroy the book? The poetry is wonderful, and surely it won't result in busloads of readers invading your quiet town. I mean, we're talking about poetry—by an obscure poet. My idea about a five hundred-copy print run may actually be rather reckless and optimistic. I usually do three hundred per book, and they take their time in selling out. I make little profit—mainly I do this because I love the work, and William Davis Manly's verse has really charmed me."

They came to a small clearing and Desmond stopped to study the slim ruddy stump of what had once been a tree. From where the tree had been severed, a single flower bloomed, its petals black and moist. He bent lower to look at the flower and wondered how it could thrive in a place that saw no sunlight. "This is a sacred spot, young man," Simon quietly spoke. "This is where the tree once stood of which the poet penned. It was destroyed by one who invaded the valley and came here with a hatchet. Alas, your kind has a destructive bent. The valley clouds itself from the outside world, but there are those who slip in nonetheless." Desmond knelt next to the stump and ran his hand over the queer paw prints in the ground that encircled it. "Yes, they still come here, to dance homage to the one your kind destroyed."

"What in hell do you mean—my kind?" the mortal asked angrily as he arose. "I don't know what your experience has been, but I assure you that we are not all monsters in the city, violent and destructive."

Simon's silver eyes twinkled with amusement. He raised a large hand and pointed deeper into the woodland. "We are almost there, to the place that I alone can locate. It is a small cabin, and yet it still contains a tissue of his dreaming. It aches for his song and alchemy. Yes, you find his poetry evocative. But that is nothing compare to him. He was the first to follow me out of the shadowland, when we were lured by the coming of your kind unto this vale. He had—*qualities* that no one else contained. But something took him from us—and with all of my power, my cunning and my craft, I have not been able to find him. And thus I dwell in his lodgings, waiting, hoping that he will return from wherever it is that has seduced him. Come, follow me."

Desmond trailed behind the strange tall man, and then he saw the place where the air looked softly bright, and finally he stepped into the clearing where a small dwelling sat surrounded by trees and shrubbery. He looked above them and saw, through treetops, the peaks of Mount Selta, which seemed impossibly near. He found that he could not turn his eyes away from the sight of that white stone.

"You are mesmerized, Mr. Peters."

Desmond smiled. "Of course I am. I've been reading Manly's poetry for several years, and much of it concerns his—relationship—with that mountain. It's weird, but I feel that through his poetry I have my own link to Selta—or, rather, to Khroyd'hon, for I visit the mountain in my dreams. I am high above this valley, close to cloud and starlight. My time among the curved peaks (and they *are* curved, just as I saw them in my dreams, like gigantic wings on a titan's shoulders!) is especially poignant, because in his poetry Manly speaks of the mountain as if it were something longed for yet forbidden."

Desmond turned and watched as Simon entered the door of the rustic habitation. Looking for another moment at Selta's white rock, he followed the beast inside. The main room was small and crowded with books and a variety of oddities. Furniture was sparse, but Desmond was too enchanted by the room's contents to want to sit down and be social. He came upon a large framed portrait of a man who could have been either the poet or Desmond's present host. Simon joined him and smiled at the painting. "Rather good, isn't it? He had such an interesting style. The way he caught flesh-tone—I've never seen his style duplicated."

"Who's the artist?"

"Oh, an obscure Boston fellow, Richard Upton Pickman. He spent a summer here, just before he vanished in 1926. Why on earth are you sniggering?"

"Sorry, I don't understand your sense of humor. This looks like it could have been painted of you last year—but you say it's you in 1925! Well, your clothes look like they came from that time. But the way you're dressed now isn't what one would call up-to-date."

"Great Yuggoth, I hope not. But, here, this may interest you. It's one of Manly's personal notebooks. You see that this one is mostly verse, while others are a combination of poetry and sketches of the valley. Ah, here's a small notebook of his drawings of the valley— you'll see that they have a carelessness about their style as opposed to the finer pieces that Vreeland published in that book."

But Desmond wasn't listening, for he was too excited by the note-book of verse. "Unpublished poetry by William Davis Manly!"

"Oh, yes—reams and reams of the stuff. But, here, close that and let me show you more of his things. No, I insist, close the notebook. Here, this should interest you. He sculpted this from a chunk of rock that someone brought from the mountain. Rather wonderful, isn't it? The design is so simple, and yet one can see that it represents Selta."

The outsider took hold of the heavy chunk of sculpted rock and admired its eerie beauty. Although the light inside the cabin was dim, this piece of stone seemed almost to shimmer in the gloom. Desmond gazed in rapture at the white rock; he could detect minute prisms of radiance within its surface, tiny particles of color that seemed as if they belonged to a spectrum not of this earth. And when he looked up at the peculiar face that hovered so near to him, he saw within Simon's queer silver eyes a similar suggestion of shimmering tincture.

From somewhere on the twin-peaked mountain, a beast raised its snout in baying. "Let's go there," Desmond whispered.

"I beg your pardon?" Simon gently took the sculpture from the mortal's hands and returned it to its place. He squinted his eyes as he studied Desmond's expression.

"I've been meaning to go to the mountain and read from Manly's poetry there—kind of a homage to his memory, his *vision*. I've done it so often in my dreams of Mount Selta, standing on the white rock be-neath those massive peaks and declaiming Manly's lines in honor of the mountain's majesty and lure. Now I can do it out of dreaming, for real. I can stand on that white rock and yell the magick of his verse to the valley. Take me there!"

"Ah, no—no. The children of shadow cannot linger near the mountain. This land has its laws, alas. Where are you going?"

Desmond vacated the cabin and walked into the late afternoon air. The sky was beginning to lose its light. He sensed that the beast of Sesqua Valley was behind him. "Yes. Manly hinted of such laws, in some of his really vague verse. And he mentioned the 'shadow children,' as you call them, with which he linked himself. That's one of the most imaginative and fascinating recurring motifs. He wrote as if he imagined himself outside of humanity. How did he phrase it?

> 'Come hither, all you voices in the air;
> Come hither, all you tremblings 'neath the mud.
> I harken to the cries of Selta's lair
> That call to me and others of my blood.
> Mauve shadow I wholeheartedly embrace—
> For such is my inheritance, my race.'"

From somewhere atop the mountain, a thing howled in answer to the mortal utterance. Simon's eyes gleamed with weird emotion. "To speak my brother's verse in this place is to conjure forth a potent alchemy. You feel it deep within you, do you not? The magick of this place? The lure that fumbled in your mortal dreams and brought you finally to us—and to your fate? Ah—Sesqua Valley! She can sense the souls who are drawn to her, those mortal pigmies who cannot resist her call. She has called to you, and here you are, your human foot pressed against her ground. You have dreamed of dwelling among the peaks of Khroyd'hon—but now you have within your reach the power to make that more than mere fancy. Open the book to its first poem— yes, that initial sonnet, and speak it to the air."

"It's one of my favorites," Desmond replied as he opened the book and scanned the lines. "Of course, the book takes its name from the title of the poem." He brought the book nearer to his eyes and began to recite in a loud clear voice.

"It stands titanic in the gloom of twilight;
Majestic, like some god beneath the skies.
You cannot turn away your spellbound eyes.
You long to kiss the stone of sparkling white."

The valley's floor shook for one moment, as if the earth trembled. From beneath them, the occupants in the woodland felt a steady pulse, as if some great heartbeat palpitated in the depths below. The sky darkened at the sound of Desmond's loud voice, and a cloud of blackness subtly formed above Mount Selta's twin peaks.

"Among the dancing trees a night-wind sighs;
It rushes 'neath the shadows of the night
And sweeps toward the antient, ageless site
Where antediluvian magick never dies."

Simon closed his eyes as the wind arose, embracing him. He opened his mouth as some thing on the mountain wailed to the eldritch cloud that wove itself among the mountain's curved peaks, and he faintly howled in answer to that other baying. He did not need to see how the blackness that spun and shaped itself above the mountain spread a pair of aether-wings and drifted toward the trees beneath which the mortal spoke the lines of enchanted posey. Desmond was oblivious to the daemonic presence in the sky. He was caught up by his passion for the poetry he uttered. Raising his voice more loudly, he continued to declaim Manly's evocative lines.

"In dreams you sense the passion of the daemon
That lures you from the slumber of the sane.
Your soul is lost and never can regain
The sanity of sweet unfettered reason."

Simon opened his eyes to the sound of tempest. Windstorm tortured the trees with heavy movement, a storm that howled all around them. Raising his large hand, Simon made a signal to the occupant in the sky, the daemon that was a portion of the mountain's shadow, the mountain's lunacy. It was a thing that had been evoked by the sound of mortal voice, by the lines of poetry that had been spoken by the lips of him who had been drawn to Sesqua Valley, the innocent young man who had ached, in dreaming, to stand on the white stone of an ancient mountain. Simon watched as the talons of that black shape above them spiraled downward and clutched at the mouth that could no longer speak. He watched as those lips drank in the ethereal essence of Selta's daemonic shadow. He watched the transformation as the human flesh darkened, as it broke into bits of transfigured tissue that was welded to the substance of the thing that lifted what remained of Desmond Peters above the trees and flowed homeward, to its daemonic place beneath the peaks. Simon shivered as he heard the baying of those things that existed thereon, those things that accepted the new one who had now joined them in their realm of rich nightmare.

The tempest subsided, and early starlight filled the sky above the valley. Simon walked to the spot where the outsider had stood, bent and picked up the book that had fallen to the ground. He turned to the opening sonnet and whispered its final couplet.

> "But never fear, you'll find your fate anon
> Beneath the ach'd peaks of antique Khroyd'hon."

The Boy with the Bloodstained Mouth

I saw him in the smoky room, leaning against the pockmarked wall, indifferent to the noise and fumes. His thick dark glasses hid his eyes. I do not think he wore them for any reason of fashion; rather, I think they were meant to conceal his eyes. Oh, how I longed to gaze into those secret eyes. Ah, what revelations might there be revealed, in the eyes of a beautiful boy? He turned his face to mine, and I felt certain that he had noticed my fascinated attention. He smiled as he studied me. Flames of mad desire consumed my weary soul.

I went to him.

His hair was chaos, a mess of black and crimson rat tails that protruded from pale scalp.

His mouth was stained with wet red blood.

Oh, that crimson liquid! How it gleamed in the misty blue light of the place. It clutched my soul.

My fingers caressed his brow, the flesh of which was like ice. He took my hand in his. Leaning to him, I kissed his lips.

I kissed the boy with the bloodstained mouth. I felt nothing as our lips met, no rush of desire, no flame of ecstasy. And when I backed away, I gasped in confusion. His expression had not altered; but his mouth, clean and unstained, mocked me horribly.

And when I licked my lips, I screamed with awful horror.

Your Seventh Eikon

with Maryanne K. Snyder

We rode beneath the vast mauve sky and its scintillating sun, she on her stallion, me on my mule. The dry wind rustled her clothing and headdress, but the latter had been securely fastened and would not fall. I opened my mouth and drank in the dry wind and particles of dust as I continued my song in honor of dark Khroyd'hon and its illicit valley, to which we journeyed. When at last we came upon a pond, we stopped to allow our beasts to drink; and when, while exploring the territory, I came upon a forsaken altar, I pulled a pinch of oakmoss from my pouch and set it alight in honor of the deity that was my especial doom. Seeing me prance about the altar and wail inarticulate psalms, Euryale laughed and tapped her brass hands together in time to my frolic. I stopped my gambol in the meadow-grass when she knelt near to me, and I lifted my face to the bright sun and shut my eyes as Euryale sliced one of her metal talons into my forehead and replenished the insignia that had been etched into my dusky flesh.

"Open your eyes, my dwarf, and read the shadows within mine own," my Lady commanded; and so I exposed my purple pupils and peered into her emerald orbs, where I beheld the coils of blackness that moved as ghosts of serpent-ink behind the surface of her organs; and when I read the secrets of their forms, I smiled and winked. "From your mask of mirth I assume that all is well, and so let us continue on our way; for the sky will soon turn to blood and diamonds, and we must reach foreboding Khroyd'hon before that instant."

I returned to my mule and continued our expedition, across the meadow-grass and over hillocks of dust, until we came to the haunted forest before which our nervous beasts hesitated. I sang with soothing tones as I hopped off my mule and led her into the dim realm of dark mute trees on which fungoid faces watched our progress. Finally we stopped, at the place where the forest momentarily ended, and we gazed down the sloping terrain, into Khroyd'hon, as above us the mauve sky darkened into a scarlet sea within which golden stars glinted as they circled the ginger moon. I walked beside my weary beast, down the inclined earth, and sang to the woman who followed close behind on her stallion. Above us the sky congealed and darkened as if composed of ingredients of antique gore in which its scab, the moon, hung like an emblem of decease. I leaned against my mule's muzzle and sighed as she bathed me with her breath. Perhaps she sensed her fate—animals are far wiser than we can comprehend.

I stared, as we descended, at the twin-peaked mountain from which the valley took its name—at the crimson stone that glistened like new-shed blood, at the impossibly high twin peaks, lean and curved like the wings on a slumbering daemon's back. The trees were now few and far between, and the soil on which we trod was chill and rigid. We followed where that soil led, to the squat neglected temple that was our destination. Its hoary stone was enshrouded with the dust of ages, and one dark vine clung to its wall in such a fashion as to resemble a fissure extending in a zigzag line from the roof of the edifice to the lush grass from out of which the temple ascended. Looking away from it, I espied the area of blue stone that was Circle of Sacrifice, and to that I led my beloved beast. We stepped onto the smooth blue stone and I knelt beside my mule, which lowered to her knees and pressed her snout to my eyes one final time. Gazing at the orange moon, I made to it the Sign of Forfeit, and I shuddered at the beam that shot from that bloated sphere onto my mule; and I wept as my beast bayed in torment until it dissipated before me as dust. Wiping woe from my murky eyes, I watched as my Lady dismounted her stallion and stood before me.

The magnificent she, silhouetted against the red sky and its golden stars. She stood tall and potent, attired in a robe that concealed most of her celadon skin. Her chiseled countenance was very proud and persuasive, and one could have gazed for an eternity into her diamond eyes. Clapping her brass hands, she pointed to the temple and hissed my name; and so I lifted to my feet, removed myself from the Circle of Sacrifice, and crept into the sanctuary. I stopped first at the pool of bones, wherein creatures had drowned themselves in honor of the Goddess; and it was in its water that I beheld my clear impression, the small thick frame of dusky flesh, the misshapen head and its grotesque face. I had been reviled as a leprous thing because of my ugliness, and had fled the people among whom I was raised so as to live a solitary life, a difficult existence. But then, one gloomy afternoon, my Lady discovered me, and soothed me, and coaxed me to follow her. And when I slept between her thighs I was enchanted with perfumed memory of things that I had forgotten or knew of in dream only.

I moved along, into the temple, where stones of fire set in places of the wall provided queer illumination; and it was in that extraordinary light that I beheld the six stone figures, the sight of which I had seen in deepest delusion. And I saw that each was of my height and form and possessed faces similar to my own. And on each wide forehead I beheld the insignia of the Goddess, cut deep into the surface of stone as mine was etched into my flesh. And as I peered at their rigid faces I felt a sense of belonging, almost an euphoria of joy. And so I took my place within their tribe, and watched as Euryale lifted her hands of brass so as to remove the covering from her serpent-hair. And I wept one final tear in memory of my beloved beast, who had been my only friend in life, as I transformed as she had. Yet unlike her, I did not disintegrate into a cloud of mortal dust to be tossed into the wind, but rather my limbs hardened as smooth mineral, kissed by the potent alchemy that spilled into my eyes as I beheld my Lady's serpent-hair. And although my eyes are things of stone, yet can they see her still, standing in all her glory; and I am happy to be her Seventh Eikon, to dwell here with my kindred for all ages.

Heritage of Hunger

He stretched onto the dilapidated seventeenth-century slab and squinted through the willow branches at late afternoon sunlight. Shadow and light played on the surrounding graveyard ground, the numerous trees, the tall iron fence beyond which he could see the venerable town of Arkham. Everything around him whispered of a time long past. Even the neighboring tree, whose trunk had nearly engulfed the unmarked slab on which he lay, was a creature of inestimable age. When Adam pressed his hand against its bark he seemed almost to touch the hoary past. As a child of Sesqua Valley, Adam was well-versed with the legends of this New England town. Simon Gregory Williams had often visited, and on returning would whisper lore of this place and its haunted past. It was a past that never died, that seemed to taint the very air. It was evident in the twisting lanes of cobblestone, in brooding seventeenth-century houses; and here, in this fabulously timeworn necropolis, it was most evident.

How many solitary souls had stretched their limbs on this aged slab of stone? He could imagine them, in the varied costumes of distant eras. And there was one he did not have to imagine at all, one whom he had known and could clearly see in memory. Adam reached into a pocket and produced a small book, its thin hardback covers wrapped in scarlet cloth that had been embroidered with squiggles of woven gold. It was Richard Lund's private diary, written in his strange poetic idiom.

"The mists of light that play upon the tombstones; a light of peculiar radiance not unlike the cadence seen in clouds above Mount Selta. O dim
light of Arkham, play on stone and dance between dates of death, of
birth. Swim through tall grass, on trembling leaf. Illume the familiar faces. They look down and would whisper what I fear to know. In dreams
of madness have they sought me and nigh they have me in this Arkham
light. Ah, dreams of Witch Town. Shake loose the clogs of mortal clay
and see one leering face. There mocks dark destiny. Born of strange
shadow, unto that shade return. I reach for thee, silent brother of decay-
ing stone."

Adam Webster returned the poet's diary to its pocket and pushed
off the slab that lacked inscription. He walked the cool hard ground
and glanced at tilted tombstone, at silent tree, at the town beyond the
fence. He saw the nearby house, a structure that had withstood the elements of two centuries. How wonderful that it had survived. Although so very old, it looked structurally strong; and it was obviously
inhabited, judging from the clean curtains and objects seen at windows. Adam noticed a faint twinkling from the high attic window, and
saw the gently swaying prisms of cut glass that hung from invisible
wire, prisms that caught the sun and reflected it as rainbow hues. And
there, just behind one shimmering piece of glass, he detected a small
pale face watching him.

But other faces were more intriguing, and to one of these he now
turned. Yes, he could see how such a thing would have so affected
Richard Lund. It was gigantic, the statue of weathered stone, an awesome figure that seemed to have shuffled forth from decadent nightmare. Its face had been worn away by elemental time, yet Adam could
just make out the remnants of eroded nose and mouth. The thing had
stood as sentinel for a long time. He turned and walked to another
statue, one that had been sculpted of newer stone; and he gasped as he
beheld its face, it so resembled his dead friend. There was the same
width of nose, the enlarged eyes, the slightly tapered ears. Although the
substantial mouth was shut, he knew that behind those lips were thick
strong teeth, the kind he had seen when Richard laughed.

Late afternoon deepened toward dusk. Adam closed his eyes and
raised his face to dim starlight. Mentally, he called to they who slept,

seeking to taste Arkham dreaming. He breathed slowly and sensed something dark and strange, a presence that fumbled in the blackness of his brain. Something near. He opened silver eyes. He had touched a sense of lurking shadow, and of stench. It was here, close at hand, a nasty bogey that had answered his mental call. Opening eyes, he scanned the burying ground; he espied the grassy hill that was almost hidden by a thick growth of trees. He stepped toward the shadowed knoll as the moon began to rise, and he hissed at the sight of the dae- monic thing that spread bronze wings to evening wind. The metallurgy of the thing was astounding, for it indeed looked lifelike. It was a blend of sphinx and crouching hound, and its bestial limbs had been posi- tioned so as to give the figure a kind of Oriental grace. Adam had seen its like before, on the pages of an elder grimoire he had found in Si- mon Gregory Williams's vast library of alchemical lore; but no diagram could have prepared him for the electric thrill of seeing this tremen- dous chimera cast so massively in metal. He observed the houndlike face and saw that it had been oddly vandalized; one of the wicked eyes had been disfigured.

He looked beyond the statue, to the grassy knoll. Approaching it, he saw an undulating blackness at its base where a flock of creatures pecked at items on the ground. Sensing him, they darted as a horde, disappearing into night. Adam bent before the mound and its cavity of ingress, moving with his shoe the scraps of stuff on which the scav- enging fowl had been feeding. A foetor exuded from the hole in the hill. Despite better wisdom, Adam moved toward the opening. He sensed the unclean thing before feebly seeing it. There was a bulky blackness, a sinister shadow that crouched and abided. A spear of moonlight stabbed the darkness; it was reflected on the wide green eyes of the face that became discernible. Chilliness kissed Adam's spine.

"Richard?" he whimpered.

The eyes slanted for one confused moment, and then grew large with violence as the beast sprang for him. Padded hands dug nails into his neck; a hungry face grimaced, then grinned at Adam's fearful panic. It bent to him, that face, and Adam gagged at the reek of rotted breath.

A gunshot sounded, and the thing, looking up in annoyance, light-ened its murderous hold. Another shot rang out, nearer, and the fiend snarled at an approaching figure. Sneering at its captive, it clenched a massive fist that savagely batted Adam's head. His sight grew static and went out.

II.

She bent to his face and deeply sniffed. Never had she smelled flesh so strangely scented. Licentiously, she smoothed her tongue against his sepia flesh. He moaned and moved. He slowly opened silver eyes. Her small round face came into focus, as did her amused smile. Adam took in the rough skin and dark hair, the thin lips and blemished eye.

"It is the beating of his hideous heart," he mumbled groggily before better sense could stop him.

"Pardon?"

"What?" he stupidly asked, and then he moaned and touched a hand to his head's bandaged bump.

"You've taken quite a thumping," she said, bringing a cool damp cloth to his sweaty face.

"Thanks," he answered, taking the cloth and smoothing it over his skin. He lifted himself higher on the sofa and looked around. "Who are you?" Then he remembered the leering face that had emerged violently from a cavity in earth. "Great cosmos, did you kill it?"

"I shot into the air. Doesn't take much to shoo them off."

"*Them?*"

"The band of vagrants who lurk in the burying ground. It's lucky you weren't robbed."

Shifting around, he put his feet on the floor. "It wasn't money that was sought."

"To answer your question, I'm Hannah Wilcox. And you—"

"Adam Webster."

"From Sesqua Valley." She laughed huskily at the look of astonishment on his startled face. "This fell out of your pocket as I was carrying you across the road." She held to him the red diary.

"Ah, yes. Thanks."

"I recognized it as Richard's. Is he here with you?"

"Sorry, no. He's dead."

It was she who then looked startled. "Oh, my. But he was so young and rugged."

"Physically, yes, quite vigorous. Emotionally, another tale. He grew morose over his mother's sudden death."

"You mean he took his life?" Sorrowfully, Adam shrugged. "Oh, how sad."

She fingered the periapt that hung from a chain around her neck. Without thinking, Adam reached out to touch the small green charm. "Not as ferocious as its bronze ancestor in the cemetery; but impressive, all the same."

"Mother fashioned it before her death, copying it from the 'ancestor' you saw tonight."

"It represents the face-eating cult of Ancient Leng."

She smiled quizzically. "How the hell do you know that?"

"From an old book."

"A book of legend?"

"Of sorts. Of course, there are numerous myths concerning face-eating cults that are supposedly scattered around the world. But why the face?"

"It houses the brain, which is rooted to one's soul." Miss Wilcox took hold of Adam's hand and touched it to her cheek. She smiled coyly. "Plus it's so deliciously tender, don't you find?" He forced laughter, which hurt his head. Moaning, he leaned back and pretended to shut his eyes, keeping them slightly open so that he could subtly study her blemished eye. He could not ascertain if the pale milky orb had been damaged in violence or was the product of birth defect. The sight of it was certainly disconcerting.

Opening his eyes, he stretched and stood. "How did you meet Richard?" he asked as he looked around the room.

"I saw him when he was sitting on that slab in the boneyard and writing in his little book. He looked magnificent and I wanted to do him." Turning, he gave her a questioning look. "I sculpt." Rising to join him, she reached toward a bookshelf and took from it a manila envelope, from which she pulled some photographs. "He was impressive, wasn't he? Such a body, such an aura of strength. I wanted him to stay and pose in the flesh, but he was anxious to leave for Boston, so I took these." She handed him the photos. One was a portrait shot of Richard's massive head; the other was of the young man's full figure, fully nude. Adam studied the portrait, remembering the gleam of Richard's green eyes, the steady breathing that issued through wide nostrils, the taste of generous lips.

A thought came to him. "Say, did you create any of those statues in the graveyard?"

"No, those are all before my time. My grandfather made most of the newer ones after moving to Arkham in 1929. Some of them are really old, as perhaps you noticed. The burying ground seems older than time, especially at night. Hasn't been a burial there for at least a century, except for one clandestine affair. Has a bit of a history, that place. Decades ago some foolhardy young fellows got it in their minds that there was valuable antique loot buried there, among the slumbering dead. There was vandalism. Grandfather Henry was very fond of that old boneyard, so he sculpted some of those stony sentinels and hired laborers to help place them among the tombstones. It was too arduous an expenditure for him, and his heart suffered. I was very young when he passed over. Mother and I buried him in there, illicitly, one moonless night, and we made one new statue to serve as his nameless marker."

"And the behemoth of bronze?"

"Now that's interesting, because supposedly it's always been there, and seems to have inspired the original town folk to have chosen that site for burial, strange as that may seem. Now if that's true, who built it? It's not like anything that I've found in local aboriginal totem art. Some say it's the work of weird cults that have been in Arkham forever. Obviously, it was built by people who knew of Leng and its infamous sect. Queer thing is, there are tales told of faceless corpses being found near the statue." She ceased her babble when Adam once more brought his hand to his head. "How's your head?"

"I'll survive. So, your mother made that amulet for you."

She grinned, wondering at his obvious though suppressed enthusiasm for this talk of legend. "Yes. She had heard stories from Grandfather. He was full of tales. Had a great library of queer old books, most of which he gave to Miskatonic in his last days. They even have one of his statuettes in their University library, some Daemon of the Ocean or some such thing."

"Your sculpture of Richard—did you complete it?"

"It's just a bust, but life-size. I keep it in Grandfather's attic study. Come on." She led the way down a dimly lit hallway, past a doorway at which Richard stopped. "That's Grandfather's library, what's left of it. As I said, most of the really interesting books are now at Miskatonic; but I managed to hold on to a few, and we can look over them later if you like. Come, Adam—Richard Lund awaits you." They climbed a narrow stairway, past vague faces that grimaced from oval portraits. He quickly noticed one singular photograph, of an older woman whose facial structure was similar to Hannah's. The dark hair was worn much longer, but the blemished eye was identical. Finally, they reached the attic, and she switched on an overhead bulb. The ceiling was low, almost touching his head. He saw the row of art books and the various macabre figurines; but it was the bust on a low and sturdy table that took his breath away, and his heart ached as he looked at it. She had caught his nigh-departed friend to near perfection. There were the sad, dreamy eyes that had in life been of dark green hue; and there was the unruly hair, worn in imitation of Oscar Wilde at the time of the poet's tour of America. And there—the wide sardonic mouth. Adam knelt before the table and touched the face of rock.

She moved close behind him. "I'll leave you with your memories. You'll find me in the library, Adam." He was surprised when she reached out and took his hand, and slightly unnerved as she brought it to her lips. The gentle kiss was a prolonged thing. Was she smelling him, tasting him? He pulled his hand away, and she departed. Raising his hand to feeble light, he saw the moisture of her kiss upon his flesh. He brought the hand to his mouth and licked, and then he touched his hand to Richard's rigid hair. Reaching into a pocket, he produced

Richard's diary, through which he flipped until coming on a sonnet
scratched in nearly illegible handwriting.

"The midnight constellation calls my face
  As I star-gaze into eternity
  Where cosmic vision promises to place
  This timeworn visage far from misery.
  Far from misery I ache to soar;
  Far from form, this sheath of mortal mud;
  Far from face, this visage I abhor,
  This countenance of flesh and bone and blood.
  This countenance of flesh and blood and bone
  That howls into the dreadful cosmic place
  Would laugh between the frigid stars alone,
  Would weep between the dying suns of space.
  But cosmic boon is all too far away.
  Among terrestrial worms I pace my play."

Adam closed the diary and leaned backward, as if to stretch away
sorrow. He listened to the sound of rising wind at a nearby window, to
the sound of tinkling chimes. He turned to see the slender glass prisms
that swung from slim pale wires. He knew what house it was he occupied. Crawling on hands and knees, he went to the window and saw
the moonlit burying ground, the stony sentinels, the bulk of a gigantic
winged hound. He noticed the small white figure that struggled toward
the knoll where he had met with violence. The childish being dragged a
shapeless burden toward the opening in the knoll. It stopped and
gazed upward, to him. Adam stared at the small pale face as clouds obscured moonlight and cast the place into momentary darkness. When
again the rays of dead refracted light illumed the forlorn place, no figure moved among its markers

III.

The ambience of the spacious library was pleasant, a climate of mellow
light that flickered from the scented candles set here and there. A child
of Sesqua Valley, Adam did not require too much illumination with

which to read over the various titles that slanted on their shelves. He stopped at one group of books and pulled out a moldy tome.

"Ah," said Hannah as she saw which book he was examining, "that's one that didn't make it to Miskatonic. Unfortunately, I can't read French."

Adam sat next to her on the sofa and thumbed through the copy of the *Livre d'Eibon*. "It's very rare. We have a Latin text that Simon found in Prague some decades ago."

"Who?"

"Simon Gregory Williams, the self-appointed mage of Sesqua Valley. He would have enjoyed knowing your grandfather, and he would love to own this. I suppose you wouldn't sell it? No, I didn't think so, it being a family heirloom, so to speak. I'm very curious about this diagram drawn in faded ink on the flyleaf. Your grandsire's work? It's fascinating. I've seen its like before, or something very similar, on a parchment in the tower room. Simon would relish a look at this."

"What's the tower room?"

"A room in an antediluvian edifice that stands in Sesqua's woodland. It houses Simon's extensive library of misremembered lore." It was bold of him to speak so bluntly of the valley to an outsider; but Adam sensed that he had found this place and this woman for a specific reason. Too, he was excited about the book, which cast a spell over him and made his mouth to babble. It is the nature of a child from Sesqua Valley to be enthralled by such a thing.

"Richard spoke of this curious valley of yours. Some of what he said seemed quite outlandish. He thought that grandfather and mother would have enjoyed seeing it because of their interest in weird cults and such. The more I hear you speak of it, the more I itch to see the place myself. Richard said something very odd, that I would feel at home in Sesqua Valley because I seemed to him as 'wanton' as the valley itself." She laughed heartily.

"That's so like him, poor dramatic lad. But, yes, he was correct. I can sense your unruly nature, a delicious wildness. That explains some of Richard's liking you, for he too was undisciplined. And Sesqua Valley—yes, it is a place of special mischievousness."

"Special?"

"Well, to those of us who are born of its shadow—and to the outsiders who are summoned to it, those chosen few."

"Summoned?"

"Called by dreaming," said his hypnotic voice. "Called by whispering wind, by the buried pulse of Sesqua's hunger." His silver eyes darkened, and beneath the bewitching music of his voice she seemed to hear another sound, of some thing that called her soul. "There are sensitive folk, Hannah, who are outsiders no matter where they dwell. They are the creatures, Hannah, who dream the dark dreams and sing the secret songs. Oh, Hannah, they are the poets of ecstatic madness who can hear beyond the rim of reason. How Sesqua Valley hungers for their lunacy and vision. The valley longs to taste them, Hannah, to claim them with her soil."

She tried to smile. "It sounds crazy, the way you tell it." Her voice was laced with queer emotion. She watched his eyes grow darker still, those metallic optics that held her in their spell. She could not move as he reached for her with his free hand and with it closed her eyes.

The heavy olden book was snatched from him and battered violently against his face. Adam raised his hand protectively, and his blurry vision saw the small pale face that hissed at him. Snarling, he arose and staggered after the imp who flew from the room and out of the house. Groggily, Hannah pushed out of her trance and struggled to her feet. She ran to the door and saw the Sesquan race across the road, into the burying ground. She followed, aware of the other things that watched, the bulky shapes that hunched and hid, creatures pent in darkness. Hannah entered the burying ground and saw the fellow stop beneath a tree. She saw the pale thing that dropped from that tree and pushed the man to the ground, and she hissed with pleasure as the small one found a chunk of broken tombstone with which to bash the fellow's skull. Reaching them, Hannah knelt next to her sister and watched the fluid that secreted from the young man's wound, the sap that spilled into their waiting hands. She saw the weird misty tendrils that accompanied the liquid flow.

"Ooh, his taste!" cried the child after dipping her mouth into cupped hands.

The sisters supped. Once more, Hannah felt the occult presence of unseen things. "Are *they* satisfied?"

"They ne'er are. Brought 'em some dead feed early on, but they twitch for more. What was this un doing to ye in the library? Ye looked all whacked out."

"Not sure." Clouds moved in the dark sky and began to obscure moonlight. "Don't matter." She brought the liquid in her hands to her face and washed it over her features; and then she bent to join with her sister in the eating of Adam's face.

IV.

After a passage of weeks, during which she had carefully instructed her sibling, Hannah departed from her home in Arkham. The journey was long, but when at last she stepped from the train that had transported her to Sesqua Valley, she knew that she had been right to follow instinct. The valley was a place of breathtaking beauty. She was especially captivated by the sight of the titanic twin-peaked mountain of white stone. And the air! To suck it deeply in was to be reminded of the scent and taste of Adam Webster's flesh. She smiled at the memory of his death, of how they had dragged his corpse to the cavity in earth and left it there to be finished by the things that dwelt in darkness beneath the ground.

After two days, she had discovered the tower in the woods, had entered its portal and climbed its winding steps. The large round room contained a treasure trove of lore, and she spent one full day devouring tome and folio and codex. Darkness came to Sesqua Valley, and at last she stretched and rose to depart. She noticed the small stand, and the book that sat upon it. Going to it, she saw that it was familiar. Picking it up, she turned the pages filled with French script; and at last she turned to the flyleaf, on which her grandfather had sketched an esoteric design. From some place atop Mount Selta, a creature bayed to moonlight. Looking out a small aperture in the wall, she saw the pale willow tree and the figure that stood beside it, watching her. Returning the book to its stand, she stalked down the winding steps, past the threshold and into night.

He smiled at her from his place beneath the white willow. She moved toward him, as underneath her feet there came the subtle pounding of the valley's supernatural pulse. "Ah, Hannah Wilcox, we meet again. And, oh, how your hunger aches within you. Did you come to my homeland especially to feed? Did your feasting of my flesh wet appetite? Very well. Come into my arms. Partake."

She answered the lure of his voice, his scent, his alchemical eyes. Consumed with unholy appetite, she licked his face and then bit into it, tearing flesh. This time there was no flow of dark liquid; there was only a flow of thick mauve mist that stitched into the violated skin and wove it whole. Hunger grew more bestial, and she raised her claws quickly; but her attack was thwarted by the willow vines that wound around her wrists and held her fast. Beneath her stance the floor of earth began to move, to divide, to pull her down. Adam lay upon the ground, grinning, pleased with her panic.

"Help me," she begged.

"Ah, Hannah Wilcox, this is beyond my control. You have fed upon the shadow spawn of this enchanted vale, a violation that must be reckoned with. But don't look so distressed—it's such a delicious fate."

She was deep inside the earth. Furiously, she screamed, but his large hand pressed heavily against her mouth and stopped the noise. He turned onto his stomach, his face now level with her own; and overwhelmed with ravenous temptation, he pressed his face to hers and tongued the blemished eye. Its taste made him moan; and turning so as to lay on his back and face dark welkin, he smiled and shut his eyes as she was enveloped by the devouring loam.

Born in Strange Shadow

Richard Lund was not native to Sesqua Valley, and yet I had always felt a close kinship with him. I liked his clumsy bulk, his large rugged hands with their thick yellow nails. I enjoyed listening as he uttered his poetry in his deep sepulchral voice. I loved the spacious face from which that poetry was spoken, that face with its thick lips and flat nose. Above all, I was seduced by his eyes, those dark green globes that caught candlelight and moonglow. Richard had come to the valley as a child, from Boston, with his wild unruly mother. She had been a great beauty, had posed for a number of scandalous paintings and photographs by the women and men who were her lovers. Truly bohemian, she had experimented with every kind of narcotic and alcohol that had been brought before her by her tribe of anarchists, the appetite for which took her over, body and soul, as inescapable addiction. Her relationship with her oft-neglected son was sad and peculiar, to the point where Richard felt an abandoned child, an image that frequently found expression in his poetry. I quote a typical example, a selection from his long poem, "The Changeling":

> "For I was in strange shadow born and bred,
> Squeezed from maternity of chilly pitch,
> And moonlight was the milk on which I fed;
> And I, the issue of a nameless bitch,
> Was hurled away from my maternal place—
> Unknown, unwanted, useless, full of brine

That seeped from out mine eyes onto my face.
I stagger in a world not mine."

I had met his mother often and pitied her. She was an absolute grotesque, her once-proud beauty now dissolved into a ruined package of withered flesh. It was horrifying to see her suddenly take hold of her massive son, press her emaciated face to his flesh and deeply sniff him, or move her tongue along his flesh. At such times Richard would look at me with an expression of such misery that it was almost impossible not to weep. He never pushed her from him.

His need to escape, if only temporary, was clear; and when he turned twenty-one, he decided to leave Sesqua Valley to visit his long-forsaken homeland. He told me of this plan with joy twinkling in his eyes; and then those eyes turned somber. "Adam, you must manage my mother while I'm away."

"I will do all I can," I promised. Thus I spent two weeks in their two-story house, sleeping in Richard's small room, in which I found notebooks filled with disturbing sketches and snatches of abandoned verse. I cooked for and cleaned after his dam, and when she called me by his name I would answer; and when she held me I did not push her away. And when, one windless night, she entered into his room and joined me in Richard's bed, I embraced her. The morning after that was when I found her sprawled on the sofa, dead, a variety of pills next to a bottle of spilled absinthe on the table beside the sofa. With wretched misery, I wrote to an address that Richard had given me.

We do not hold funeral services when outsiders to the valley pass away. The dead are taken to the mass of land in which the dead are planted, sans ceremony. Richard, however, refused to follow custom. Having had the corpse embalmed in a neighboring town, he brought it to their home and kept the coffin in an unfinished cellar room. He then went into seclusion. Even I was kept at bay; but I would not be so ignored, and after one week I made bold enough to pound on the front door and yell his name. Finally, I heard the fall of muffled foot-steps, and then the door opened. Richard, shirtless, a candlestick in hand, gazed at me in silence. I was horrified at his alteration. He was beginning to resemble his deranged mother. He was thin and haggard, depleted of the vital strength that I had found alluring. My horror must have been obvious, for he smiled and then coughed laughter. The smell of absinthe mingled with bad breath.

"Let me see your arms," I demanded as I rushed into his abode. "And why is it so dark in here?"

"Adam Webster, how like a mother you sound."

I grabbed his arm and examined it angrily. "It's obscene enough that she brought that city filth into these sacred confines, but that you . . ."

He stopped my mouth with a kiss, and then held out his other arm. "What, did you think I needed her stimulates? Don't be absurd." Freeing himself from my hold, he wandered into the living room.

"You've been imbibing," I lectured, following him.

"Yes, I made a solitary toast to Wilde's memory. Come, have a little yourself. No? As you like. Then sit with me on the sofa and we'll pose as the absinthe drinker and his sober wife. Do you know the painting by Degas? As for the darkness, you know that I suffer from an ailment that makes bright lights a torment on mine eyes. Of late the condition has escalated. Thus is darkness my domain. Do sit, Adam."

I remained standing. Richard poured some green liqueur into a glass and sadly drank. "You look tired."

"Yes. Quite, quite so."

"We need to talk about . . . arrangements. You cannot keep her down there, she requires proper burial."

He sneered. "There was nothing 'proper' about her when she lived. Why should it be otherwise in death? We'll not discuss it."

"Oh, but we will . . ."

Suddenly snarling, he hurled the glass at me. "I said *enough!*" The glass smashed against the fireplace behind where I stood and shattered. Rising, he rushed at me and wrapped his hand around my throat. "I don't need to be lectured by you, child of valley shadow. Your kind knows nothing of mothers."

"Do let go, you brute."

Roughly, he pushed me from him, and I had to hold onto the mantelpiece to keep from falling. "No more about my mother. She was an outsider and is no concern of yours. I'll bury her when I've a mind to do so. I am not now in the mood."

Peevishly, I turned my back to him and began to brush shards of broken glass off the mantel. As I did so, I noticed for the first time the picture that was hanging above the hearth. I had not seen it before. I raised my hand so as to brush away an accumulation of cobwebs from one corner of the frame. Richard's low voice filled the room.

"I found it in an old shop in Boston, a neglected place along a narrow cobblestone alley. A homey place, so it was. The charming proprietor was a quaint gentlewoman in her twilight years. She seemed as dusty and faded as so many of the objects in her shop. She couldn't remember how the painting came into her possession. There's no signature that we could discern, although we found a title on the back— 'Gallows Hill.' I gave her a little money for it. I gaze at it continually. It haunts me."

I leaned nearer to the painted surface. Its colors were very dim, perhaps from age, but I sensed that it was due rather to artistic intent. The scene was a lonely hill. A semicircle of baying creatures paid tribute to a corpse that hanged from a sinister gallows. Sensing Richard behind me, I did not move when he placed a heavy hand on my shoulder.

"I love the subtle use of color. See how the moonlight lingers just over the crouching beasts, as if afraid to get too near? The shadow of night blends with those powerful daemonic limbs, seeming to become one with their flesh. Do you see how the dark sky contains just a hint of purple, a delicate bruise of color to distinguish it from darker shadow? And most marvelous of all, observe how the moonlight is reflected in the staring eyes of the dead hag, those wide green eyes. See, too, how a darker hue of emerald is caught in the eyes of her hunkering compatriots. Rather superb, eh?"

I stared at the image of the woman's dead face as Richard leaned closer. I felt his warm breath on my neck. "Do you see how her rigid visage subtly resembles those baying physiognomies beneath her? Wonderful."

But I could not listen, for my mind was whirling with what I saw and numbly recognized. I turned my startled face to the creature at my side.

"Yes, dear boy," he said. "Odd, isn't it? That face, that stiff dead canine countenance encased in a shaft of yellow moonlight. I noticed it straight off, and thus I had to buy the painting. Why, that dead hag resembles me more than my own dam!"

II.

He led me, gothic candlestick in hand, to the cellar. We entered the squalid room that had been transformed into memorial chamber. Richard smoothed the wood of his mother's small coffin. He slowly opened the lid. A variety of unpleasant odors assailed my senses. Richard inhaled the engulfing foetor as if it were some succulent bouquet. "There she be, finally at peace. Almost as fresh as when she lived, eh?" Ghoulishly, he smiled.

"Richard . . ."

"Hush, child. Look upon her husk of death. I've lived with her all my numbered years, and yet she looks to me like some stranger. Did we actually know each other? Betimes, especially when drunk, she would penetrate me with intoxicated eyes and ask, *Who are you?* I ask that very question. From what did I issue? Her loins? Did she birth me, or find me in some shadowed place? Why have I always felt so miserably alone? So alien?"

I reached for him. "Darling . . ."

He took my hand and touched it to his face, beneath the wide green eyes. "Hush, dear child. We all have loneliness and sorrow." Releasing me, he went to the coffin and reached in. He held his mother's hand and brought it to his flat nostrils. Deeply, he sniffed. "I don't smell like her, don't look like her." Pressing lips to her chilly hand, he kept them there for many moments. "I don't taste like her."

I tried to take his hand away. With savage fury, he shoved me from him, with such force that I knocked against a table and crashed with it to the floor. Wickedly, he smiled. I saw his dark tongue lick the dead skin, saw the crooked teeth nibble a thin slice of flesh that tore from the corpse's hand. I had never seen within his eyes such rapacious frenzy.

"I wish to spend some private time with my mother."

I slithered on the floor in outraged anguish, clawing the cement until my fingers were raw. Sucking in the foam that coated my mouth, I pushed myself to my feet and climbed the worn wooden steps out of the cellar. I staggered out of doors and cursed the refulgent moon. The haunted woodland called me, and I crept into it. I found the place of pale willows and danced within the glade around the weird figure that nestled there, the thing that raised it hands to dark heaven. I raised my hands as well and yelled curses to whatever gods might hear me. Pulling tough vines from a willow tree, I wove the tendrils into a crown and then placed the garland haphazardly on my head. Like a lunatic fool, I danced in moonlight, until I fell to the ground, exhausted.

The garland had loosened and slipped around my neck. When I tried to pull it free, the tough vines wound tight around my throat, reminding me of his hand that had so forcefully choked me. From some place atop Mount Selta, a beast howled to lunar light. I rose and walked to his house, timidly tiptoeing into the living room, which was empty of inhabitant. I saw the weird painting that rested on the sofa, went to it and picked it up. The dead hag's face was moist where he had kissed it. Again, from the twin-peaked mountain, I heard the wailing beast. The noise was a signal that something untoward had happened in the valley. Silently, I climbed down the weathered steps into the cellar. The coffin lid had been lowered. A song of wind began to moan at the trapdoor that led outside; going to it, I pushed it open and widened my jaws so that the banshee wind could wail within me. With a voice like storm, I cried his name.

I saw the tall oak in their backyard and its platform that Richard had built when very young, as a place where he could escape. From one of the tree's study branches hung a length of rope whose burden moved in violent wind. I approached that swaying figure and knelt beneath it, as leaves and other debris were tossed at me by the storm. His dark green eyes were open, their dead surface reflecting the merciless light of moon. I raised my silver eyes to that globe of lifeless dust and bayed in desolation.

An Imp of Aether

for August William Derleth

I.

When Jacob Wirth returned to Sesqua Valley I barely recognized him. He seemed much altered, older than when he had departed six months gone. His epicene face, more womanly that I remembered, gazed at me with brilliant flamelike eyes. Those eyes alone were familiar, yet even they contained an alien alchemy; they seemed the eyes of one who had beheld and remembered weird wisdom. Jacob stepped from the train in a cloud of steam, his tall frame elegantly draped in a flowing coat. His face smiled beneath a wide-rimmed hat, beneath which he had hidden his long dark hair. Tightening a light scarf that was wound around his long throat, he held to me his welcoming hands.

"My dear Adam. Ah, home at last. But what a time you've suffered! Your melodramatic letters moved me to tears. I did not admire Richard Lund's poetry, the little of it that you've shown me; but why the morbid boy should take his life is beyond conjecture. Perhaps it is the price of romantic entanglement with you." He chuckled as I scowled.

"Let's get your luggage to the cab, dear. You look tired, and I'm certain you want to get home."

"Tut. I overflow with energy." The day was very hot, and I could not help but notice how queerly he kept looking at the sun. "How it burns in cosmic vacuity," he mumbled, "like some bubbling throne of

Azathoth. What does the *Cultes des Goules* say of the sun, that it is but a spark compared to the supernal chaos of the Daemon Sultan? Yet what an inferno it feels upon one's eyes."

"I'm surprised you know the heretic ravings of the Comte d'Erlette. Rumor has it that he was a secret papist, despite his over-exaggerated anti-Catholic zeal. He was little more than a self-indulgent ghoul. His theories concerning the Old Ones have long been exploded by serious scholars."

But Jacob was not listening to me as he kept staring at the sun. I looked up at the disc of yellow fire for an instant, but its glare so hurt my eyes that I quickly turned away. Jacob chuckled softly. "No, your silver eyes cannot gaze for long upon its volcanic splendor, my child of valley shadow. That sphere of living combustion has blazed for a billion years. We live by its light—we mortals, I mean. Beyond it, oh, there are other spheres of fire, strange alien globes dominated by solar deities."

I looked at him and laughed. "How curiously you speak, my chuck." In answer he kissed my cheek, and then we linked arms as a pretty boy carried his bags to our waiting taxi. I was a bit annoyed when, after we had arrived at his spacious house, he rushed out of the car and into his abode, leaving me to pay the fare and handle his luggage. I found him in his spacious library, devouring the pages of some ancient tome. Setting his bags on the floor I sat in on a wooden chair and waited patiently. He had thrown open all the shades of the many windows, which otherwise he would never allow because of the condition of so much in his athenaeum. I watched him, studying his face, trying to understand its subtle alteration. He had yet to remove his hat, which was curious, for his coat had been thrown off and dropped to the floor.

"I've told you that my maternal ancestors are Dutch Jews," he suddenly spoke. "I've long been fascinated with Dutch culture. A queer people, with queer elder secrets." Rushing to one of his bags, he unzipped it and took from it a book; and opening the book he took from where it had rested between the leaves a piece of yellow parchment. Back he hurried to the book he had been studying, seeming to compare its text to that of the parchment in his hand. I could contain my curiosity no longer, pushed out my chair and stalked to him, snatching the parchment from his fingers. How mischievous was his smile.

"You know I cannot read this," I admitted.

"No, poor child, language was never your *forte*. That's the province of Simon Gregory Williams." Taking the parchment from me, he held it to sunlight and examined it anew. "I found this in a forgotten hillside tomb, a place that has slept undisturbed for centuries beneath a Holland hill. Curious, the sacred things buried in hillsides. On thinks of Cumorah or Qumran. Within this neglected—shunned?—sepulcher I found buried a woman of delectable legend. From certain papyri entombed with her I discovered her succulent history. She was known as the 'fire hag,' and her legend is whispered still. Those who crossed her met with a fiery demise. One stupid fanatic condemned her to the stake. Oh, how the embers devoured her bonds and danced into the frothing crowd, igniting them. They left her alone after that."

He sat into a chair and gazed lovingly at the parchment, and then he turned to stare once more at sunlight. His hushed voice came again, little more than whisper. "The language is in a forgotten dialect, and it took me forever to find the woman who helped to decipher it, an Italian whore whom the locals call 'la strega,' with good cause. We thought at first that it was some kind of poem or unholy psalm; but with further study we discovered it to be a prayer to something called Cthugha, supposedly a fire elemental. You know the idiotic notion that the Great Old Ones represent terrestrial elements, as if these cosmic creatures could be molded by corporeal law. Bah! However, in this case, there seems to be some sustenance. I journeyed to Miskatonic on returning to the States and found an explanatory tome in its special library. But it was not really required, after all. I had merely to wait for the dreams."

"Ah," I suspired.

"Ah, indeed. I beheld her marbled coffin, which had no lid. She was remarkably preserved. Seemed to be waiting, so she did; seemed almost to beckon. Her perfumed hair—how intoxicating! It seemed, her hair, to shine with ethereal radiance. I caressed it with my hand, watched it shimmer with light beneath a candle's puny blink. I bent to kiss it, and as I did so a thick strand came loose—a gift from the grinning ghoul."

"A fascinating dream," I responded.

"Dream, dear boy? Mmm. I saw my exit from the tomb, my walk to my rented room in Arkham, that old witch town. I spent the evening twining the bright dead hair into my own, and I fancied I could feel it weave into my strands and root seductively into my scalp. There came to me a series of peculiar memories, and I knew that I had somehow been conjoined with the hag, rooted soul to soul. I went to the mirror and saw the softening of my features. I saw . . ."

Dramatically, he removed at last his hat. Soft fragrance wafted from the thick dark hair that fell to his shoulders. I arose and went to him. I touched the length of pale yellow hair that seemed to oddly catch the light of sun. Lowering my face to it, so to sniff its weird aroma, I shouted as the strands moved so as to meet my face.

"Rather wonderful," Jacob sighed, "what a witch's hair will do." Turning from me, he peered at blinding sunlight.

II.

I spent most of the next day in the round tower wherein is collected the massive occult library of Simon Gregory Williams. Although I searched thoroughly, I found no reference to an Old One aligned to fire. At last I leaned against the brick wall and searched my dreams. Hazily, an image came to me, but of what I could not apprehend. It was dark and formless, like some ash-hued offspring of Shub-Niggurath. As I saw this thing in inner-mind, my senses seemed tainted with a smell of incineration. Perhaps some candle had extinguished itself. From a patch of darkness in the tower room, something drifted near me and oozed out of one of the slender openings in the wall that served as window. The patch of darkness subdivided into particles of melting residue that vanished when it touched the wooden floor. I sat where I was, watching the place where the stuff had deliquesced, for untold moments; and then I heard the footfalls that climbed the winding steps that led to the tower room.

"Adam Webster, I thought I might find you here. And what a strange expression sits upon your charming face. Come, link your arm with mine. I've been too long away, I want your company tonight. Let us wander the woodland of this enchanted vale."

I let him led me from the room and down the small stone steps. "We've missed you, Jacob."

"We? Oh, you refer to Sesqua Valley—that prodigious entity. I took a portion of it with me, in my dreaming. No matter how far I wandered, the valley had its influence over mind and body. Yes, this frame of flesh. I could feel the valley's rhythm coursing through my veins and pump my human heart. It's interesting, how we outsiders become adopted into your obscure pack. We discover Sesqua Valley— by chance? We experience its wonders and we are seduced by its shadow. Of course we have had a penchant for the esoteric realm, which acts as part of our seduction. We come; we smell the sweet cloying air that slips between our lips, that sinks into our souls." He stopped our movement and kissed my mouth. "We are seduced by the spawn of mauve shadow, you few creatures with sepia skin and silver eyes. You lovely beasts." He kissed me again, passionately. His hot mortal mouth pressed against my ear. "But just as we are bewitched, we are disturbed. In time one of you will go away forever. If we are among those especially confided in, we are told that the vanished one has 'returned unto shadow.'"

Roughly, he pushed me from him and frowned at the moonlight that silvered the tops of trees. "Pah, such a dead light. So pallid, lacking luster. Yes, it makes one dwell on death. Do any of we outsiders expire by 'natural' means, Adam Webster? I cannot think of one. We are somehow—consumed—in water or in earth. Or we are swallowed by shadow. Most peculiar. As peculiar as the knowing smile that curves your lips, dear boy. But—behold!—my smile is just as knowing; because I will *not* be consumed by this preternatural vale, delicious an experience as that might be. This valley is your temple and your god; but there are other gods, who also call in dream."

"You speak riddles, Jacob Wirth."

"A fascinating sphinx am I." I saw him shiver at the growing cold, wrapped my arms around him and led him homeward. We made love in a pool of moonlight that stained the library floor, and as I lay beneath him his hair wound into my own, caressingly. Wakefulness was ushered by the whispering of a husky voice, and I smiled to hear Jacob speaking in a Dutch dialect. I pushed his hair away so as to put my ear nearer his lisping lips. His mouth was still, unmoving. Disturbed breathing was all that issued from it. Yet still I heard the whispered language, from a corner in the spacious room. A potent fragrance wafted toward us from where darkness sibilated. A patch of churning murkiness detached from other blackness and drifted to us. It spread its formlessness above where we lay, and I pressed my arms protectively around my friend. I felt the thing's hot scented effluvium on my face as it turned to me its cauterizing eyes. Pale streams, like strands of spectral hair, floated eerily to Jacob and touched his amber tress. I could not turn my Sesquan eyes from the burning yellow eyes until my own eyes felt on fire and began to blur.

Jacob moved and moaned, pushing off me and writhing on his back. He sighed, in ecstasy, an alien name. My clutching fingers found him, pulled him to me; my mouth touched the salty fabric of his flesh. His mouth touched mine and spoke, so seductively, the weird name, and in answer came the whispering of a thing my blindness kept from sight. Again, he sounded the daemonic name. Seduced, I moved my lips in imitation of his talk. Sensation poured like lava into my bubbling brain, and then came darkness absolute.

III.

I awakened, in his bedroom, consumed by fever. Jacob bathed my face with cool wet cloth. "You'll be fine," he reassured. "Do be still, Adam. It came for me, to teach me the way to cosmic domicile."

"It was *she!*" I wailed. "I knew her scent from your length of haunted hair. It was an essence of the hag!" I noticed the dark bruise on his throat, and touched its ashy substance. Jacob pushed my hand away.

"No, lad. It was the fire vampire, an essence of the Old One that burns in Fomalhaut. You looked too long, too deeply, into its ember eyes. You cool silver orbs are slightly scarred, so potent was your engagement with the valet of Cthugha. *Do* stop twitching!"

I rubbed my eyes and thought I saw an alteration on his face, imagined that his features were more feminine. "What did you mean, it's come to take you otherwhere? I won't let you go without a fight. You belong here, with us."

He shook his head. "Not so. I leave—some *portion* of me anyway—to seal the covenant. I will sit in rapture beside the blistering throne. The rapture will flame in me forever!" He chanted words that were a mixture of Dutch and elder language. His yellow eyes penetrated me with fiery beams. With some new possession of power, he enchanted me toward slumber. When again I awoke, I was alone. A heady redolence issued from some place below the room in which I had slept. It was the scent of that enchanted hair—tenfold. I kicked damp bedclothes from me and staggered to my feet. Like one lost in cataclysmic nightmare I stumbled down the stairs and into the library. Jacob lay on the floor, yellow parchment in his hand.

The thing, dark and formless, hovered above him. It raised its smoky head to me and hissed. I could not help but peer into its voracious eyes. Turning its attention to Jacob, it spread like liquid smoke over his trembling frame. He pushed the yellow parchment into the things insubstantial face and cried an invocation in antique Dutch tongue. His dark hair began to move as if in water. I watched the slim strand of yellow hair that snaked to his lips, which kissed it.

I watched, as the parchment that had been thrust into the daemon's head turned charcoal, as did the hand that held it. I watched in horror as that hand blackened and turned to ash. Oh, how his flesh crumbled. Ah, the hot burning wind that came from nowhere, that encircled Jacob and the thing to which he was yoked. A cyclone of ash churned toward the ceiling, and within its storm I could see the lustrous face of an ancient woman. Haughtily, she smiled. I watched the poisoned lips pucker and exhale. A flake of ash flew from out the tempest, drifted to me and sailed into my heaving mouth.

The storm grew tempestuous, and then it died. Simply that. I fell, exhausted, to the floor. I wanted to call his name, as if to summon him back from wherever it was that had swallowed him; but my tongue would not work. For on that fleshy organ I could taste the thing that had sailed into my mouth, that flake of ash that tasted of my friend's beloved flesh.

The Horror on Tempest Hill

in memory of Adam Niswander

I. The Shadow on the Chimney

We drove through the quaint center of Sesqua Town but did not stop, and I smiled, charmed, at the rustic nature of the habitations. All the buildings looked incredibly old, and one or two so slanted in the sunlight that one fancied they were but peripheral inhabitants of mortal time and space and that soon they would fall into some unknown pocket of the past. There was a sharp sense of bygone eras in this enchanted vale, and the thing that we journeyed to was, by all accounts, a spectacular symbol of elder time. My fellow at the wheel continued to chauffeur us toward the titanic twin-peaked mountain as the road we were on began to rise and enter a region of rich woodland. Our destination was a tall, domed hill directly below the white mountain, and the hoary mansion atop that hill. My love of the grotesque and terrible mysteries of the world had resulted in this newest of many quests for strange horrors in literature and life. I had found, in an odd private journal, mention of Sesqua Valley and its peculiar ancient mansion, and of the nefarious legend surrounding that construction. What increased my fascination was the enigmatic nature of this unheard-of region, a place that no one in my circles seemed to know about. It was only by chance that I met Edwin Pratt, an obscure and elderly painter who had connections to an occult group I used to frequent. Visiting him in his home in Providence, Rhode Island, I found myself beguiled by a painting in his drawing room. He caught me staring at it and nodded his head.

"Captivating, isn't she? I call the piece 'Sesqua Mountain,' as I can't quite remember the mount's actual name. It's a strange thing about that valley—I know that I spent time there with a witch of my acquaintance, and I have some hazy recollection of fantastic adventures. I know it's located in the Northwest, in a region that resembles a primeval forest. And yet it's like trying to recall a dream that is but a haze of impressions in the back of the mind, ephemeral and impossible to connect as concrete memory. One feels an allure about the valley, and yet the memory of it is also laced with a vague sense of . . . of intriguing danger. At times that sense of menace is so acute that one simply stops dwelling on it, stops trying to conjure it in reminiscence."

I went to the painting and raised a hand that almost touched the canvas. Praising his technique, I made comments on certain aspects of the terrain depicted, and thus I got him to talk more about the valley, offhandedly, guiding his replies so as to inform me of the area in the Northwest where the place could be located. Eerily, the more I gazed at the image of the mountain, and the more I got him to chat about his visit to the valley, the more concretely I seemed able to imagine the region myself. I could almost taste the fragrant air and feel the cool green shade upon my eyes. As my fancy played with these sensations, I felt as one who was being summoned, either by the mountain or by the valley over which is towered. Or both. I had spent a year in the Pacific Northwest and had a vague idea that Sesqua was located in the foothills of the Cascade Range. Once my two husky companions and I began to drive from Seattle toward the area where we imagined the valley was sequestered, I felt like one being supernaturally guided, a sensation that I had never before experienced in all my dealings with hauntings and macabre horrors.

We had been driving for over an hour along a busy freeway, passing woods and pastures and small towns, when I suddenly announced that we were to take the next exit. Mateo, who was driving, turned around to scowl at me but obeyed my instinct, and we found ourselves passing along a winding road that cut through thick woodland. And then the trees stopped as we began to descend into a valley, and for but a moment we were astounded by the magnificent beauty of our destination. The sun was low, about to set, and Sesqua Valley was bathed in a lovely amber light. My attention was riveted to the towering twin-peaked mountain, and then the woodland returned all around us, blocking our view as we continued our descent. I took the private journal that had first alerted me to Sesqua Valley's existence and carefully studied its description of the hill on which the haunted manse stood. "We must follow the main road through town toward the white mountain. Eventually we will find a road leading up an extremely high hill that is almost a mountain in itself, and at its apex we will find our target. Do you smell that?" I rolled down the window and pushed my head out of the car, opened my mouth and gulped the rushing air. It tasted very sweet, as if a person was burning some saccharine-scented incense. My first impulse was to try and expel the syrupy stuff from my lungs, its sweetness seemed so excessive; but the longer it floated within me, the more pleasant its sensation became, and I did not heed the others as they tried to coax me back into the vehicle. Quinn Archer finally pulled me back to my seat and placed his heavy arm around my shoulder as Mateo Crux, up front, guided us toward the high domed hill that rose near the base of the white mountain. I frowned at the sudden change of odor in the air and rolled up my window.

The shunned and deserted mansion was an outrageous sight. Reading the unknown gentleman's private journal had prepared me for something menacing, but I wasn't expecting the aura of the place to be so immediately fantastic. It looked as if it had been designed for sinister effect, a Cyclopean construction of immense proportions. The building's dark stones, of irregular size, contrasted sharply against the shimmering white rock of the mountain that rose directly beside it. I turned to look at the valley outspread below us, most of which was covered with woodland wild, although just beyond one particular grove of enormous trees there was an ugly spread of diseased land that was spotted with clumps of colorless grass and a number of black, twisted trees. I quickly turned my eyes away and regarded the mansion once again. My two muscular companions had already approached the wide double doors of the structure, and Archer pushed at one of them with his boot. There was no eerie creaking of rusty hinges, but I imagined that a charge of chilly air emerged from the pile, and I shivered with nervous anticipation. We entered a phantasmal chaos of dust, of thick cords of cobwebs, of the rotting carcasses of disused furniture. There was something else as well—something inexplicable. Although I was a connoisseur in horrors, I detected here an atmosphere of such foreboding as I had rarely experienced; indeed, never had the word "unearthly" defined so precisely anything previously experienced as it did the atmosphere now confronted.

My hearty companions had returned to the vehicle and brought from it a supply of bread, cheese, and wine. We had brought plenty of candles, as well as three kerosene lamps, but the mansion itself was littered with an abundance of stout candles composed of amber wax, and so we lit a number of them and enjoyed our repast in their mellow glow. Archer, who possessed an over-keen facility of smell, complained of their bitter odor, but we others could not detect it and chided him for his sensibility. I watched the coils of combined smoke rise from the little flames that burned steadily upon their wicks, coils that drifted into the upper darkness of the high-ceilinged hallway in which we gathered; and as I watched weariness overcame me, so that I decided it was time for us each to choose a room in which to spend the night. Picking up one of the kerosene lanterns and one plump candle, I crept through the hallway and stepped into the first-encountered room. It was an apartment that measured twenty feet square and contained a number of bookshelves, with some old titles still intact. Using my candle, I set my lantern alight, and with its more generous glow I examined the entered room. I liked the immense east window, which still contained panes, and discovered a comfortable leather bench that would do as impromptu bed. I set my candle on a low table and went to gaze out of the large window, and then turned to examine more of the room. Away from the window, at the opposite side of the chamber, was a magnificent Dutch fireplace with tiles embossed with simplistic images that I thought, at first, were religious; but the more I scrutinized their art in the dim light of my lamp, the more I discerned disquieting aspects in what was represented. I would have to investigate those tiles more specifically in the morning light.

Rummaging into my pack, I retrieved the private journal that had been the nucleus of my coming to Sesqua Valley and opened to an oft-read passage:

"Never—never have I dwelt in a more lonesome place than this accursed mansion, this cesspit of disease and death. The silence has been absolute, except for the two times I have called out to the valley with psychical calling. The earth shuddered, and the white mountain cried in response. Having perused the books on the shelves of this room, I have shuddered too. The clan of devils who built this nauseous pile of stone was among the earliest to settle in this valley, and I have little doubt that it was their treacherous trafficking with black magick that awakened shadow's brood. What else could have caught the peculiar attention of shadow's first-born beast and lured him from that realm of mist and gloom? They won't come here, the shadow children; for this mansion sits too near the accursed mountain, from which they keep apace. The beast has told me that he never dreams, and I am envious of that. Would that I could discard the dreams that have tormented me in this place, my dreams of squalid ancestry, in which I quaver to stretch my jaws and gnaw upon a human face, to sup as fiend and thus acquire the intelligence and torments of that which is my repast. I have come to pluck down these stones, to dismantle this refuse of lunatic sorcery. My fear is that it is I myself that will be the first to experience disassembly."

I thought that I could detect a distant rumbling, a suggestion of sound that was not repeated. My eyes had grown heavy, and so I extinguished the light and stretched my limbs on the long leather bench. If I dreamed, I dreamed of darkness. I was startled into wakefulness by a flash of brightness that was followed by low rumbling in the sky. Heavy rainfall came toward the mansion like some wave of liquid sound. I had left the candle lit on the table some feet from me, and it had burned down to almost nothing, its diminutive illumination quite useless; yet there was light enough for me to notice the silhouette that blackened the brickwork of the chimney just above the fireplace, an outline that I thought was not a stain of age on the ancient brickwork. A second lightning bolt electrified the outside air and sharpened the outline of the creature that stood before the hearth, a being oddly attired in clothes from some past decade, its dome covered with a large slouching hat that hid the topmost portion of the face. Frail candlelight sputtered toward extinction and all was darkness again—there was naught but the sound of storm and the shadow on the chimney, the shadow with silver eyes.

II. A Passer in the Storm

I sat in silence for many moments, and my eyes adjusted to the gloom. The dark figure moved from the hearth toward where the lantern sat on the bare floor, bent and struck a match. I could smell the lamp's kerosene as its wick was lit, and I watched a large hand move the knob so as to adjust the brightness of the flame. Observing the top of the hat as the creature worked at the lantern, I was somewhat taken aback when the head swiftly lifted so that I could see the face beneath the hat's wide brim.

"Your arrival comes unannounced, sirrah." The voice was what one called sepulchral—full of dismay and doom, its low tones echoing within the chamber. I couldn't help but gawk at the misshapen mouth that uttered those words, at the uncanny assembly of facial features that, in the lamplight, did not seem entirely human.

I tried to laugh, a feeble effort. "To whom should I have 'announced' myself? We're merely passing through."

The figure snorted disdainfully. "I think not. This hill is too out-of-the-way for that. No, you are here by design." He espied the private journal on the floor, swooped to take it up, and perused its opening leaves. "Aha, all is explained. I knew that Timeus had kept a journal—a pox upon his soul!"

"You knew him."

"Naturally. Timeus Martense, whose wretched ancestors built this manse while clutched by red madness and the mockery of diabolism. Dutch, of course." The fellow slipped the small book into a large pocket. "I'll just keep this, I think. It was folly on your part to find us. This place is insalubrious, and you will be wise to leave it now."

"That book is mine, you have no right to confiscate it. Nor have you 'announced' yourself or explained your sudden presence here."

He laughed like one who is showing great patience with a troublesome child. "I am Simon Gregory Williams. My sudden attendance is due to the storm, which your being here has beckoned. We never suffer such storms in the valley unless this edifice has been trespassed. Again, you will not want to linger here for long, your health will be infected, and your dreaming."

He sounded so superior that I became hotly annoyed. I answered as nonchalantly as possible. "Oh, I've had some experience with such things. I'm a searcher after horrors, a haunter of weird places. You smile, but I assure you it's quite true. You see before you a connoisseur of unnamable things. It's more than a hobby—it's a grand compulsion, and I can afford to gratify it. Being here pleases me extremely—I've never experienced the intensity of the uncanny that I have encountered here. Rarely have I felt so haunted."

A new expression filled the fellow's face, one of growing interest. "Hmm. Then we have a thing in common. But come away with me now, out of this place. I assure you, one single hour within these walls will completely unsettle you."

"I can't leave without my companions."

"They have already deserted you."

"What?" Rushing from the room, I ran down the hall and to the huge double doors. Wind and rain lashed my face as I stepped outside. Archer's car was nowhere to be seen. Scandalized, I returned to the hallway, where on a low table I found the other two lanterns and a supply of cash. Mr. Williams walked toward me down the hall. "This is terrible," I said. "I can't account for it. Those guys have been with me for two years." I took up the wad of cash and pushed it into a pants pocket.

"Come, follow me. I have a fellow awaiting us." Not even thinking about collecting my things, I walked with Williams into the storm. Car lights flashed on, and I saw the old Ford that indeed awaited us. Williams opened the front door for me, and I slipped into the passenger seat. The young man at the wheel looked pleasant enough. "This is Arthur Munroe," Williams informed me as he sprawled onto the back seat. "You'll find him quite amusing. Let us leave this wretched place and the Martense stain."

We passed through the violence of storm, away from the high domed hill and toward the main section of town. Turning to peer out my rain-drenched window back toward the hill on which the mansion stood, I saw the dark silhouette of the twin-peaked mountain; and then everything was blocked by a growth of woodland, through which we drove until I saw the lights of habitation ahead of us. Munroe parked the car and I stepped out onto a plank sidewalk. The rain continued to fall in torrents, and my new acquaintances rushed me inside an establishment that proved to be a quaint lounge with beamed ceiling.

"I expect you're hungry. What's your name?"

"Notis Angelis. Actually, I'm suddenly starved and soaked. That's quite a storm."

"It'll pass now that we're away from Tempest Hill. Let's sit here at this booth. Simon, are you actually going to join us? How rare!"

The other gentleman had seated himself across from me and was flipping through pages of the journal he had stolen from me. "I shall have coffee." I studied his unfathomable face and was struck again with the idea that this creature was more than human—or less than human. His eyes beguiled me, being slightly slanted and of a silver hue that seemed to contain particles of other shades in their pale irises. I watched as, at times, those eyes flashed with emotion and the creature laughed out loud. "Whatever happened to this precious fool Martense, I wonder? He seemed so resolved to pull down his ancestral haunt. Wherever did you find this sensational diary, Angelis?"

"I stumbled upon it in an antique shop in Providence."

"Hey, that's where I'm from," Arthur chimed in as he returned from placing our orders. "It wasn't the Kiernan shop on College Hill, was it?"

"I believe that it was. She has a great collection of those kinds of unusual things for which I have a passion." An unattractive woman approached with a tray of food and beverages. I watched as she set a cup of steaming coffee before Williams, who paid her no heed, and I noticed that her eyes were of a similar hue as his own. How strangely she gazed at him! I suspected they had perhaps shared a romantic moment, the memory of which haunted her still. She then set ample plates of sandwiches and potato salad before Arthur and me. He smiled and reached for the two stout glasses that were the tray's last items.

Simon Williams shut the journal and pressed its cover to his wide nostrils. "So you were guided to where this journal was sequestered within a hidden shop in Providence. I know the establishment, of course. It's secreted down a kind of alley between two other business-es. Not easily observable. Yet you were lured to it by some kind of in-stinct, and thus you found this journal and its captivating references to our valley. Yes, that's the way it often comes to pass."

"Oh, I knew about Sesqua Valley before finding the journal. I know Edwin Pratt and saw his oil of your twin-peaked mountain. He spoke so strangely of his time spent here." I flinched as a fist crashed onto our table.

"*Who* in the name of Yaddith is Edwin Pratt?"

Arthur Munroe, unfazed by the other fellow's explosion, took a calm sip of brew and smiled at us. "He's a painter who accompanied Sarah Susan when she returned after her time away. It was a few years ago, during your extended stay in Greece."

Williams pointed a cruel talon to Munroe. "*That* is when it hap-pens—when I am away, and none of you check it. They *flock* to our terrain. More and more. Worse than hordes of night-gaunts, and equal-ly odious."

Munroe picked up his sandwich and motioned for me to experi-ence mine. I was indeed hungry, and this was a wonderful repast. I could not decide what the main patty was composed of but thought it was some kind of perfectly seasoned fried curd. Munroe flashed me his sloppy smile. "Great, isn't it? Try the salad. And Sesqua grog will forti-fy you, mark my words."

Simon Gregory Williams pushed away from the booth and sneered at us. "I will let you mortals take pleasure in your repast. I shall just take this new item to the tower. Good day."

I watched the creature stomp out of the establishment. "Damn, he's unpleasant," I offered as I took up my mug and sipped the delicious brew with which it had been filled.

"He's brusque, that's all," Munroe responded dismissively. "Actually, you've caught his interest more keenly than you realize. He shares your passion for inexplicable lore. Were you actually going to spend the night on Tempest Hill? That's insane!" He raised his eyes to the ceiling in an aspect of listening. "I don't understand it, the storm has yet to pass."

"We need to return. I've left some valuable items there, and I wanted to look over some of the books in that room. Will you accompany me, or may I borrow your vehicle?"

"Damn, you *are* mad! We'll wait until morning."

"Oh, come on. It's a ten-minute drive, and then another fifteen minutes inside the mansion. It won't kill you."

He stared at me so abnormally that I looked away from him and finished my beverage. Then I stood and patted my belly. "Thanks, I'm quite fortified. Is there a local place that rents out cars? Or a taxi company?"

He pushed his plate away. "Oh bugger, I'll take you. But we won't linger." We exited the establishment and stepped out into torrential rain. "It hasn't come down like this in quite some time. You've triggered something."

I didn't understand him and kept silent as he led the way to his car. Secretly, I wasn't really interested in repossessing the items that I had left behind. My experience of the mansion had been interrupted, and I meant to complete it. It was my destiny, to which I had been supernaturally guided. Perhaps my entire enthrallment with strange horrors in literature and life was leading up to this magnificent moment, to my discovery of the Martense mansion and its furtive legend. What eerie elation I experienced at the sight of the high domed hill set against the pale rock of the twin-peaked mountain! I was but half-aware that I was muttering, "Yes, yes, yes." Then I noticed the way Arthur Munroe was looking at me as he parked his car. I cleared my throat and assumed a sophisticated tone. "Quite right. This won't take long at all. Join me if

you like, or you can wait here." What a funny expression he gave me—
it was almost a sneer, and something in its nature made me uneasy.
Not waiting to reply, he stepped out of the vehicle and ran to the double doors of the mansion, one of which we had left open. However, he
did not enter, but rather stood there in the door frame like some uncertain sentinel. I pushed out of the car and joined him, as from some
place over the valley we heard the sound of distant thunder. He gave
me his odd look again, and I laughed. Playfully, I began to speak in a
macabre voice. "What a sense of violation fills the air, eh, Munroe?
Something has spilled through right here, some stain from the trans-
cosmic gulfs, an unearthly blemish. It fills one with vague and novel
fears, and with a kind of zeal for discovery." I took a deep breath and
stepped into the gloom, but he did not follow me. Removing a squat
candle from its sconce, I ignited its wick with my lighter. When I
turned to look at Munroe, I saw that he had touched one hand to one
of the frescoed doors. Returning to him, I ran my hand over the very
faint image of hooded figures.

"I've never been inside, and I don't want to join you. By god, man,
can't you sense the peril into which you have placed yourself? Do you
think this storm is a natural occurrence? This site is shunned—even
the shadow children avoid it."

"What a curious phrase, 'shadow children.' It's in the journal as
well, along with something about 'the shadow's brood,' or some such
thing." I stepped again into the dark hallway, holding my tiny flame before me.

"What journal is that?" Munroe had waited for one second before
following me into the gloom.

"The private diary that served as my guide to your valley. Your
unpleasant friend appropriated it. To answer you—yes, I can feel an
electric sense of hazard on this dark hill. I have been aware of little else
since entering Sesqua Valley. It is the epitome of what I have experienced in my quest for the horrific and grotesque in literature and life. I
want to touch it—it's like some deadly panther that invites my hand to
stroke its pelt, at the risk of losing that hand to fiendish fangs. I relish
it, and I shall pursue it, with or without you." So saying, I found the

table on which my past companions had placed their two hurricane lanterns. Discarding my plump candle, I took one lantern by its handle and touched my lighter to the wick. Shadows danced upon the hoary walls as I traversed the hallway toward the room that I had claimed earlier, and I smiled at the furtiveness of the footfalls that followed me. Entering the room, I went immediately to the fireplace so as to study the macabre imagery of its tiles. Those images, however ceremonial, were not religious. Many of them showed a series of robed figures whose faces were concealed by hoods. One hooded form held a body in its embrace, and my flesh tingled when I saw that the held one's head was faceless. On one tile, a cowled subject held arms up to a mass of darkness from which a crooked line of light erupted. The largest tile had been placed at the center of the hearth, its scene being a row of figures standing by a long table on which a woman's corpse reclined. One of the hooded creatures, bent over the cadaver, looked as though he were placing some kind of mask onto the prostrate figure's head; and then my blood chilled with horror as, studying the image perceptively, I realized that it depicted a face being removed from its possessor.

Munroe, who had been pacing the room nervously, went to the window to watch the storm. A terrific bolt of lightning flashed like white fire, followed by the sound of shattering glass. Yelping, my companion staggered from what was left of the window, and when he turned around I saw that his face was a mess of dripping gore.

III. The Horror in the Eyes

Running to Arthur Munroe, I removed the shard of shattered glass that had been embedded in his brow, just above one eye; but rather than letting me assist him, the fellow clutched at my lapel and pushed me from him with a force of violence that sent me hurtling to the floor. I yelped in pain as the piece of glass cut into the hand that held it, producing a pain so severe that my eyesight blurred and I was but vaguely aware that Munroe had vacated the room. Staggering to my feet, I removed my handkerchief and wrapped it around my wounded hand as I stalked into the hallway. I could hear the man stumbling down the hallway, but in the opposite direction from which we entered. Not bothering to fetch my lantern, I crept down the hallway, tripping now and again over discarded pieces of rotting furniture. A rush of wind was my guide, toward which I moved as a rectangle of night formed before me. I was gradually aware that the storm had stopped, and at last I stepped into a moonlit garden at the back of the mansion. It came upon me suddenly—a sense that the place wherein I stood was horribly diseased. Baleful trees of unholy size stretched skeletal limbs toward windswept clouds and starlight, and grotesqueries of marble formed an assembly of cowled figures that might have been a coven of petrified effigies. I peered at the hooded statues but turned away in horror at the facial expressions that moonlight dimly revealed.

Pale movement caught my attention, and I looked to where Munroe knelt on the ground and dug with frantic hands into a low mound that rose in what looked like a ruined area of the extended garden. It was a place polluted by white, foetid vegetation, by malformed growths of sick fungi. I saw that there were other low mounds in other areas of the yard, and I wondered if I stood upon a plot of private and illegal burial, wherein the Martense ancestors had planted their dead. Munroe's arms had sunk inside the earth, struggling to bring forth an object from the cavity he had created. Yelling his name, I hurried to him as he pulled a large ceramic urn out of the pit. Before I could reach him, Munroe smashed the urn onto a boulder, and then he rose to his feet and kicked the debris of death with which the urn had been populated.

"Man, are you mad?" I yelled as I grabbed hold of his arm. He turned to me and snarled, and for a moment I expected him to strike my face. I saw that his wound had split wider and that he had been bleeding into the shallow pit, onto the broken pieces of urn and its cremains.

Seeming to regain his senses, Munroe raised a hand to the cut on his forehead and gawked at the redness that stained his fingers. Looking down at his act of violence, he turned deathly pale and pushed me away from the place. "Run," he urged, and then scampered away without waiting for me. I began to follow him, stopping for just a moment when I heard a strange sound coming from the place where we had stood. I thought it must have been the howling wind, and this seemed corroborated as I beheld the blue ash and bits of brittle bone that had been inside the urn rise as a kind of whirlwind. Something in the sight so chilled my blood that I took flight, not stopping until I had leapt into Munroe's vehicle and slammed shut its door. The man gibbered in a low voice as we made our hasty escape from Tempest Hill.

Munroe parked the car and sat at the wheel, panting and mumbling to himself. I reached out to give him a reassuring tap on the arm and then yelped as he started violently. When he turned to glare at me, I did not recognize him as the happy-go-lucky fellow I had met earlier that evening. As we sat there, some few figures emerged from a distant door and moved toward the vehicle. As they neared us I could just make out their strange repulsive faces and silver eyes. One of them opened the car door and helped Munroe out onto the wooden walkway. Exiting the car, I followed them into a building that proved to be the establishment where we had eaten earlier and quarreled with Simon Williams. My companion, weak and disheveled, had been guided to a table where a large glass of some dark liquid was offered him. He drank greedily and seemed to regain composure. I stood a little away from him, not knowing what to do, until he looked up and motioned for me to join him. "A glass of grog for my friend, please. And we'll need one of the upper rooms for a night or two. Sit down, Notis." Moaning, he ran his hands through his hair, and then smiled as the others joined us at the table and offered me a mug of the delicious beverage that I had had with my lunch.

I confess that I was disconcerted by the others who had joined us. I like to assure myself that I have no racial prejudices, but there was something in the facial features of these persons that unsettled me and aroused an almost instinctual dislike. I assumed that they were related, their facial characteristics being so similar. Like Simon Williams, they possessed the oddest eyes, eyes that were slightly slanted and of a silver hue. "Notis Angelis," I uttered, lifting my glass to them in uneasy salutation.

"It was you who violated the Martense mansion," the smallest of the three strange ones stated.

"Yes. I have an interest in its history."

"We do not trespass there. The air is unhealthy."

"What a remarkable phenomenon," I shot back, feeling defensive. "Yes, the air there has a rancid taste and smell, as if it had been polluted by dead and rotting things. Have you noticed those malformed trees with their swelling black trunks? In my imagination I thought, at times, that they shuddered, as if consumed by some malicious contagion. Worst of all, a part of me, that part of my nature that is drawn to monstrous things, felt a keen desire to press my face against those malformed trunks and catch their nameless fever. I am bewitched by your haunted valley! When I gaze at that titan of pallid rock I feel that it will stretch its twin peaks over me and cast a shadow from which one can find no escape. What is it in the air down there, that sweetness that creeps onto one's tongue and rises to the area behind one's eyes? It's so different from the rotten air atop the ghastly haunted hill."

I became aware of how intently the others in the room were listening to my discourse. Munroe peered at me in silence for some moments, and I detected a kind of frenzied worry in his eyes. "How did you come to learn about Sesqua Valley, Notis? What is your interest here?"

I took a sip of the excellent brew, wiped my mouth, and tried not to let on that I had noticed their intense scrutiny, uncomfortable as it made me feel. "I have a *keen* interest; indeed, I have a *passion* for the grotesque and terrible things that haunt our little globe. This enthusiasm has evolved into a career. My circle of other like souls is now quite wide, and they bring items to my notice. From one such compatriot I obtained a private journal that had belonged to Timeus Martense. It was his ancestors who built the mansion of the hill, as I'm sure you know. I suspect that they were very early visitors to the region. Simon Williams, or the journal, I can't remember which, has hinted that their coming to the land resulted in some kind of weird disturbance—an awakening of aboriginal forces."

"That was in the early or mid-1870s," Arthur Munroe informed us. "The Martense cult was the first potent clan of sorcerers to be lured to Sesqua Valley, and they were attracted to one of the valley's tainted spots. Their black magick was of such a diseased nature that it resulted in awakening the children who slept within the shadowed realm. That's how it all began."

"The shadow children," I whispered. "I keep hearing that repeat-ed. What the devil does it mean?"

The youngest of the other fellows gazed at me and smiled. "We are the shadow children, we with silver eyes. No, don't hush me, Am-brose. He won't remember once he's left the valley—unless he, too, is keeping a journal. Are you?"

"No. I remember things through dreaming. My line of work brings me such fantastic dreams. Yes, I was given the journal by a person who finds rare things for me. And I saw a painting of the twin-peaked mountain shortly afterward, the image of which captivated me."

Arthur Munroe drummed his fingers on the table as the young Sesquan continued speaking. "It sounds like eerie fate. I think Notis was lured here by restless necromancy. Something is agitated atop Tempest Hill. Notis, here, has been affected by the fiend."

"Not I alone!" I countered, turning to Munroe. "Whatever were you doing in that garden, digging up and then smashing that urn? It was crazy behavior."

"I . . . cannot remember doing any such thing. Damn, my head hurts."

Reaching to his face, I pushed his hair from his forehead and ex-posed the scar. "A window shattered in the storm, and you were sliced by a shard of flying glass. You should probably have that looked to." Pushing away from the table, I stood. "Did I hear mention of a room? I'm in need of solid sleep. I'll want to get up early and return to the mansion to get my belongings."

"You will not return to Tempest Hill, sir."

"I most certainly will. I have much more to explore. And I think I want to trek up that twin-peaked mountain a bit: the view is probably splendid. Now, is there someone here who can show me to a room?"

The youngest of the strange ones arose. "I'll take you. Come, follow me."

I was led to a stairway near the back of the establishment, and I liked the smell and feel of the old wood as we ascended and I ran my hand along the wall. We reached a second floor and I was ushered into a small room, and the sight of the bed made me realize how very tired I was. Going to it, I sat on the mattress and was about to ask the young man some questions, but he had gone. Kicking off my shoes, I stretched out on the bed and shut my eyes. I could feel the curious dreams that coiled beneath my eyes and whirled within my brain; and their motion reminded me of the whirlwind I had witnessed in the mansion's garden, that unexpected tempest of blue debris and bone that had lifted from the earth and spread into the air. I witnessed it again, in dream, and saw it shape itself into a hooded figure that glared at me with alabaster eyes. There came the spectral sound of Sesqua Valley's wind as it fluted musically in the air—such a seductive sound. Moving my mouth, I tried to speak to the hooded figure as it bent over me, as it spread as a bank of shadow in which numerous points of shimmering silver observed me. Something in the nature of those many eyes unnerved me, and I was suddenly overwhelmed with terror. Frantically, I struggled to push myself from the bed and thus escape the room and its devilish inhabitants. Hands pressed down on me and retarded my effort of flight. I could discern, vaguely, shapes within the bank of shadow, and saw one that was familiar. Simon Gregory Williams floated over me, a reed at his mouth from which the musical airstream issued. Removing the flute from his monstrous maw, yet continuing to expel breath, he covered my mouth with his own. His ghastly silver eyes shimmered with daemonic vim and they drilled into my own, and I began to weep with fear as other mouths pressed against my ears and whispered esoteric language. I felt one nail of his horrid hand begin to etch into my brow, painfully—and then I succumbed to nothingness.

IV. The Scream of the Dead

I awoke to a memory of a mouth stretched wide in fury, a maw that dripped saliva onto my eyes. I awoke and pushed the tears from my eyes, the sweat from my brow. My fingers touched the place upon my forehead that had been defiled. Dazedly, I lowered my feet onto the wooden floor and worked to regain a sense of equilibrium, and then I pushed myself off the bed and staggered to a wall where a mirror hung. The wreckage that regarded me in the glass was appalling, and I moved my hands to my face to make certain that the creature beheld was indeed myself. My face had never been such a wan pallor, my eyes had never been so marred with red lines. My mouth was numb, as if it had known a serpent's kiss, and a thin line of drool slipped from one corner of it. Pushing hair away from my eyes, I saw the place on my forehead that had been marked by some phantom in the night, a phantom with silver eyes. Although my career as a hunter of horror had made me familiar with many esoteric signs and symbols, this was one I could not identify.

My clothes were shabby and askew, but I did not bother to straighten them before exiting my room and trotting down the stairs to the lounge area. Arthur Munroe, seated at a booth, was devouring a hearty breakfast. He had regained a bit of his jocularity and chuckled as I sat across from him. "You look awful," he chirruped.

I was about to scold him when I noticed the unusual thing—the mark on his face, where the shard of glass had embedded itself, had been altered. "What the hell?"

He chuckled again and tapped a finger to his forehead. "We wear the mark of the beast."

"It's Simon's work," I said.

"Just so—a sigil of his own invention, found in his book of spells or whatever it pretends to be."

"His what?"

Finishing his food, he pushed the plate from him. "His personal grimoire. He wasn't content, you see, merely to study the alchemical tomes of other sorcerers—he had to create his own. Quite potent it is, in regard to things that occur within this valley. I don't know that his magick has much significance outside of Sesqua. What is this expression on your face, Notis? I thought you made a career of this sort of thing."

"I've never encountered such a . . . a blatant exposure of it. Part of the allure of my career is that I unearth secret things, rare distortions and perversions in reality. I chase after nebulous things, phantasmal stains, weird dimensional rips in the fabric of reality. Here you speak of such things as you would of walking the dog."

He grimaced. "Dogs are not popular here. This is cat country." He leaned forward on his elbows and pierced me with his eyes. "You'll never know a realm rarer than this, Notis. How exceptional, your discovery of us. How extraordinary, your time within our air. Almost feels like fate, doesn't it? I've heard it from outsiders often, how they 'chanced' upon a mention of the valley, how that revelation worked on them in an almost maniacal manner until it became an obsession that resulted in their locating Sesqua Valley. Like some extraordinary destiny, eh?"

I leaned back and folded my arms. "You love being mysterious, don't you?"

"*Au contraire*—I've never spoken so plainly. You see, it's been my experience as well. I found a book of verse in Salem, by a poet named William Davis Manly. Most of the poems concerned a haunted supernatural valley, a place called Sesqua. The verse intoxicated me, and I began to work on a sequel to it, a series of sonnets that I had published as a very limited chapbook. I'd never written a line of verse before; my work was always in the plastic arts. But, man, I felt compelled to write those poems! Three months after their publication I began to have vivid dreams about the things Manly and I had written of, and three months after that Simon Gregory Williams located me and played his role as pied piper. We've touched on something with our art, with our senses, and Sesqua Valley has touched us in return. We swallow the lure, and thus are we reeled in. Never to escape—not that we ever care to."

"I have no art," I informed him. "I have my intellectual work. I don't dabble in necromancy—I study it, and record my findings."

"How very sane. Well, maybe you'll be able to escape once this is all over."

"Once what is all over?"

"The disturbance your being here has resulted in. Damn, the dreams I suffered last night. You've triggered something unpleasant."

Rising, I shook my head. "If that's so, then I mean to explore it. Such is my vocation."

"Simon wishes to commune with you. He's in his tower."

"Lead the way, Munroe," I said, waving my hand in invitation for him to get onto his feet.

"Nope. He wants to see you alone. Just find any pathway leading into the woodland. You'll find your way."

"What, I'll sense it 'supernaturally'?" I mocked.

Instead of answering, Arthur Munroe gave me a most perplexing look, an expression so intense that my blood seemed to freeze momentarily. Nonplussed, I shook my head and blew air through scowling lips, then turned to exit the place. It was early morning, and mild sunlight warmed the valley wonderfully. The air still contained its surfeit of sweetness, but I had grown used to its taste in mouth and nostrils and rather liked it. Looking around at the surrounding woods, I could not decide what direction to walk in, and so I strolled down the road until I caught sight of a curious sphinx statue, a mammoth creation, before which a young woman was sitting on the dirt ground. Casually, I walked to the statue and pretended to examine it as I slyly studied the girl. She was obviously very young and possessed a very pronounced Sesqua Valley physiognomy, her features almost resembling a curious blend of frog and wolf. Sunlight shimmered on her silver eyes. I saw that she was drawing in the dirt with a short stick.

"Do you write a riddle in the sand?" I inquired.

She did not look up at me as she answered. "It's an ancient Egyptian symbol for 'mountain.' It has twin peaks. I like that." She then looked up at me and frowned. "You're the fellow who has caused all the commotion."

"What commotion is that?"

"The dreams of the screaming dead."

"Have you suffered this incubus?"

"I haven't learned how to dream yet. I'm new to the mortal realm." The young woman raised her head in listening. "Simon's calling for you. You don't want to keep him waiting."

"I have no idea where this tower he presently occupies is at. How am I to locate him?"

She pointed beyond a nearby graveyard that was surrounded by a low stone wall. "There's a lovely path over there, just beyond the Hungry Place. It's my favorite. Follow it to the beast: he grows impatient."

"Thank you," I said; and then, strangely, I was inspired to kneel before her and touch her etched hieroglyphic, and although I didn't turn to look at it, I was heavily aware of the mountain that towered over the valley. "What's your name?" She did not speak; rather, she pressed her stick into the yielding dirt and began to write. "Isola," I whispered, reading the name she had inscribed. Pressing a finger into the dirt, I wrote my name.

"On your way, Notis Angelis—the beast awaits."

I rose and watched as she ran her hand over my etched name, erasing it. Looking at the cemetery, which she had oddly named the Hungry Place, I walked toward it and slid over the low wall. A cloud curtained the sun, and the atmosphere chilled. I walked slowly, observing the markers and tombstones, one of which affected me violently, for instead of a name and dates it had engraved on its stone surface the symbol of Simon's that had been cut into my forehead. Lowering to my knees, I traced the carven sigil with my hand and shivered as the chill in the air increased. Strangely compelled, I poked a finger into the earth and spelled my name in the Hungry Place. I thought, as I knelt there, that I could sense a faint subterranean pulsing beneath me, and I was overwhelmed with a longing to dig my hands deep into the cemetery sod. My brain then erupted with the sensation of someone calling my name, and so I lifted my limbs and leapt over the low stone wall at the other end of the graveyard. I walked into the woodland and began to follow a wide path into its depths, pausing now and again to admire the workmanship of the occasional statues that had been placed along the path. These sculptures showed tremendous talent and imagination, and I hesitated for quite a while to admire a life-size replica in ebony stone of a beautiful woman who, in my imagination, might have been some awesome Egyptian sovereign. I watched the dapples of sunlight that fell on statue and mossy earth. As I continued to walk the path, the woodland darkened for a while as trees grew closer together and shut out daylight. I then saw a raised area, brightly lit, before me, and walked into a cleared vicinity in which the tower stood, an erection of ancient brick that towered seventy-five feet above the ground.

I approached the metaphorical arched entryway, around which emblematic symbols had been embossed. I felt, as I passed through, that I was crossing a kind of threshold from one sphere of existence into another. Atmosphere certainly altered; even the silence of the valley, which I had noticed offhandedly, became heavier, more solid and intense. One was almost afraid to breathe and thus become detected by some spider in its web. I ascended the curving steps, advancing past small square window slits through which daylight feebly lit my way. Finally I saw a golden glow ahead of me, and the air became warmer. I moved into an enormous circular room that was cluttered with immense tables littered with books, scrolls, and manuscripts. Simon Gregory Williams was a regal sight ensconced in his antique English Gothic-style nineteenth-century bishop's throne, a thing of magnificent workmanship complete with griffin finials. He leered at me.

"The valley reeks of nightmare."

"From what I've seen of Sesqua Valley, nightmare is its natural state."

"Something has been reawakened and unearthed. It thrives on terrestrial environment and aches for corporeal breath. It has a taste for mortal blood. I have evoked protection of a kind, but this thing is a mighty force."

"I saw something at the mansion when Munroe smashed the funeral urn or whatever it was. There was a shape that looked like a combination of shadow and black sand. It was nebulous but seemed to be summoning a kind of sentience. I've investigated my share of haunting, but this—"

Simon made a mocking sound. "Your 'investigations,'" he scoffed. "I entertained, for one mere moment, that there may be something to your 'career,' as you call it, something that would assist me in my art. And yet, search as I may"—and he waved his hand so as to indicate the myriad bookshelves in the room—"I find no mention of you in the annuals of supernatural investigation. Have you written no books?"

"Not yet, and not for many years hence. The cases I work on are often delicate. I wouldn't want to discourage clients by having them worry that their lives will be put on display in a record of my work."

Simon tutted. "I fear, sirrah, that you are a bit of a charlatan. That you have been a pawn among us is evident; but I do not think it was the valley that summoned you. That is unprecedented. You need to depart; your presence here poses a threat to my kind."

"Your kind," I echoed as I stepped toward him. "What exactly *is* your kind?"

"Why do you come so near? Move away, sirrah. Pah, I can smell your human pant. Why do you study me thus?"

I picked up on his phrasing. "You're not human, are you? Your eyes—no human could possess such eyes. They own degrees of silver hue, with an iris in which weird particles of queer color swim. Why do you and your kind possess such eyes?"

His voice, when he spoke, overflowed with menace. "They were fashioned to look upon our realm of mist and shadow. They are the one element of our being that is difficult to disguise as we roam your temporal plane."

"You're an Immortal."

The beast leaned back into his throne and shut his eyes. "I exist differently, and indefinitely." His eyes opened, and I thought they were of a darker hue, more menacing than before. "None of this avails me. You are quite useless, and your being here awakens unwanted things. Under other circumstances we would welcome such paranormal anarchy, for we love magick and its wanton ways; however, this force is monumental. The Martense warlocks were the first to settle in this vale. They were instinctively lured to one of the poisoned spots in Sesqua

Valley, those places that even we, the shadow children, avoid at all cost. Do move away from me, Angelis. You infiltrate my air."

I backed away and sat on one of the long tables, and there I opened an ancient book that was filled with diagrams and charts. Its text was in Latin. "Rather dangerous, isn't it, spilling the secrets of your race into my ear?"

"You won't remember once you leave our demesne. Selta will remove the memory of your time here. That is one of her functions. And if she doesn't, then I will pay you a personal visit." I knew that what he spoke was truth, and I shuddered. "You will leave the valley tonight. Munroe will drive you to a town where you can rest overnight. You will be given sufficient funds for returning to your city."

I held up my hand. "I have plenty of cash."

He shrugged. "Excellent. Go now, our conference is ended. Pray to whatever god you will that we never meet again."

I winked at him and got to my feet, then sauntered to the stairway and progressed out of the tower. There was one thing that I had cultivated in life, and that was a ferocious sense of individualism. I had needed it when I left my job in a bank and began my career as a seeker of horrors. My family had mocked and threatened me, proclaiming that I would bring infamy upon our name. When, at parties, I had been introduced as a 'ghost hunter,' I was asked the most insulting questions and laughed at behind hands that concealed mouths. Initially filled with a sense of defiance, I gradually mellowed into a kind of serene practicality whenever confronted with mockery. I neither explained nor defended my life, yet pursued it with a quiet conviction that others came to admire. Gradually, I gained a reputation for success, although I was careful to avoid unwanted notoriety. My life was calm except for the cases with which I was involved, and they were often thrilling. But mostly I pursued my interests for their own sake, and for the knowledge and pleasure they gave me. I had compiled notebooks that overflowed with memos of things that were of especial significance, and there would one day be a book, but that was years away.

All this weighed on my mind as I followed a pathway through the forest, and then I realized that I was lost. The trail that I had been fol-

lowing began to rise, and the growth of trees thinned a little so that
what was now late afternoon light spilled onto the ground before me. I
approached a hilly area that was covered with shrubs and thin skeletal
trees of white bark. Tall megalithic stones stood in formation, smooth
and gray and formidable. I had seen similar sites in portions of New
England; but there was something about the shape of these tall stout
stones that dismayed me, for they seemed like the frozen embryos of
stillborn monsters that had been sequestered to this deep spot in the
woodland so as to conceal their progenitor's shame.

I went up and stood among the stones, which seemed situated
haphazardly, with no occult significance. There was a cool breeze playing between the standing stones, and I opened my mouth so as to
drink its syrupy elixir. From some distant place, a beast bayed to the
dying light, and I smiled as gathering shadow coaxed my limbs to settle
and my eyes to shut. Leaning against one sturdy pylon, I slipped onto
the ground and dug nails into the sod, and then I lifted one filthy nail
and stabbed it into my brow, disfiguring Simon's sigil on my flesh.
How strange, that even with my eyes closed I could still see the swirling shadow and those things that inhabited it! One terrified visage ma-
terialized and split open its mouth—and its terror was so intoxicating
that I wanted to stretch my dreaming mouth and scream in unison. I
watched a red cloud spill from the phantom's orifice, a cloud that
boiled and dissolved the specter's face. Other faces, twisted in death,
pushed out of nothingness and screamed in agony before melting into
featureless slates of gore. The sweet savor of Sesqua Valley was replaced by a revolting taste of carnage. An intense bolt of light awakened me. For some few moments I stood not knowing where I was,
my startled eyes adjusting to darkness. Gradually, I realized that I must
have been walking in my sleep. Drops of moisture began to fall on me
as the sky rumbled overhead. Another flash of lightning assaulted the
sky and illuminated the sight before me, the pale twin-peaked mountain and the dark hill that rose below it, the haunted hill with a mansion at its apex.

V. From the Dark

I moved through gale and rain and shadow toward Tempest Hill, following the dirt road that weaved upward to the mansion. Wind and water lashed my face, which I covered protectively with both hands, although doing so seemed to throw my balance off so that I often stumbled and came close to falling. As I neared the hill's summit a monstrous bolt of lightning exploded nearby, striking a tree that burst into bits of flying debris, some few of which struck me. The sky rumbled with diabolic satisfaction as I found the gravel path that took me onto the Martense grounds and led to the ruined edifice. The great double doors were shut, and I noticed for the first time the black streak on one of them, which I assumed to be the mark of a lightning bolt. I stood before those portals of metal and ancient timber and then pressed my palms against their surface, trying to sense the aura of the sphere beyond them. I had never pretended to possess psychic powers; my attraction to the grotesque and uncanny was aesthetic and intellectual, and I used my mental prowess during my sessions of investigation to root out the truth concerning hauntings and paranormal disturbances. More often than not the trouble I encountered had a human source, however psychic the manifestation may appear. What thrilled me, and formed an absolute passion, were those very rare encounters that involved the Outside. Certainly, I have never felt the presence of the Outside more vividly than I did in Sesqua Valley. As my palms pushed open one of the weighty doors I was overwhelmed with a plethora of sensations, all of them fantastic. Terror held me in its thrall, exquisitely.

I walked to a door just past the vestibule and entered into a main sitting room of colossal size. Although the dusky room was littered with deteriorating furniture, my focus was on the seven strange statues that stood in the center area. For the longest moment I couldn't decide why those towering figures—and their arrangement—disturbed me with a sense of familiarity; and then I realized that they reminded me of the monolithic site that I had found in the woods, with its standing stones, which had been positioned almost exactly as these seven statues had been placed. I stood and looked at them for quite a while, shivering in the cold wind that blew into the room, probably from some storm-violated window. I sensed, somehow, that these figures had stood here for a very long time, perhaps since the erection of the mansion; and yet they looked pristine, untouched by time, their forms smooth and absolutely intact. I drifted to them and moved between their number, amazed that the breeze that chilled the atmosphere seemed more vigorous among the ghostly effigies. The room was too dark for me to make out the features beneath the sculptured hoods, but like the other rooms I had lurked at in the manse, it was littered with a number of thick sallow candles. I bent and picked one up, then moved out from among the statues so as to find a spot that wasn't so breezy as my hand rummaged in my trouser pocket for my lighter. Hearing the patter of rain, I went to a window to observe the storm, and I saw that the windowpane was intact, suffering no breakage. The gust that had chilled the room did not come from that window. I moved to another window and saw that it, too, was undamaged and shut. The current of frigid air did not issue from any window, nor did it assault me as pointedly as it had when I stood among the statues. I lit my candle, the wax of which felt oddly soft against my fingers, and wrinkled my nose at the unpleasant odor of its smoke. My imagination had certainly been infected by the aura of the place, for as my candle-light grew in brightness the entire room darkened all around me, until I could see nothing but my candle and the hand that held it.

I moved timidly toward the center of the room with my free hand outstretched, guided by the soft moaning of the wind. I touched a smooth, cold, solid thing and held my candle to its hooded counte-nance. It was then that I experienced the velvet kiss of fear—for a draft of icy air was spilling from the parted lips of the frozen mouth, and the more I listened to that unfathomable current the more I imag-ined that it articulated my name. Numb with a lurking fear that blos-somed in my bosom, I held my candle higher so that I could scrutinize the daemon's satanic countenance, and I shuddered as the flickering light so played with moving shadow that the statue seemed to fluctuate and bend its head so as to regard me. The chiseled mouth parted and a stench poured forth, as if a pile of corpses had been spread upon the creature's tongue. That churning mouth moved toward me and I clamped shut my eyes as I awaited the kiss of death.

Something tightened onto my coat's collar and tugged violently, and I nearly fell as I was pulled away from the group of statues. Arthur Munroe, a lantern in hand, pushed at my back and guided me from the room. I still clutched my candle, although its wick had extinguished, and I looked to see why so much wet wax had stained my hand; but as I brought the candle nearer, I saw that it wasn't wax that covered my hand but rather a secretion of semi-human sweat that perspired from the candle's husk. I hurled the thing from me.

"Come with me now," Munroe commanded. "The storm grows in fury, and the valley is tormented with audacious nightmare. Damnation, what a monstrous catalyst you have proven to be, what a pawn! I'm returning you to the city tonight. Your coming here has been a mistake, and Sesqua Valley has been poisoned. You were quite deluded to return to this diseased pile—utterly deranged."

I spat. "You're the fool who's been duped, by Simon and his brood. They're the source of all the chaos of this valley. They're not human; they're some kind of demented changelings that have infiltrated the sane world. They've filled your mind with nonsense and convinced you of its truth. Whatever is happening here tonight, it's a part of their design."

With a cry of fury, Munroe smashed me against the wall and screamed at my face. "You've been here one day, and you know better than *we?* Fool! You think you're so well-versed in occult matters, and yet here you are, their stupid puppet. Can't you perceive the darkness that has fallen over everything? Do you think that's a natural occurrence?" I sniggered at the audacity of his charge, at his use of "natural" in this forsaken land. "You have yet to encounter those famished statues that bend their hoary limbs and tilt to eat your face! God, you're ridiculous—insanely stupid!"

It was my turn to be violent, and I shoved Munroe from me with such force that he stumbled and smashed his head against a marble table as he crumbled to the floor. I shook and heaved anger and did not try to assist the man as he turned onto his back and moaned. The wound in his forehead had split, thus disfiguring the symbol that had been etched therein. Outside the mansion, I heard the sky rumble, and thus I rushed out of the manse, into the air that smelled of thunder. I was bewildered by the thickness of the darkness that covered the realm—even the white mountain was completely blocked from view. Like some drunken thing, I moved toward the back of the mansion and the area where Munroe, in his delirium, had unearthed a funeral urn. A desire burned deep within me, to sink my hands into that earth and see if I could find other buried relics. I knew that I was mentally unhinged and found it an extremely liberating experience. Stretching my mouth, I bayed laughter to the unseen sky. Tripping over a nauseous-looking shrub, I crashed onto the earth, and my face fell into rank diseased vegetation that seemed like something from lunatic nightmare rather than rational reality. Pushing my heavy frame upward on my elbows, I continued my crawl on hands and knees. There was unholy movement all around, and the stout feverish trees, some horribly lightning-scarred, swayed with sinister motion, as if their limbs hungered to clutch at me and tear me apart. Although semi-blinded by blurring eyesight, I struggled on my way, and at last I could feel the fleshy tissue of the garden's sickly growths. Creeping further, I moved into a shallow in the earth and knew that I had located Munroe's pit.

A swaying spot of fire approached from the distance. Arthur Munroe was advancing through the peculiar darkness with a lantern in his hand. Before he could reach me, I felt the substance that accompanied me in the shallow cavity sift and rise and shape itself. A coiling phantom lifted its unholy essence, a horror darker than the supernatural pall that enshrouded Sesqua Valley. It elevated itself out of earth and billowed gigantically before me as one upper portion of it formed a daemonic face. I watched, hypnotized, as the fiend reached for the other fellow and lifted him from the ground. Munroe swung his lantern wildly and shrieked at the spectre in an extraordinary tongue that I could not comprehend. He thrust his lamp into the apparition's face, illuminating it for one brief moment. I quaked with inexplicable dread as I looked upon the ogre's countenance and realized that it resembled that of the seven statues that lingered in the chamber we had but recently vacated. I saw the airy maw that churned with noisome appetite as an essence of that phantasmal mouth stretched toward Munroe's face.

A bolt of lightning illuminated the plot of land behind the mansion, and I saw the figure of Simon Gregory Williams with his hands held high. His bestial visage was twisted with vehemence as he thundered language. Rods of electricity flashed crazily in the darkened sky, and I watched them in amazement as they stayed alight and formed themselves into the sigil that the beast of Sesqua Valley had etched onto my forehead. The glyph sizzled in the sky, a sky that lost its element of unholy blackness and began to twinkle with wondrous starlight. The dark covering that had consumed all else melted from the valley.

A foul whimper sounded above me, and I saw that the mammoth phantom was beginning to break apart, to dissolve utterly. It released the human in its hold, and Munroe's body crashed onto the earth near to me. Pushing out of the pit, I crept to Munroe as moonlight began to bath the valley. Reaching out to him, I called his name; but Arthur Munroe did not respond, for he was dead; and when I turned his body over I saw, illuminated in the lunar light, that on what remained of his gouged head there was no longer a face.

Child of Dark Mania

for Frank Belknap Long

I.

My weird and amusing cousin, with whom, in childhood, I was very close, wrote to me one late September day, asking if I would set some time aside and visit her. The letter's tone was warm and easy, yet something between the lines worried me. I had not seen Diane since her return, eight years previously, from Greece, to which she had journeyed with a gang of lesbian witches. A creature of wild abandon, she was always on some exotic journey to some strange land. I have a collection of postcards from every corner of the world.

She shocked us all by becoming pregnant and settling in a place called Sesqua Valley. I had, when her letter arrived, been recovering from a serious epistolary row with my publisher. My last two novels had sold amazingly well and it was time, I was informed, to drop the reclusive author "pose" and go on an extended book tour. I absolutely refused. My solitary ways, I wrote them, were not a pose but a way of life. I saw no one, I went nowhere. I would not own a telephone. If my books were selling briskly, I told them, there was no need to journey hither and yon to pitch a popular product. These battles with my publisher left me extremely distraught, and I felt need for escape. Thus, one splendid morning, I boarded a bus and journeyed to the mysterious Sesqua Valley. I felt an almost criminal thrill in making my escape. No one had been informed of my sudden departure; no one would be able to find me.

The motion of movement soothed me, and I napped. On awakening I found that we were entering a valley. Hugh hills, thick with evergreen, rose all around. I gasped at the beauty of a magnificent twin-peaked mountain of white stone. The bus pulled into a rather tiny depot and stopped, and I saw her smiling as she stood next to a wide clean wheelbarrow. Diane's blond hair, faded and streaked with gray, moved lightly in the wind.

"Sonny," she said, using my childhood nickname, "you look great, exactly as a distinguished writer should. And how kind of you to have more gray hair than I." We got my luggage, which she placed inside the barrow. I was a bit perturbed to discover that we were to walk the distance to her house in the hills, and acquiesced when she insisted on pushing the barrow all the way. My city senses seemed to come more fully alive as we trudged along the rutted road. I could actually hear the soughing of the wind as it brushed against treetops, something I never knew in town. I could smell nature, a captivating aroma. There was a singular sweetness in the Sesquan air. The verdant beauty all around us felt cool and soothing on my eyes. We came at last to her yellow house, and I was delighted to see the wide porch with its swing and rocking chair. I longed for easy comfort, to sit and smile and do absolutely nothing. We carried my luggage to an upper room, and then went to the kitchen. A tray of fruit and cheese was set on a table before me. I ate slowly, drank fresh hot coffee, and felt indecently at home.

"I'm glad, if a bit amazed, that you've come."

"Amazed?" I queried.

"Of course. In every review of your books you're always described as 'the reclusive author.' Makes you sound difficult and distant."

I smiled. "I insist on being so described. It is my little theory that doing so will discourage visitors. I never answer knocking at my door. I need peace and quiet in order to write. It feels at times like an obsession, my insatiable need of solitude."

"Then you've come to the proper place."

"I would have come before now, but you've been rather distant yourself, these past many years."

She hesitated and thought. "It comes from being the oddball of the family. Whenever I was with kin I felt the need either to explain or to defend my actions. Especially after Melissa's birth. So I finally found this place in which to hide."

"You never get lonely?"

"I do feel a bit lonely, at times. That's why I suddenly wrote. I think Melissa is soon to leave me. We've become distant, but the idea of losing her has me a bit flummoxed."

I pushed away my empty plate. "It's natural for her to one day go her way."

She folded hands and stared at nothing. "Yes. Yes, I'm being silly. Well, you must be tired after your long trip. Go relax. No publishers or door-knockers will find you here."

I kissed her hand and rose to my feet. Looking at the crinkles that lined the corners of her eyes, I felt a tinge of sadness for our lost youth. Her pale eyes seemed to betray a sorrow of her own. Silently, I turned away. The autumn day was mild, and I opened my bedroom window so as to enjoy a refreshing breeze. Stretching atop my soft bed, I shut my eyes and placed hands on chest. I could feel the hypnotic pulsation of my heart, and soon I must have slept, for suddenly I was awakened by an awful sound. Groggily, I got up and stalked to the window, through which I espied the black valley with its pointed silhouettes of surrounding trees. The full moon looked down on Mount Selta, the twin peaks of which so sparkled that it seemed they had supped upon the moonlight and caught its radiance.

It came again, from the darkly shadowed hills: low unnatural baying. From somewhere underneath me, some place in the silent house, came an answering howl.

I shivered as my flesh prickled with unfathomable fear. Timidly, I turned and left my room, walking down the carpeted steps and entering the kitchen, from which there shone soft silver light. My cousin sat at the table, drawn and pale. She tried to smile.

"What was that unearthly sound?"

She bit her lip and furrowed her brow. "It's happening more quickly than I expected. I was wrong to bring you into it. I didn't want to face it alone. I'm not like you; I can't abide the solitary life. And you've such a wild imagination, which is obvious from your work, and so I thought perhaps you'd be a comfort and not condemn me." She stopped as I stood behind her and stroked her hair.

"I have never done so, nor shall I."

"The worst is that I feel almost apathetic. I knew that He would come for her—eventually."

"My dear, your enigmatic talk is less than elucidating."

"Yes, of course. I'm blathering. Melissa has asked to see you. Go through that doorway and follow the stone steps that lead to her dungeon. I'll be in my room if you need to talk afterward." With this she rose and departed. I hesitated, for the creepiness of the situation was confusing and uncomfortable. Quietly, cautiously, I opened the door and stepped down the narrow way, pressing palms to the rough concrete wall so as to support my weak legs.

The creature awaited me. She wore a simple dress of amber cotton. Her hair was long and dark. Gray eyes regarded me from behind the cloth mask that completely covered her face. The eyes seemed to smile. "Francis, how good of you to visit. I've been rereading your early work." She gestured to a small pile of softbound books. "I prefer your shorter tales to your novels."

"As do I; but novels are ever so more popular with the public herd. They are the necessary bread and butter."

Not rising from her chair, she indicated that I was to sit on the bed. I tried but found it impossible not to study the grotesque cloth mask, and the bizarre shape that moved beneath it. I had known that Melissa had been born with birth defects, and we had assumed that this had been the result of Diane's consumption of foreign opiates. I had always supposed that this was the authentic reason for Diane's not having anything to do with her family. She felt that we would look at her with blame for the defacement of her offspring.

Melissa gazed at me in silence, and I blushed, imagining that my expression betrayed my thoughts. "My mother was mistaken to ask you here, but I'm happy to meet you at last. Diane's always been such an impulsive woman. I like that, usually; it's made for a remarkable existence, an excellent adventure. She is, at times, an amusing companion. Perhaps she's told you that I'm leaving? My sire comes to claim His own. Mother's just a tad bit nervous now that the stars have come right."

"You and your mother have the most extraordinary way of talking! I cannot understand either of you."

"Oh, but you will. And it won't seem outlandish to you. Surely you've done much research into dark lore so as to display the outré knowledge evidenced in your fiction."

"*Fiction*, my dear."

She licked her lips and grinned. Rising, she picked up one of my books and opened it. I felt a sickness in my stomach, for I *loathed* hearing my prose read aloud. She raised a hand, as if to still my agitation, and began to read in a strong clear voice.

> "What was this thing before me, this sick pulsation from diseased dreaming? It seethed in midair, an incongruous mass. A multitude of mouths split open and sang my name. I shuddered that this chorus of damnation deigned to know me."

I could not help but slap my hand against my forehead and giggle. "God, what rot."

"Where did those images come from, Francis?"

"They came from silly dreams."

She sighed heavily, an exhalation that caused her mask to billow. "And dreams are such curious things, containing knowledge we did not know that we possessed. And deep within our subconscious dreaming there are other layers of vision, unremembered and unsuspected. Sometimes we need assistance to unlock those compartments of arcane sight." She went to a stand and unwrapped a piece of plastic, from which she removed a small cone of incense. This she placed next to me on the bed, along with an incense burner shaped as an Eastern deity, an elephant god whose name I could not recall. "These will help you to understand. Burn the incense before you go to sleep, and concentrate on mother and myself." A note of sudden tenderness entered her voice. "Please take care of her, she can be so childish at times.

You'll find that Sesqua Valley can be a happy home, especially for one of your imagination."

It came again, from some distant place outside: a low and inhuman howling. That now-familiar chill pricked my flesh, and I shivered. I watched the woman's eyes and shuddered at their fervor. She closed them dreamily and tilted back her head. The bizarre shape that bulged beneath her cloth mask expanded, and from it there came spine-chilling ululation.

Clutching the tokens she had offered me, I leapt from the bed and fled the nightmare chamber.

II.

My bedroom was cool and welcoming. Not undressing, I sat on the bed and placed the figurine on the bedside stand. Studying for a moment the cone of incense, I detected strange minuscule symbols that had been etched or printed onto its surface. I placed it on the burner and, with matches used for lighting candles, set the cone alight. Musky smoke found my nostrils, which I breathed in deeply. Leaning my head against the bedstead, I thought of my cousin and her daughter. The disturbing cloth mouth with its moving mound of unseen flesh plagued the dreaming into which I fell. From some distant place in Sesqua Valley a thing wailed to darkness, accompanied by a vague beating sound that seemed to come from beneath the house, from some core of valley earth. The noise entered my brain and coaxed manifestation.

Blurred lines and muted moving spots writhed before my shut eyelids. They moved with shaping, gradually forming an image of ancient ruins standing on the apex of a black and hoary hill. I floated nearer to the ruins and saw the spot of unhallowed ground wherein a woman danced with jerky motion, as if suffering some epileptic fit. This woman was Diane. She danced with provocative grace before an enormous statue of an elephant god. Dream had altered the features of the silent deity—horribly so. Its ears had lengthened, as had its monstrous trunk. Trunk and tusks and ghastly mouth dripped with gore. Diane was nude, and I was disconcerted at the way her nimble movement, her almost exotic beauty, aroused me. I was not the only creature thus affected. My blood froze as she bent low and kissed the shadow of the rigid god, and I inwardly cringed when that blasphemous silhouette began to blur and bend. Sinuously, behemoth arms began to move, and taloned hands reached for my kinswoman. I watched in terror as the daemon lifted Diane to its writhing trunk, that shaft of grisly flesh that ended in a moving maw. I watched the trunk move over the woman's nudity like some ravenous lover. The creature raised its hateful eyes to me. Atrociously, it offered me the writhing body of my blood relation. I gaped at her blood-soaked limbs, at the heaving swollen stomach, and I stretched my mouth with howls of protest.

I awoke to baleful wailing, and at first I wasn't certain if it were an actual sound or a tissue of clinging nightmare. Gathering wind whimpered at my window. I glanced through the pane, toward the black hill that rose behind the house. I saw Melissa moving toward it, as winds pushed clouds from before the moon. She turned to gaze at me, and my blood froze at the sight of her unmasked face. I rushed from the house, into yellow lunar gleam, unearthly bright. I saw the girl move with dancing, like unto the memory of her mater in my dream. Her head hung low as she capered toward me, and her lank hair draped her visage from my view. I took her in my arms and pushed the strands of hair away from her face, as her writhing trunk rose to meet my mouth. Beneath that stem of distended flesh her own mouth chortled.

"He calls, Francis! He comes! Can you feel them, the shifting stars? They tug my blood, my brain. Oh, Francis, can you taste the cosmic wonder? Delicious, delicious!"

I placed my hands onto her head and gazed into delirious eyes. She clutched her breasts and shook with crazy zeal. Passionately, the maw of her trunk fastened to my lips. I drank my blood. From somewhere on the black hill there came a tremendous sound, and pushing me from her, Melissa turned to answer the summons. She ran to the formless shadow that awaited her, that shadow that was not of this world. I shrieked with rage and grief as she vanished into it, and wept to realize that she was gone forever.

Pale, Trembling Youth

with Jessica Amanda Salmonson

ykes, kikes, spics, micks, fags, drags, gooks, spooks . . . more of us are outsiders than aren't; and *that's* what the dear young ones too often fail to understand. They think they've learned it all by age fifteen. Perhaps they have. But they're not the only ones who've learned it.

They're wise, these youngsters, no doubt about it, and I wish them all survival, of one kind or another. They're out there on the streets at night; they've spiked their hair and dyed it; they've put roofing nails through their earlobes and scratched their lovers' initials on the whites of their eyes. And they're such beauties, these children. I have empathy for them, though by their standards, at thirty, I'm an old man. Am I a dirty old man? Perhaps. But I keep my hands to myself and am outraged by the constant exploitation I have seen. I help who I can, when I can. They laugh at me for it; I don't mind. Much as they hate to admit it, they appreciate the helping hand; they assuredly need it.

The new bands have power. They have raw, wild, gorgeous, naive energy. The temporary nature of these bands, the transience of the sound they create, the ephemeral nature of their performances *and their youth* have a literal and symbolic truth to it that breaks my heart. Ah, the dear young ones! Their own parents hate them. Their parents hate themselves.

But I have my criticisms. I don't tell them what to do with their lives, but I do tell them they're not the first and only ones to *know*. They all think they've invented it; invented everything. Twelve year-old artists of the street—don't ever doubt that some of them are geniuses.

Their music, dress, and Xerox flyers are undeniably brilliant works of art. Stripped of technical gaudiness and the veneer of social dishonesty, these kids and their art alternate people because of the reality that's exposed.

Reality is pain.

But none of it is new. A punk who's a good friend, a good kid, I gave him a rare old Dada poster for his birthday. He loved it. He thought it was something new. "No, sir," I told him. "It was printed before World War I." He was impressed. He got some white paste and smeared it onto the window of an uptown jewelry store. What brilliance! It breaks my heart.

So there's nothing new. Least of all pain. It's the oldest thing around. I want to tell them, "Yes, you're outsiders. Yes, this thing you're feeling really is pain. But you're not alone." Or not alone in being alone. A poison-bad planet. For everyone.

On the north side of Lake Union, visible from about any high point in and around the city, is a little spot called Gas Works Park. Considering how visible it is on the lake's edge, it's rather out of the way. It has the appearance of war's aftermath—a bombed factory. When the gasworks closed shop several decades ago, no one knew what to do with that extraordinary network of chimneys and pipes and silos. For years they sat rusting. Then someone had the fat idea of painting the whole thing, laying a lawn, and calling it a park. It looks good. It looks monstrous. It is urban decadence at its best and worst. It's not much frequented at night.

A pathetic old faggot took me across on his sailboat. He's not only pathetic, but rich; spent his whole life "buying" his way to the inside. But he's an outsider, too. We met in a downtown park in the days of my own alienated childhood, when he wasn't much younger but his gums were less black; and we've pretended we're friends ever since. I'd been on his boat most of the late afternoon and early evening, until the sun was going down. Then I said, "I don't need to go back into town. Let me ashore at Gas Works Park."

He let me off. I stood on the concrete landing and waved to the old man, who looked almost heroic pulling at the rigging—but not quite.

The sun had set. The last streaks of orange were visible beyond the city's silhouette. Skyscrapers south of the lake were shining like boxes full of stars. I turned my back, climbed the grassy knoll and gazed toward the antiquated gasworks. The garish paint had been rendered invisible by darkness. Breathing deeply of the cold clean evening air, I felt invigorated. The decayed structure before me was huge, the skeleton of a gargantuan beast. Its iron pipes, winding steel stairs and catwalks, variety of ladders, planks, chains, and tanks had a very real aesthetic charm. "Danger—keep off," a sign read on a chain-link fence. Even in darkness, the evidence of the structure's conquerors—their graffiti—was palely visible on the surface of its heights.

Hearing footsteps in the gravel behind me, I turned and saw a tall skinhead punk shambling toward the fence. He nodded and smiled at me, then leaned toward the fence, curling fingers around the links. I thought I detected a sadness in his eyes. He was looking upward into one particular part of the gasworks with such intensity that I could not help but follow his gaze. It seemed that he was staring at a particular steel stairway that led up and into a long pipe.

The sound of his deep sigh made me look at him again. He had taken a pack of cigarettes from a pocket in his leather jacket. "Smoke?" he offered, holding the pack toward me.

"No, thank you," I replied. Kindness and gentility, contrasted against a violent image, no longer surprised me in these youths.

"Something else, ain't it?" he said, nodding at the structure.

"It is," I replied.

He continued: "My band used to come here at midnight to record tapes of us banging on parts of it. You get some awesome sounds."

"You're in a punk band?" I asked lamely.

"Naw. Industrial. Kind of an offshoot of techno and hardcore. You know, a lot of screaming and banging on pipes and weird electronic rhythms. Makes an intense noise."

"Hmmm," I said, having trouble imagining why anyone would want to sit around banging on pipes and screaming. I must, occasionally, admit to a gap between this generation and mine.

"But we broke up," he continued in a quiet voice. "Our singer hanged himself—up there." He turned to gaze once more at that particular section of the structure. I felt a chill. Talk of death was unpleasant to me, and this was too sudden an introduction of the subject.

"I'm sorry."

"Yeah, it's sad. He had a great voice. He could scream and make you feel like you'd die. The he could sing so tenderly that you couldn't hold back tears. But he was messed up. His dad was always beating on him, so he took to the streets. Came to live in a squat with me and some mates. We called him Imp, he was so small. He'd never eat, just drink coffee and do a lot of speed. He shook all the time, and he had so little color to his skin that we took to calling him 'the pale trembling youth.' He didn't like that much."

He paused to take a drag from his cigarette. The night had grown especially dark. The gasworks stood silently before us and seemed to listen to the young man's tale.

"He really loved this place. Used to come at night with a wrench and investigate sounds. He slept here a lot. But he was a lost soul. We knew he had talked about doing it, but . . ." He tossed his cigarette to the ground and pushed on it with his boot heel. "They found him swinging from that pipe, his studded belt around his broken neck."

"How old was he?"

"Sixteen. Well, it's getting chilly. Think I'll head on down to the District and find me some anarchy and beer." Nodding to me, he turned and sauntered into darkness.

It had indeed grown cold. Yet as I turned to look once more at the weird structure, I felt drawn near. Looking with dismay at the fence before me, I took hold of it and began to climb. Reaching the top, I groaned at the difficulty of climbing over and down the side. I felt cold air against my neck. Looking at the section of the gasworks where the kid had ended his life, I thought I saw a shadowy figure watching me. Then the shadows blended and the image was gone.

With sudden resolve, I climbed over the top of the fence, nearly falling down the other side. I stood near a huge rusted pipe, perhaps forty feet long and five feet high. I felt a boyish excitement, for I have always had a love of tunnels. Going to one end of the pipe, I looked inside.

I entered.

My footfalls echoed weirdly as my boots hit the metal surface. The sides felt chill and rough. When I reached the middle, I sat down, bending knees to chest, and listened to the night. Then I heard a pinging, coming from the end of the pipe that I had entered. I looked and saw a small person standing there, watching me. It held something in its hand, which it slowly struck against the pipe. Then either my vision or the figure began to blur. I rubbed my eyes with shaky hands; when I looked again, I saw nothing.

I sat for what seemed endless moments. Finally I began to raise myself on unsteady legs.

From above came a sudden banging, horrible and ferocious, as though a madman were leaping from place to place and violently striking the pipe with some implement. The sound of it shook the pipe, and I felt the reverberations like a throbbing pain in my skull. Shouting in alarm, I fell to my knees and covered my ears. On and on it went, until I was certain that I would lose my mind.

It ceased. For some moments all I could hear was the ringing in my ears. Then another sound came to me: low sobbing. I have never heard such misery and loneliness in any voice. It tore my heart to listen to it, and froze my soul. Gradually it faded into silence.

I was too weak to rise. When at last I found the strength, I crawled out of the pipe, into the waiting dark.

Your Kiss of Filth

We wandered beneath the arsenic moon, to the place just outside the city where the long canal stretched darkly. Randy walked a little before me, silently leading the way, the tatters of her queer clothing moving in the slight wind. An ashen night bird, crying, darted above us, and I stopped to lean on my walking stick and watch its aerial progress; and then I continued to gaze skyward after the whitish creature had passed from view, for some aspect of the nighted heavens disconcerted me.

Randy stopped and turned to me. "What's the matter, tired already?"

I raised my walking stick so as to point it to the sky. "The stars, look you; how tiny they appear, how far removed, compared to the largeness of the lunar sphere. I've never known the stars to look so distant and so small. What is it that they fear, I wonder? What keeps them from drawing nearer to our dull world? And yes, I grow weary. I am over sixty years of age, and my bad leg aches painfully from all this walking. We have wandered far from city lights, and I do not like the natural darkness of this forsaken place. Nor do I care for the stench of this sluggish canal beside which we wander, nor the blackness of its liquid; nor do I care for the pastel things that float, barely discernible, here and there beneath its surface. This is a vile adventure."

The young woman shook her head and spoke from beneath her sallow mask. "You wanted to know where Todd had destroyed himself. We're almost there. You said you wanted to know the places where homeless punk kids dwell, so that you can write about it with authenticity in your new novel. Shall we continue, or are you going to be a crybaby and have me escort you back to town?"

I refused to listen to her, turning my face to the city instead and frowning at its silence. "Why is the city so noiseless? Why do its nocturnal revels make no sound?"

"Hesketh, it's three A.M. in the middle of the week. The revelers have gone to bed." She seemed to notice at last that I was shivering. "Button your heavy coat if you're cold. Follow me if you want to, or go home." I frowned at the frozen mouth of her pallid mask, at the taint of bitterness in her impatient language. She shook her head and turned from me. Sighing, I followed her until we came to an antique bridge that spanned the vile canal. I watched her step onto the arched structure and climb to its middle point. She stopped, leaned against the parapet, and stood like some inanimate thing that aped human form. A vigorous breeze began to rustle the leaves of the o'erhanging tree branches, and I felt a desire to gag at the increased stench of the grotesque canal thus aroused. Stepping onto the stone firmament of the arched bridge, I stalked to where my young companion stood. Standing beside her, I turned my eyes to the city, which seemed impossibly far away.

"How beauteous are the city lights, twinkling like diamonds in their oblong black boxes. How we have journeyed so far I cannot comprehend; surely the city isn't as distant as it seems. How horrid, this lonesome place to which you have lured me. Yes, I can't see clearly why he would destroy himself in such a wretched place, overwhelmed by its atmosphere of isolation and lack of style."

A sound of mocking laughter hissed behind her mask. "You really are a freak, Hesketh." Then she turned her mask to mine of antique flesh. "But such a wonderful writer." Her faux-face lifted a little, and I bent so as to kiss its brow. "Your round face looks so large in this moonlight. Really, you could be the moon's cousin, your flesh as pale as she. I'm trying to be poetic, to speak your language. You don't seem impressed."

"I am bored and uncomfortable. It was a mistake coming here to this sequestered spot of suicide. I did not need to see this squalid habitation to write about his death, I can do that with pure imagination."

"That's not it," she said, removing the mask and holding it over the stagnant water of the canal. "You thought it would be romantic to see the place where your beautiful boy breathed his last. You're so naïve that you think you can make suicide romantic. You cannot. He walked into those waters from the place beneath this bridge, and in their depths he gagged to death."

"How poorly you understand the artist," I sniffed. "I have no desire to paint suicide as some quixotic instance. I wanted to be here so as to feel the totality of him, in realistic terms. It is true, I thought perhaps that being here would help me to understand, somehow, his senseless need of extinction. I feel nothing. I feel naught but void."

"Ah," she answered, smiling sadly, "then you understand him completely, if that's what you sense."

I felt suddenly ridiculous as a teardrop escaped one eye and slid down my face. Removing a handkerchief, I wiped my face and blew my nose. Randy released her hold on her mask and watched it float to the water. Moving from me, she walked to the other end of the bridge and disappeared beneath the structure. I stood for some few moments gazing at my beloved city, but then the fear of being alone assailed me, and I stumbled across the bridge, and then climbed to the slanted area beneath it, where the punk girl sat on the hard cold dirt that led down to the water.

"Is this where you propose we slumber?" was my incredulous question. "I shouldn't sleep a wink in this frightfully chilly air."

"It's the middle of August, old man. Imagine sleeping here in winter. He did, often."

"It was too absurd. He could have slept on my sofa any time he wanted."

She placed her hand over my own where it pressed against the compact earth. "He didn't want to break your heart. He knew you were in love with him. You wanted to turn him into some kind of fantasy, into something he could never have been. The gap between you was too wide, and I'm not talking about age. You live in a cozy world of fantasy, safe and secure, where you cannot imagine what it's like to be threatened by the world. Do you know why he became homeless?"

"We never discussed it," I said.

"He left home at thirteen because his dad would always get drunk and beat the crap out of him. He moved into the abandoned house and started doing heavy drugs. Then he discovered your books and was beguiled by the beauty of your writing. We all knew that you were a local punk legend from thirty years ago, and so he went to you, to learn from you and be your friend. You ruined it all by being stupid and falling in love with him, and that added to his sadness."

How odd, to feel words like a brand, burning into one's soul. "It's frightfully cold," I replied, shuddering. "And the stench is too much. But I grow drowsy. I'll just recline here for one moment and shut my eyes. If you've any further cruel philosophy, keep it to yourself."

I rested on the earth, my walking stick in my embrace. The horrid dream came like some diseased fever, burning behind my closed eyes. I heard the liquid cries of lost souls and felt the chilly wind cut deeper into my flesh. Lifting so as to rest on my elbows, I peered at the stagnant canal water and its disquieting surge of movement. Formless portions of its slime crept out of it and onto the slanted earth. I watched as these enormous slugs of stinking grime oozed toward me, slowly, inexorably. The one nearest me raised what might have been an amorphous head and mewed; and then I felt its weighty chilly substance wash over me, pressing heavily at my chest, as if to hear my heartbeat. It oozed like mire to my throat, against which it pressed wetly. I watched as it lifted its formless head before my own, and I fought not to gag at its appalling foetor. What was it about its shape that haunted me? Why, when its lower portion seemed to curl into a smile, did my heart break? It was his smile there on the wet black surface, the smile of the boy I had loved and lost. But when I lifted my lips to kiss it, I was overwhelmed with nausea, and I shuddered as the vomit spilled from out my mouth.

I was awakened by the sound of a heavy splash. Groaning, I struggled to sit upright. I turned to look at my companion, but I sat beneath the bridge alone. Turning to look at the canal, I saw that its surface had been disturbed. For one moment I feared that loathsome formless things would crawl out of its depths and claim me. Instead, I saw the pale thing that lifted itself from its liquid and floated upward. I thought a night bird cried to moonlight. With difficulty I crept from underneath the bridge and returned to the path beneath the trees. Again some sentient thing cried in the night, and I raised my eyes so as to watch the pale entity above me. No, not a bird. Rather it was my young friend's mask, drifting above me like some poignant pallid face. It cried once more as if to call my name. I watched as it drifted away, over the trees, away from the city. Holding tightly to my walking stick, I followed the floating thing, into darkness.

Old Time Entombed

Noah and I stood beside our bikes and looked over the area of destruction. That which would be known as the Great Seattle Fire of 1889 had damaged an area of around twenty-five blocks. One of the buildings destroyed had been the small vacated meeting house that we had turned into our temporary temple, and my companion smiled slightly as he scanned the area where our tiny group had once convened. The summer weather had been balmy, with no wind for three days since the fire; the air was still tainted by the stench of smoke and charred wood, and the populace was praying for rain to come and clean the sky.

"Should we search that area, just to make certain that the small sarcophagus has been buried in the destruction?"

I shook my head and sucked the smell of destruction through my nostrils. "We did all that has been required, and the first portion of ritual has been accomplished. The city was unprepared to face this kind of devastation. Let's walk a little before we mount our bikes. I like the looks of grief on the faces that we encounter. The waves of shock and agony that ripple in the atmosphere please me in an enigmatic way. How little they comprehend. This ruin is puny compared to the calamity to come."

Late afternoon had melted into twilight, and we slowly climbed the hill toward home. I stopped to look out at Lake Union spread below us, at the few buildings with their red roofs and the distant neighborhoods across the water. The city was certainly growing. I watched the moon as it rose above the water; and as always, when I look at that globe of dust, I felt the age of the universe, and of the things that it contains. I thought of cosmic secrets and insanities, as they had been whispered to us by our enchantress. Then Noah and I boarded our bicycles and headed home through encroaching darkness, to my secluded cottage on the hill. The place had been a very private, very quiet home—and then its aura had completely altered with my acquaintance of the sorceress who now held dominion over our very lives.

I had been involved with ceremonial magick for many years, and during my time in Europe had trafficked with the Hermetic Order of the Golden Dawn; yet I had never actually experienced supernatural manifestation until encountering Guan-Yin during a meeting with a group of political activists who had formed after the nauseating Chinese riots that had plagued Seattle some years before. Guan-Yin was one of the few Orientals who had stayed in Seattle in the aftermath of the violence, in which her father had been one of the few casualties. I sensed, on first meeting her, an intense connection, even though I had no idea that she, too, was involved in esoteric ceremony. Although she had a distrust for most white men, Guan-Yin warmed to Noah and me, perhaps because we are both Jewish and have had personal experience with ethnic bigotry.

Parking our bikes against the small tool shed at the side of the cottage, we advanced toward the front door, and I hesitated momentarily before opening the door and entering. I can't quite explain the emotions that were stirred by our enchantress. We were beguiled—and slightly fearful, because of her quiet intensity and her profound knowledge of occult things. She was young, but his wisdom was as deep as the ages, and it cast a peculiar light inside her jade eyes. You almost felt ashamed at times when she gazed at you, because she seemed to unclothe your soul and reveal elements of psyche that seemed perverse. She aroused unholy appetites, and was expert at quenching them.

I felt Noah behind me and could hear his asthmatic breathing. Quietly, I pushed open the cottage door and sighed at the smells that wafted to us—the scent of incense and fragrant candle wax. Soft light illuminated the living room, which we had made our altar to the Old

Ones, and the young woman knelt within a circle of pure white sand, in a fetal position so that her forehead touched the floor. She wore a black gown that completely covered her figure and into which diagrams had been sewn with dark red silk. Her length of hair was worn up, wound upon her head and kept in place by shellacked ebony chopsticks. I allowed Noah into the room and closed the door, and then we removed our shoes and knelt before the woman in her circle of sand and listened to the almost indecipherable words she whispered to the wooden floor. Slowly, she lifted head and torso. Her eyes had been shut, but now she opened them, and I felt a thrill of fear and wonder that human eyes should look so bestial and ravenous. It had surprised me, when I first met Guan-Yin, that her skin tone was so pale, whiter than my own. When I once was bold enough to ask her about this, she replied that dark skin was for "peasants," which I did not understand. I never asked again, although I wondered if she was a partaker of arsenic or mercury.

"What news, gentlemen?"

"The city is already planning renewal. We saw no sign of the sarcophagus, it is buried beneath heaps of ash. The destruction was extensive. They say a million rats perished in the holocaust."

With graceful motion, Guan-Yin stepped out of her circle of alchemical sand. "One rat yet remains. We will extinguish him tonight, with the aid of the dead-yet-dreaming. It slumbers now in a field of destruction, and from that debris it will rise to do our wreckage."

"How do we awaken your ancestor?"

She smiled and shook her head. "The thing in its small stone coffin is not my kindred. It is a superior mage of the Miri Nigri, an antediluvian race. Its ashes have been combined with relics of sacrifice and slaughter, and with the sacred earth of an antique Roman temple. It delights in destruction, and will have relished the chaos that surrounded it during the inferno that we kindled. We will stir it toward wakefulness now, with our ritual of blood and water. Noah, fetch the black window and join us out back."

The beautiful woman took my hand and led me out of the cottage, to the back yard and the ritual pool that I had constructed there. We could not detect many stars, but the moon beamed its chilly glow on us, light that was reflected on the pool's water. When Noah joined us, he held a circular pane of black glass that was half the size of a carriage wheel. Our enchantress had informed us that this "window" had been part of a shrine in Malaysia that had been destroyed by her cult's enemies. It was through this window, during certain times of ritual, that the cosmic deity worshiped by the cult would manifest its icon.

"Raise the portal above your head, Noah, so that it may drink the moon," out enchantress spoke as she began to undress me. "I have spoken obliquely about the Outer One—his name is not something one carelessly speaks, for there is power in naming and potency in uttered language." There was no wind, and the summer night was warm. I drank the perfume of her flesh, her hair, as she undressed me, and I sighed when, finally, she unfastened her robe and let it slide off her frame to the ground. She watched me silently, like some abiding beast that contemplated prey. When she lifted her eyes to the object that Noah raised to moonlight, I turned to him and studied the black circle of glass. Behind me, Guan-Yin whispered words in a language that sounded alien and insane. I saw two red stars awaken as glowing embers on the surface of the window, and then a semblance of a monstrous and malignant face began to form as our enchantress took my hand and conducted me into the pool. Following her, I studied the grotesque tattoo that covered the entire area of her back, an etched image that resembled the Hindu deity that wore an elephant head; yet this image on Guan-Yin's flesh was far more sinister and bizarre than anything I had seen, and I trembled at the sight of its ravenous mouth and wicked tusks. It was disturbing, staring at the tattooed image as the woman moved, like a lithe panther, into the shallow pool; for as she swayed her hips and shoulders, the image of the beast seemed almost to take on an uncanny sentience. Again, I thought of my long acquaintance with occultists and their covens, and of how paltry their ceremonies seemed compared to the potency of this woman and her sorcery. I entered into the pool and stood beside her.

"Lift the window higher, Noah, so that moonbeams may pierce through it and touch our nudity."

Turning again, I peered at the black circle of glass and its spots of red illumination, and I saw the purple hue that oozed from it, onto me. Ah, that chilly light, as cool and smooth as the lips that kissed my back, my throat. I turned to face our enchantress and brought my hands to her breasts. She lifted one hand as fist from which the index finger protruded, and I saw the purple light play upon the ample length of fingernail, into which small diamonds had been implanted. I watched, as the woman touched that fingernail to her mouth and slit her lips, from which drops of blood began to drip into the pool. My hot phallus erected as our loins met, as her fingernail slice my mouth. We kissed and sipped each other's blood, and when she moved her slightly away I heard the name she moaned orgasmically—"Chaugnar Faugn."

Pushing away from me, Guan-Yin walked out of the pool, past Noah and into the cottage. Stepping out of water, I picked up my discarded clothing and followed her into the house, where I could hear her moving about in one of the two small bedrooms. I dressed, and then she emerged from the room in masculine attire, her hair and the top of her face covered by a hat. Spectacles with thick lenses hid the Asian features of her eyes.

"We'll walk to town and complete our ritual," she commanded. Nodding, I slipped on my shoes and escorted her outdoors. A black haze still hung over the area of destruction to which we journeyed, and I was curious as to why the entire scene had taken on a vague violet hue, as if I were looking at it through some tainted piece of gauze. We finally drew near the blackened area of ash and charred wood, and my enchantress sniffed the tainted air.

I kicked at a portion of the tarnished ground and frowned. "How do we find the sarcophagus?"

"There is no need. It is here, the antique thing entombed. You must summon it with the new properties of your alchemic eyes; for the radiance beyond cosmic space and time that flowed to us through the black window now glistens on your orbs, and from you that prehistoric illumination will awaken the Outer One. By our combined alchemy, the beast will rise from this debris of destruction. Summon it, Wilfred, so that it may break the walls of its tomb and conjoin with your flesh."

Unable to understand the full meaning of her words, I compre-
hended my task instinctively. Moving further into the fuliginous mass
of ruin, I gazed over cinders and burnt rubble that poked out of the
ash like blackened bones of some incinerated beast. I soon detected
movement. A thing that lacked substantial form began to creep toward
us like some monstrous caterpillar. I could not make out what it was,
for its elastic shape refused to become one solid entity. Finally, the
creeping thing stopped just at my feet, and I saw that it was an amorphous mass of odorous ash and shards of blackened bone. Mingling
within its accumulation of horror were tarnished relics of golden metal
into which strange sigils had been engraved. The sentient nightmare
quavered before me as a mortal mouth touched my ear.

"This old one reigned, in prehistoric time, and moved in ritualistic
orgy beneath our moon. Murdered, it was folded into its tiny coffin of
stone, with those vestiges of worship, those icons etched in gold. In
slumber, forgotten by most who had once diabolically adored it, it rotted and became this heap of ash and bone. Now, by magick and new
adoration, it awakens, in answer to the power from Outside that has
been caught in your transfigured eyes. You must feed it with your
crimson kiss, Wilfred." Her lips bit into my ear, my throat; they found
my mouth and chewed into the area where my lips had been split by
her fingernail. Beside me, she knelt before the leprous thing. I lowered
to my knees next to her. Winding the slim fingers of one hand into my
hair, she pushed my face to the mass of ruined onto which my mouth
bled. My countenance burrowed into the monstrous mass. Fingernails
that were talons ripped the fabric of my shirt from me and etched a
sigil into my back; and then those talons tightened into my hair and
tugged as I shuddered at the chilliness of the alien flesh that crept onto
my back and mingled with the blood of my new insignia. The sorceress
yanked my head upward, and the mass rose with me, conjoined to my
flesh into which it sifted. I gagged and screamed in pain as the relics of
gold embedded into my altered flesh. But with pain there came a kind
of strength such as I had never experienced, and the taste of blood in
my mouth was intoxicating. I erected my limbs, stretched my hands to
moonlight, and moved weirdly in the place of destitution.

"Smell the air, Wilfred, and detect the one who murdered my sire."

I peered through purple vision. "He is not far. His flesh and sweat insult my nostrils. Let us follow his stink of mortality."

Guan-Yin genuflected before me, and then we moved together, to another part of town and its thin alleyway. Sheathed in shadow, we watched the doorway of a sequestered tavern, through which various figures staggered. Finally, one wretch emerged and leaned drunkenly against the doorframe before shuffling through the alleyway, homeward bound. I planted myself in the man's path and ignored his cursing as he bumped into me. He glared at me, and then his eyes grew wide with terror, and I saw, for just one moment, my altered image on the surface of his orbs. A strangled scream began to formulate within his throat, but my tusks found that throat and robbed the fellow of his voice. I shuddered is ageless ecstasy as my ravenous mouth feasted on his gore.

Guan-Yin knelt before me and dipped her hands into the mess I had created and its pool of spreading blood, with which she washed her facade. "This is simple murder," she spoke in her low voice. "Satisfying as it is, true sacrifice is finer. It is through sacrifice alone that we rend the veil and split the cosmos, so that our dread lord may filter through and feast until fulfilled. He waits for you, Wilfred, to locate his realm beyond the rim, beyond the stars, to the Great Outside. Look into the dark abyss, brother-fiend, and find Chaugnar Faun, so that he may filter again to our demesne and bring his icons with him. Summon him from beyond time and space and let us glory in his magnificent destruction."

I raised my transformed eyes. I tasted the crimson stain that slipped down my tusks into my famished mouth. I scanned the haunted sky.

The Barrier Between

The ancient oak was a freakish thing of monstrous size and shape. Its trunk was of an inordinate breadth, and yet it seemed, seen from a distance, stunted, as if the thick and weighty limbs expanding over it had caused the trunk to shrink into yielding earth. In one place at the base of its trunk a gathering of bumps or small burls formed what resembled a weird crouching beast, and something in its form so disturbed onlookers that they were unwilling to approach the patriarch of wood. There were some few, however, who found the mammoth tree so compelling a sight that they found the courage to draw near and touch its bark; and they were puzzled by the litter of small animals' bones scattered around the trunk, remains of what might have been beasts brought as votive offerings. On this late afternoon, some few of those white bones had been strewn onto the small cot that had been set up beneath the tree and played with by the bending toes of the nude creature reclining on the mattress.

"I want your head hanging over the mattress and your hair falling to the ground, as in Fuseli."

The reclining figure frowned. "I thought we were replicating Abildgaard—isn't that why I'm naked?"

"I'm combining the two—they studied together in Rome, you know. Fuseli's influence was profound; you can see it in Abilgaard's painting of Culmin's ghost, where the specter's pose is similar to the woman in Fuseli. Just a few more shots, Basil, while we have this light. That's an odd glaze up yonder, isn't it, shimmering just behind the sheen of muted sunlight?"

The lean fellow on the cot used his feet to push his body nearer to the rim of the mattress and combed fingers through long pale hair so that it billowed to the ground. Dashen Wilcott pressed his eye to the camera lens and studied his model, intrigued once more by the almost macabre image of the lounged figure that almost resembled a fresh cadaver. The camera clicked and whirred a few more times, and then Dashen stepped to the cot and bent to smooth his hands through the mass of hair. A whitish appendage reached for the photographer's face and stroked it. "Look how black your skin looks compared to my bleached hand—black as midnight. You smell strange."

"That's not me. There's something in the air, some piquant aroma that you can almost taste." Distant thunder sounded. "Damn, a storm is approaching. I wanted to change lens and try capturing you in shadow. Slip into your clothes and help me carry this cot to the pickup." They worked together, taking the lightweight cot and its small mattress to the bed of Dashen's dilapidated truck. By the time they were seated inside the vehicle the first heavy raindrops began to fall onto the windshield.

"What are you doing?" Basil asked as Dashen opened the door and climbed out of the truck. Not answering his friend's query, the photographer went to stand before the tree and study its sinister appeal. Below the long thick branches just above the width of trunk—limbs that were themselves of an uncommon width—was a cluster of very thin and long branches adorned with small bright auburn leaves. Dashen watched the leaves begin to tremble in the rising wind; and then he studied the lower section of the immense trunk, where the curious mass of bumps formed what seemed the semblance of a crouching beast. As he studied the thing it began to blur, like some form composed of coiling smoke and shadow. He became conscious of the figure that knelt beside him and watched as Basil rose to his feet with a small fragment of bone clamped between his lips. Behind the young model, the curious sheen of queer color that had earlier been noticed slowly rotated, like an image seen through a kaleidoscope. Dashen stepped backward, slowly, until he felt the heaviness of the freakish tree behind him. He pressed his back against the tree as the texture of its bark softened and allowed him entrance. Raising his arms, he watched the small red leaves that adhered to them twitch in moaning wind.

*

Dashen pushed through the crowded gallery until he was able to link arms with Arcadia Tallow, who stood before the gigantic print that was Dashen's contribution to the evening's exhibition.

"This is superb, my dear," the patron told him as she motioned to his work. "The rich antique brass tone of your tree is very fine, especially as it contrasts so absolutely with the deathlike tenor of your model's skin. Is the bone in your model's mouth an aesthetic nod to Ardois-Bonnot's series of 1928?"

"Who?"

"The French painter who did a series of canvases showing cadaverous females who all had human bones clamped between their lips. No? How strange. I do like how you've used Weisel's nightmarish imp there, with that queer hazy effect that makes the creature so indefinite. Oh dear, you're looking confused again. Have you been drinking? You know how that affects you." She moved nearer to the print and motioned to the figure composed of burls on the monstrous tree's trunk. "That's Mr. Shugoran, isn't it? I didn't know you two were acquainted. He's right over there, in the Hildegaard Alcove." Clutching his small hand, the woman tugged him to a long narrow room that was oddly bereft of people. "Not a very popular exhibit, eh?" she murmured to him. "But, oh, isn't it sublime!? It copies, of course, Thrivier's *Le Cauchemar,* although replacing white marble with black. Weisel's model here doesn't look *quite* as orgasmic as her French sibling—and his devil lacks wings, as does yours. Are you all right, dear? You look rather queer."

Dashen moved past three others who were looking at the sculpture and raised a hand, as if preparing to touch the female figure that reclined on its bed of ebony marble; but then he backed away from the sculpture and gazed in silence at the daemon depicted as squatting on the woman's stomach, and as he observed the thing he shuddered.

Feeling eyes upon him, Dashen looked up to see two persons who were staring at him; and then the smaller of the two turned to Arcadia, acknowledging her with a smile as she stepped beside Dashen and placed a hand on his shoulder. With the assistance of a short cane of crimson wood, the figure hobbled toward them. Dashen, who was himself of small stature, felt his flesh chill at the sight of the runtish figure that limped nearer.

"Dashen, let me introduce you to Zaman Shugoran. Zaman, this is Dashen Wilcott, the photographer." Shugoran held out a limp hand, which Dashen clasped as he took in the full-length fur coat in which the dwarf had draped himself. Eyes of yellow tinge shimmered within deep sockets, and twisted teeth marred what was supposed to be a smile. The little hand suddenly tightened its hold, and Dashen winced as that hold became painful. Yet he could not force his hand away, for he was riveted by the cruel expression on the imp's hateful visage. Shugoran's lips curled in mirth, as if the fellow recognized Dashen's unease and delighted in it.

"Pleased to meet you," the tiny creature said in an accent that the photographer could not place. "You see what sly Weisel has done with me," and he indicated the sculpted fiend. "How like him to be late for this unveiling."

They were aware of some new person entering the small room, and Dashen quivered a little when he saw that it was Basil. Escaping Shugoran's grasp, he rushed to the model and guided him out of the room.

"That was rude, Dashen, not to introduce me to your friends. Wasn't that the wealthy patron Arcadia Scott?"

"Never mind that, I had to get away from that fiend. By god, it's like meeting Fuseli's devil in the flesh! That fur coat could have been his hide."

"What on earth are you muttering about? Gracious, you're rattled. Have you been drinking? Not wise, considering your past. Come on, I want you to introduce me to your friends."

"No friends of mine," the other answered; and then he stopped and gawked at Basil's hair. "What the devil have you done?"

"Don't you like it? I suppose you didn't notice me collecting some of those smaller bones near the tree at our shoot. I thought it would look rather goth to tie them into my hair. I've had any number of compliments."

"You look damn silly."

Basil's eyes narrowed in annoyance. "You're in a dreary mood." Sweeping past the photographer, he disappeared into the display room.

"Damn silly fool," Dashen muttered, and then he espied the refreshment table and went to grab a plastic cup of peach champagne. That first cup was drained too quickly, and so he picked up another and downed its contents. A couple came to greet him, and he mumbled replies as he reached for a third cup. Leaning against a wall, he watched the room's light fade to a soft blue glow that reminded him of a tinted print of *The Cabinet of Dr. Caligari* that he had screened at some art cinema house. He could easily be in such a film now, given how the walls around him were beginning to tilt. Carefully pressing one hand to the wall so as to secure his posture, Dashen made his way to the small chamber where he had encountered the outré dwarf. Yet he hesitated uncertainly; for there was a light oozing from the room, and it reminded him of the unearthly sheen of extraordinary color he had witnessed during the photo shoot at the monstrous tree. He moaned a little as the place before him began to gyrate.

Cautiously, Dashen crept back to the gallery where a few souls still gathered. At first he didn't recognize the indistinct figures before him, and the scene seemed more hallucination than sane reality. He had a hunch that his senses had been infected; indeed, the silence in the chamber felt like a heavy and oppressive weight inside his ear, causing his brain to ache. He nodded to two acquaintances whose features solidified before him, Gabryel and Isola, and thought that Gabe, with his hatchet face and red goatee, looked especially satanic in the queer illumination of the room. Turning to look at the figure reclining on the stone bed, he was confused to find that it was white, where before it was atramentous. The cloudy form that squatted on the pale figure's chest was dark indeed, and its face seemed to shift and coil. The eyes within that formless face contained the perplexing shimmering anticolor that seemed to be hunting Dashen. The fiend's tapered ears twitched a little as it bent to untie one of the bones attached to the reclining figure's mauve hair. The oppressive quietude became a spear of silence that stabbed into Dashen's brain, causing his quivering lips to part. His oppressive howling was but a momentary thing, for it was stopped when the dark devil pushed a glistening white bone into the mortal's wretched mouth.

*

Mild electric light greeted his opening eyes, and Dashen found himself in his own small bedroom, the walls of which had been painted dark red. Long green curtains before an opened window moved in silent breeze. Isola was perched beside him on the mattress, and Gabryel occupied a wooden chair that had been placed beside the bed. The young woman's gypsy face broke into a smile. "Ah, there you are, back with us." Dashen tried to speak, but his confused brain could find no language. The woman shook her head and ran a soft hand across his brow. "Just rest. We had the devil's own time maneuvering you to your apartment."

Gabe leaned forward a little. "I thought you'd given up the booze, my brother."

"No—it wasn't the champagne. It was that damn imp and that unwholesome wheel of light. God, my head is still spinning."

"You need to sleep a little more. We'll leave you alone, unless you feel the need for company."

"No, I'll be all right. Basil will probably show up eventually. He always does."

"Who?"

The boy I used as model in my photograph—there." Dashen pointed to one wall, the majority of which was taken up with an enlarged print of the photograph that had been his contribution to the gallery's current show.

"You mean the mannequin? The one you keep in your grandmother's wardrobe closet?"

Dashen frowned in confusion. Gabryel rose and walked to a tall cabinet that had been painted a pastel yellow and opened one of its slim doors, and the room's unnatural light reflected on the sleek plastic of the figure that leaned inside the armoire. Clutching at the figure's throat, Gabe shook it playfully and then lifted it out of the cabinet and waltzed with it around the room. Isola then helped him to place the thing beside their friend in his bed.

"When died you weave those bones into its hair?" Isola asked. "Looks rather macabre."

When they saw that Dashen could not reply, the girl patted his head and bent to kiss his brow. "We'll leave you with your plaything, dear. Get some rest." Reaching out, she took hold of Gabryel's hand, and Dashen watched as they backed into the shadows of the room and disappeared.

He moved his head a little and hated the nearness of the manne-quin's face to his, the pale plastic of which seemed lurid in the unnatural light of the chamber. With jerky movement, Dashen covered the faux countenance with a hand and was about to push the object away from him when its surface seemed to ripple slightly beneath his palm. Something kissed his hand.

"Take away your hand, for pity's sake," spoke a muffled voice.

Oppressed with sudden fear, Dashen jumped from the room and fled to the wall that was covered with his photographic art. Basil smiled, lifted himself from the bed, and floated to him. He touched one hand to the image of the monstrous tree. "Such a magnificent an-cestor, lad. How fortunate for you to be numbered in its family."

"I have no family," Dashen moaned, turning away from the wall and noticing the dark mound that huddled on his cot. He whispered, "There's someone in my bed."

"Oh, don't disturb him," Basil responded. "He's dreaming."

The boy suddenly loomed before the photographer, so near that Dashen could see the wheels of strange color that gyrated in the youth's eyes. Dashen shut his own eyes as that unwholesome glow be-gan to leak from Basil's eyes and permeate the place. There was a noise of clacking, and intoxicating fragrance that swam through nostrils. Lips touched his eyelids, which then lifted. They stood within a field, as-saulted by windstorm that caused the bones in Basil's hair to swing against one another. The noise thus produced might have been some dainty danse macabre, and Basil, seeming to take his cue from the clattering, waltzed away from his companion, toward the monstrous tree and the dainty cot below it. Walking to that cot as Basil reclined upon it, Dashen saw that it was littered with bits of bone. Basil took up one shard of death and began to weave his hair around it.

The tree had altered, horribly, now being composed of what looked like the conjoined bodies of burnt corpses, each of which had one clean white bone clamped between its jaws. Dashen thought the thing resembled a ghastly cousin to Dali's *In Voluptas Mors,* one that was completely lacking voluptuousness. One lower section of the thing separated from the rest and crept onto Basil's chest, where it squatted and winked at Dashen.

"Good day, good sir," was Zaman Shugoran's greeting. "Come nearer, we have your gift." Dashen could not move at first, for his eyesight had become transfixed on the distant wheel of coiling light that coaxed him toward it. "Oh—the lurid light of reason," sneered Shugoran. "It so mars the madness of this place, don't you find? Ignore it. Here, let me give you this, and then you can find your place within the puzzle."

Dashen knelt beside the cot and leaned his head to the cloudy fiend, from which the rich perfume of the place seemed to emanate—that sweet stench of rot. The piece of bone looked unnaturally bright in the devil's dark hand, so bright that it hurt to look on it; and so Dashen shut his eyes as the black cloudy hand pushed the bone between his lips that did not protest. When something touched his face, Dashen parted his eyes once more and saw that the splintered hand of one of the corpses that composed the tree had fallen to him. Taking hold of that hand, the dark man allowed it to lift him into the company of carnage.

These Harpies of Carcosa

I smiled at the canvas on the wall, and felt the shadow of its artist at my left. "It's interesting, isn't it?" I told the fellow without turning to him, not wanting to take my eyes from his painting. "I've never known buildings to look so—tattered. The city itself oozes of self-extinction, although how a city could commit suicide is a perplexing puzzle. There is not a trace of life, except for the two sirens in the sky; and yet they look so fantastic that one guesses that they may be mere figments of twisted dreaming. Look how they hang there in the air, horribly illuminated by the lifeless light of the twin porphyry moons, those globes of ghastly reddish-purple rock. Finally, our eyes take in the figure in its yellow robe, with its pallid artificial face and arms outstretched. I cannot comprehend why his hands should be so crimson."

I turned my head slightly and looked at the artist; and although his eyes were fixed onto his creation, I knew that he listened to my language. "Now," I continued, "there is one minute glimmer of natural light, and yet it emanates from an artificial relic. Do you see it, there, in the corner of the canvas, like something dropped onto the road, forgotten and forsaken? Yes, the brass crown with its synthetic jewels. One feels that it sits in proxy for something more authentic. And that long knife sitting beside it looks so nasty, doesn't it, like some implement designed exclusively for mayhem? It all makes one shiver and wish for movement, for some shifting of starlight or some song of wind. But those obsidian stars in the painted sky do not crawl, of that I am certain; and the air of that deserted city, one knows, is dead and still. And yet—and yet, how *captivating* it seems, this painted image, how it tugs at the brain and makes one wonder how it would feel to weep beneath those black stars, to inhale the lifeless air. However did the artist come up with such an image, one wonders?"

"It's from a play," my companion finally spoke.

"Indeed? And where would one find this play?"

He did not hesitate in his reply, and yet he spoke as one who had lost his way in reality. "I read it in a dream. I read it aloud, and the dream took on solidity. I could hear the waves of the lake breaking on the shore, and when the wind arose I could hear the flapping of the tatters of the King, that flapping that should never be sounded. They had such a strange rhythm, and I tried to sing in accompaniment; but my mouth was dry and my voice was dead, like the lost city that festered all around me. God, the *hard* light of those twin moons, burning their essence onto my eyes. And when I finally awakened, I could still feel that acidic impression on my eyes; and the world looks weird, and its inhabitants look like puppets." He then turned to me, smiled and chuckled. "Sounds completely kookoo, I confess."

I shrugged and returned my attention to his creation. "The fantastic artist sees the world in singular ways, divorced as he is from the dull world of dreary reality. How far more creative and captivating, to live within a dream."

He turned his gaze again toward the painting. "I really *would* prefer to live there, godless region though it may be. I wouldn't have to pretend all the time. So, you like this?" He motioned to the canvas.

"Oh yes," I assured him, "for I long to live there myself." Bowing to him, I walked to the door and exited the gallery. The sun was beginning to set, and the sky was a gorgeous bouquet of color. I stood there and admired the mixture of gold and mauve and amber, and I felt his shadow blend into my own.

"Are you an artist?" he asked.

"I exist within a realm of Art," was my esoteric response. We walked away from the city, toward the hill that rose before us. It was early spring, and the trees that lined the lane were sweet of fragrance and delicate upon the eye. We had almost reached the apex of the hill when we encountered the murdered thing. The artist knelt before the feline corpse and studied it for a little while as the sun continued sinking; and then he removed the long knife from the cadaver and wiped its blade on a patch of clean grass. How deftly he handled the implement. Rising, he held the knife with hands that were clasped together as if in prayer.

We stood atop the hill and watched the death of day. He shut his eyes for a moment, and then he flinched as his body began to tilt. Sheepishly, he smiled. "Sorry. I'm feeling a bit faint."

"When was your last meal? Your face looks haggard with hunger."

He shrugged. "I'm an artist."

Reaching into my pocket, I took out a folded piece of paper. "I don't have any money on hand, but perhaps this will aid you." Putting the knife under his arm, he took the paper and unfolded it. I do not think he understood the Yellow Sign traced onto the paper. Folding it again, he placed it in his bosom. The moon rose within the darkening sky, and we noticed the distant artifact that reflected the lunar light. "Ah," I sighed, "it's your brass crown. How golden it looks in this unearthly light." We walked to it, and he bent to pick it up. "Yes," I continued, nodding my head, "it is quite golden, and its diamonds are authentic. Will you don it, the golden diadem?"

How near the white moon seemed to the hill on which we stood. Its dull light shimmered on the crown as he lifted it above him and then placed it on his head. The leaves in one nearest tree began to rustle in the rising wind, and the branches of that tree began to sway. I could not help but warble.

> "Atop the hill he makes his stand,
> In wind that sings a saraband,
> And we uncover
> Lost Carcosa.

> "There are no stars on this strange night,
> Just one strange moon that sheds its light
> Upon our dream of
> Lost Carcosa.

"See how the moon divides its sphere
Into twin globes that mock and leer
Above the streets of
Lost Carcosa.

"Ah, double globes, grotesque, divine,
Evoke the ageless Yellow Sign,
Return of hearts to
Lost Carcosa."

I moved in little steps to the music of the wind and clapped my hands as he removed the long knife from under his arm and held it before him. Reaching into my bosom, I removed what was folded just above my heart and held it before him, winking. He watched as I unfolded the pallid mask and fastened it to my face. I think he shuddered just a little as the moon began to darken and divide. I watched the division of those spheres and listened to the sound of their wings unfolding. He turned at last to face them.

"They come to adore you, these sirens of suicide. They come to take ye home. You hold the key. Will you plunge it into place?"

I danced toward him and hummed a little song, unable to contain my joy. His length of hair moved in the wind aroused by daemonic wings, and his mouth began to hum in accompaniment to my noise. Lowering his eyelids, he raised the knife and thrust it into his throat. Shouting in ecstasy, I moved to him and caught his flow of blood with greedy hands. Somehow, he refused to fall. I stretched out my arms and offered my wet red palms to the creatures of nightmare, and laughed as they floated to me and kissed my offering. Their attention was then caught by the wobbling of his body. Licking their moistened mouths, they flocked to him and caught him by each arm. Bending, I picked up the fallen knife and raised it to their nebulous forms, as they conjoined once more into one solid sphere.

In Blackness Etched, My Name

I had scrutinized the directions of my great-uncle's crude map, and I had memorized his words of recollection as he whispered of the hills behind ancient Arkham, and of the region that had been settled by maternal ancestors in the late 1600s. The road I followed was old and grass-grown, and as my car drove over it I had the oddest feeling that I was journeying out of modern time, into a realm of mystery and wonder. I imagined that this particular region had altered little since the time of Randolph Carter's disappearance in October of 1928, and finding myself in the area now felt like a fantasy of dream, as if the hills contained secrets of dark magick that awaited my mortal presence. The Carter legend, whispered by my family, had long intrigued me, and I had used my heritage as an Aspinwall to secure certain papers and books that had belonged to my forebears.

It was while I attended a private university in Boston that I became obsessed with the history of Randolph Carter and his association with the baffling mystic, Harley Warren. I sought and found an ancient soul who had, as a youth, associated with Warren, and from him I gathered occult gleanings acquired by Warren's infernal clique. Discovering covens in Salem and Kingsport, I came to realize that I had a natural affinity for what I came to understand as Outside Things, as though my ancestral blood were pulled to arcane matters. Not being social, I came to practice the dark arts alone, and that was when my sorcery thrived. Contacting a great-uncle who was rumored to have trafficked with outré things, I began to practice magick with him and to discuss our family history. His attempts to dissuade me from dwelling on the legend of Randolph Carter had the opposite effect, for I could see in his filmy eyes that I had aroused his curiosity as well, one that had been dormant for decades. Against his better judgment he showed me, one evening, the hand-drawn map that indicated the way to the old Carter property in the hills behind Arkham. That evening, he revealed to me a potent ritual; yet the excitement that his recitation evoked proved too heavy for his frail heart, and he expired. However, he had revealed all that I needed to know.

Thus, on the seventh of October, I navigated my old car up Elm Mountain and drove along the climbing road until coming to a pile of ruin that had once been a cottage. From a notation on my great-uncle's map, I knew that this had once been the dwelling place of a solitary soul who had won, through malevolence and witchery, an outrageous reputation. I spoke the woman's name in a whisper—"Goody Fowler"—but could not evoke her image in my mind. Parking my vehicle, I got out and stalked nonchalantly to the pile of rubble. A scented breeze brushed my face, and I gazed at a distant group of giant elms, the bright green leaves of which rustled in the growing wind. Something in their movement, and in the queer sparkling light all around, proved alluring, and I thought that it might be pleasant to skip toward those elms and dance among their assembly. Then the wind, rushing through the ruins, carried the smell of strange spices that I knew, from my traffic with witchery, to be the debris of magick that had been spilled in the destruction of the cottage. I knelt before the rubble and communed with extinct time as I touched my hand to rotten wood and shards of splintered glass. The shards, I knew, had once been part of small-paned windows, and as I picked one up I pondered its quality of darkness, which was perhaps the taint of toxic fumes from Goody Fowler's ominous brewing. Laughing lightly, I pushed one sharp point of the shard into the tip of a finger and watched the rising bubble of blood; and then I pushed that finger into dirt and wrote the woman's name.

The coaxing wind whispered at my ears and pushed me toward my car; and I frowned slightly at the sight of my old vehicle, which seemed somehow to mar the timeless wonder I had mentally summoned from entering the region. The sound of ignition, as I turned the key, was wretchedly loud. I followed the grass-grown road and ascended the steep slope until I arrived at the place marked on the map with a large red X. I espied the knoll on which an ancient house had been erected. Yet everything was wrong—for my forebear had told me that I would find nothing but the wreck of the homestead and an opening in the earth that was a portal to its ruined cellar. How, then, could the sight before my eyes be real—the venerable gambrel-roofed house that wore an air of incredible age? I experienced, as I looked on it, a beloved sensation, a soul-linkage with the hoary past and its secrets. I had known this sensation when reciting certain passages from antique grimoires and crumbling scrolls, when to form archaic language on my mouth was almost to taste old time. Stepping out of my hateful vehicle I spoke the remembered formula, pushing spectral language into the hungry wind; and the sparkling light of day transformed, thickened as semi-darkness, yet glistened still, as might some pearl of twilight. I clamped eyelids and harkened to the wind, in which I detected a multitude of tones. When at last I lifted my lids, I saw an assembly of souls on the veranda of the ancient house—those still forms that regarded me with charcoal eyes.

I watched, as the slits that were mouths began to twitch with movement, and although those lips moved in unison, I heard neither chant nor song. Indeed, even the wind lost its voice, although I felt its force all around me. The smallest of the figures stepped from the group and glided toward me, a diminutive creature in quaint attire. Stopping just before me, she took the map from my hand and studied it with eyes in which darkness and light coiled, and then she tore the paper to pieces that were scattered in the silent wind. There was something coy about the slight curl of her lips, and her fantastic eyes seemed to contain such qualities that I felt I mustn't gaze into them too deeply, else I would drown within their depths.

I spoke, hoping that the sound of my voice would break the spell that threatened to bewitch me utterly. "I wasn't expecting to find a house still standing. This *is* the old Carter residence, isn't it?"

She hummed softly to herself and took my hand, turned it over, and studied its lines. Then she clapped one dainty hand against my own and whistled at the wind. I was guided northward, down the sloping hill toward thick woodland. How curious that it had grown so suddenly late, so that some few black stars glimmered above high autumnal boughs beneath which I found myself. Stopping to root myself to the ground, I stretched my limbs skyward and watched heaven revolve as time ceased to exist. Turning to the woman beside me, I wound the fingers of one hand tightly into her hair.

"You seem material enough," I told her as I tugged at her pale strands. "I thought perhaps you might have been a conjuration of dream or delirium."

She placed one hand over mine and said, "You etched my name in earth, with bloodstained flesh. Thus am I evoked out of miasmic moment."

"A revenant from the past," I concluded, nodding my head.

Oh, her sinister smile. "The past is real. 'Tis all there is." With her free hand, she pointed to the ground. Looking down, I saw the large hourglass, one bulb of which was shattered. Untangling my fingers from the wraith's pale hair, I fell to earth and studied the black sand that had spilled from its broken container, and I was mesmerized by the quality of that debris, which reminded me of the shimmering black stars above me. I reached into the ruined bulb so as to bring forth a fistful of the stuff and hissed as one finger was sliced by an edge of broken glass. The fistful of midnight particles that I lifted out of the ruined timepiece sifted through my fingers, onto earth, and liquid pearls of my blood dripped onto them.

Once more she placed her hand onto mine, and together we wrote my name in the bloodstained sand. The wind grew in force and snatched at my hair, into which it weaved. I was pulled to a standing position. The woman waltzed from me, drifting away like some eidolon of smoke and fire, her pastel hair shimmering in darkness. I followed her, through the woodland, up the slope and to the antique house where her acolytes awaited us. Their mouths moved still, but this time I could hear their noise, an inhuman din that shocked my being and seduced my soul. Ah, that puny soul, linked solidly to my heritage, to the secrets of the past, to a realm beyond dreaming. The witch stopped just before the steps of the veranda and held to me her hand, and I marveled at her ghastly beauty. Staggering to her, I touched my hand to hers and was pulled into the crowd.

This Weave of Witchery

with Maryanne K. Snyder

It came as a wall of liquid blackness, an inky abyss in which he felt he would be drowned. There was something almost beguiling in its churning sentience, and he felt the need to speak to it, to name himself. Parting lips, he moaned his name as the blackness spilled into his mouth and shook him awake. Thorley Wakefield found himself in bed in an unfamiliar room. Rising, he glanced at the photograph of his mother that he had placed on the bedside stand, and then he put on shoes and exited the room, following the steps that led to the ground level of the building he had occupied. Early sunset washed the sky over Sesqua Valley with muted color, and Thorley stood for a little while to appreciate the orange and pink effects that tainted the white stone of the titanic twin-peaked mountain. He had never thought to see that mountain again, and did not remember its effect on him, how it captivated one part of his mind and troubled another. He gazed at it until he felt himself grow faint, and then he remembered his mother's words of caution, "It's not wise to stare at Mount Selta for too long a time. Turn your eyes away."

It was because of his mother's disappearance, when he was seventeen years of age, that he left the valley and journeyed to Arkham, where his mother had attended Miskatonic University. Thorley did the same, although he never could get used to the commotion of city life and its hurried inhabitants. It was while attending Miskatonic that he learned of Dunwich Village, and it was to that small and neglected town he finally journeyed and took root, spending the last of his inheritance of a small farm, the land of which he worked alone. His queer solitary ways seemed entirely natural in Dunwich, where people tended to keep to themselves, and no one bothered him about his growing habit of climbing the domed hills and daydreaming on stone altars as he whispered to the faces that churned above him in the sky. It was there, on one hill, where he had lost his ability to dream, after having fallen asleep during a thunderstorm, during which he fancied that his mother called to him from some unknown place in the gulf of night. His dreams had always been a special release for him, and to have them replaced by a wall of inky blackness oppressed him. He grew despondent and neglectful, and his farm began to die. It didn't take much persuasion for him to sell the land to a neighbor, for the idea came to him again and again that perhaps it was time for him to return to the place he had known since childhood, the place that had planted a kind of influence in his mind and called him during dreamless nights.

Thorley sighed and smelled the air, which contained an element of sweetness that calmed him. The silence of Sesqua Valley was similar to that of Dunwich, as both places seemed to have shunned modernity. There were very few vehicles on the roads, and the sidewalk that Thorley walked on was composed of wooden planks. He felt as though he had stepped into what Shakespeare had called "the dark backward and abyss of time," and it was a sensation that he relished. Yes, it was good to return to this secluded realm. Were his emotions grounded enough for him to confront the one place in the valley that tugged his heart and soul? His mind was uncertain, but his feet seemed to have decided for him as they took him up the slight hill to the ancient house where Thorley had spent his youth. He stopped and stared at the weathered building, the unpainted wood, and tried to remember if it had looked so ancient when he was young. It certainly looked much smaller than he remembered it. He saw that its front door was open and that a small sign hung just above the porch. The last remnants of daylight were fading fast, and he had to walk to the porch so as to read the sign, on which one word, "Apothecary," had been painted. A fragrance of incense spilled out to him through the open door, an odor that was so inviting that he passed through the threshold, into what once had been a small living room. Soft candlelight played among the dusky corners of the place and fell on the assortment of curious objects. He reached out to fondle the black candles that filled one wire basket, then ran his fingers over smooth soapstone amulets. It was when he saw the primitive spinning wheel that he cried out, a noise that was answered by two figures that entered from an adjacent room.

"I beg your pardon," Thorley muttered. "The door was open and . . ." He stopped as he studied the tall gentleman who stood behind the black woman. Something in the man's fantastic face perplexed him, for it seemed vaguely familiar. Thorley had never seen an uglier face, although some of the inbred cretins he had met in Dunwich came close. The face before him now was more than ugly, however; it was bestial, in a way that seemed to mock humanity. The eyes seemed like two slits of quicksilver, liquid orbs that caught the candlelight in curious ways, so that they shimmered with minute particles of alien color. The wide nose and expanse of mouth seemed malformed, and the sallow shade of the gentleman's flesh made it appear more like animal hide than human tissue.

The other person was a black woman of exceptional beauty. Despite the color of her skin, her features were not African; and Thorley thought that she was, perhaps, of Egyptian or Greek origin. There was something noble about the way she carried herself, and her green-hued eyes were certainly captivating. Her dress of yellow silk clung to the contours of her superb body, and her red hair hung in coils that reached to her waist. Her voice, when she spoke, was the most soothing sound he had ever experienced. "You look weary and distraught. Sit there." She indicated a wide wooden chair as she stepped to a table and choice a small jar of ointment, the lid of which she unscrewed as he sat. Thorley could smell the medicated substance of the jar as the woman dipped her fingers into it and then went to him and placed those fingers on his temples. Her full bosom, just beneath his face, smelled of spice that he could not place but which was entirely agreeable. Warm breath fanned his face and he closed his eyes. "How can we assist you?"

"Oh, no one can do that," he mumbled. "I seem to have lost the ability to dream. And my recall of memory has been debauched."

"What is your name, sirrah?" asked a deeply toned masculine voice.

"I am Thorley Wakefield—sir."

"Ah! I thought I detected something familiar. You lived in this house as a child, with your enchanting mother, until her queer disappearance. You left the valley abruptly and we never heard from you again. You never claimed property—all very mysterious."

Thorley opened his eyes. "That's my mother's spinning wheel. Do you use it?" he asked the woman.

"I do. It was here when I moved into this abode. I have lived here some few years."

Thorley smiled. "It makes me happy to know that someone still uses it. It's quite an antique, but it worked beautifully. Mother used to hum a song when she was using it."

"How charming. I am Simon Gregory Williams." The weird fellow's smile was an awful thing. "But what is this you have told us—of an inability to dream?"

"My ability to dream has deserted me, and I have difficulty remembering things. I was once a fantastic dreamer; it was an ability I shared with Mother, and we would spend evening after evening recounting our splendid visions. I have a vague memory of it now, being here. She used to visit me in dreams. But suddenly it all stopped. Now all I 'see' is a barrier of darkness, an undulating void of nothingness."

"Undulating?" the woman asked as she ceased her ministrations.

"Yes, like an ocean of pitch that would swallow me if I succumbed to its lure."

Simon Williams whistled. "Do you speak to it?"

"What? What could one possibly have to say to a void of obscurity?"

"And you see nothing more in the bone-pot of your skull?"

"I've just told you so."

"How fascinating. And you've returned to Sesqua Valley in order to relocate your dreaming. Fantastic. I wish you luck." So saying, the queer fellow removed a thin black flute from an inner coat pocket and exited through the door onto the porch. When the low music issued to where Thorley sat, his blood froze at the sound. Gently pushing the exotic woman from him, he moved to the door and stepped onto the porch. Simon was leaning against a tree some few yards from the house, his instrument at his lips. He did not watch as Thorley stalked to him.

"Where did you learn that tune?"

"From some other dominion, a realm of shadow absolute that I sometimes see in my imagination. It's a captivating song, isn't it? Your mother found it quite evocative once I taught it to her. Do you recall if she was singing it on the eve of her curious disappearance?"

Something in the fellow's face as he asked the question so disconcerted Thorley that he turned and fled, returning to his little room above the general store. Weariness oppressed him, and he stared at the small framed photo of his mother until he fell asleep. He slept deeply, until the darkness sought him once again, the illimitable abyss of utter obscurity that seemed to call his name with sound of cosmic wind. When he awakened he could hear that wind still, a tempest that raged outside the small room's window. And just beneath the sound of storm he thought he heard another song: his mother's voice chanting her sorrowful lullaby. He had not bothered to undress after returning from his visit to his shop, and thus he was fully dressed as he stood, walked out the room, and vacated the building. Sesqua Valley was alive with delirious movement, with swaying trees that bent to the force of storm, with dark clouds that were pushed before the moon and caused shadows to creep along the floor of earth. He heard the sound of lullaby again and followed the stealthy shadows that led him to his childhood home, where soft light moved in the room just beyond the open door. He floating along the gravel path that took him to the porch, the steps of which he climbed. He paused before crossing the threshold, so as to listen to the low humming that wafted to him from the room, accompanied by the sound of the spinning wheel at work. Thorley walked into the room and saw the exotic woman seated on a stool before the spinning wheel, her foot at the treadle. Something clutched his heart as he watched her, but soon the wheel stopped its spinning and she lifted the black scarf with both hands.

He advanced and knelt beside her. "Tell me of your life in Dunwich Village," she commanded.

He shrugged. "I was a simple farmer, with a little land and some livestock."

"And did you desert it as you did this place?"

"No, I sold it to a neighbor who was worried about the way I was neglecting the place. I fell into a funk once my dreaming stopped."

"Did you never climb the hills and dream among the stones, or call to the sky as the rumbles sounded beneath the earth? Did you never smell the thunder?" Thorley frowned at her, perplexed. "Simon took me to spend some time there. A fascinating village. Did you never call to the sky, Mr. Wakefield? Is that when your dreaming altered?"

Something stirred within his mind, like a memory that began to flex. Turning to face him, the woman lifted the black material that she held before his eyes, and then she tilted toward him and pressed the fabric against his face. His eyes, remaining open, peered at the waving blackness as a mouth from the other side of cloth pressed against one eye. "Your dreaming has not stopped, Thorley Wakefield; you simply do not understand your current vision. The void that you have pierced hungers for you, perhaps as it did for your mother before you." The fabric fell from his face. Her own face was very near to his. "Rare dreamers can conjure infrequent realms and walk uncommon pathways. Look into the wheel, sir, and tell me what you see."

Her hand reached for the treadle, and the wheel began to spin. He could feel its movement in the air just before his face, and his bewitched eyes gazed into the blur of movement. The woman began to hum, accompanied by a sound of flute-like music that drifted to them from some place outside the house. Thorley watched the blur of movement darken, until it transformed into a churning void that seemed to summon his soul. From somewhere within that dark abyss another sound came to him, an echoed humming in his mother's voice.

Someone breathed against his ear, and the mortal man turned to see the green-hued eyes that shimmered in the shadowed realm. He saw the lithe arms that lifted so that a soft black scarf could be wound around his throat. He marveled that the woman's black skin so resembled the texture of the abyss that roiled before them. Her hand clutched his own as her green eyes flashed with witchery.

"Come," she summoned, "let us cross the threshold and step into your dream."

To Move Beneath Autumnal Oaks

I stood in the Hungry Place and watched as shovels dropped dirt over Catherine's lowered casket. A sudden breath of wind playing with my hair made me raise my eyes to the pale September sky, and I marveled again at the misty light of Sesqua Valley, how soft particles of daylight seemed to sparkle as they drifted high above our little congregation. Dante Chambers, attired in his clerical adornment, smiled sadly as he stepped to me and shook my hand.

"Thank you for your uttered prayers," I told him. "She loved the sound of Latin, and you spoke it beautifully."

"Peace be with you, Charles." As Dante turned to glance at the fellow nearest me, his mouth turned down with displeasure. "Good day, Mr. Williams," he intoned, and then he moved away from us and walked solemnly out of the walled graveyard. I turned and frowned also at the creature near me, noting how the fragrance emitted from his sallow flesh was similar to the sweet scent of the valley. The breeze moved the strands of dark hair that escaped from underneath his black Fedora-style hat, the rim of which partially concealed the fellow's fantastic silver eyes. The grotesque features of his face seemed, in some weird way, an actual assault on normalcy, and filled one with the outrageous idea that Simon Gregory Williams was not entirely human. His misshapen mouth suddenly curled and moved.

"Why do you gaze at me so, Stanton?"

"Do I? Sorry. I was trying to remember something from my childhood—something about this graveyard and how it was, in some odd way, disliked by you and your kind."

His eyes slanted. "My kind?"

"You silver-eyed children of the valley. What did my father used to call you? 'The shadow-spawn of Sesqua Valley'—something like that. And there was something about the ground of the Hungry Place being forbidden to your kind."

"Pah. Nothing is forbidden me. You've been away for so long a time, perhaps you have forgotten there are places in the valley that wear a kind of taint, where the ground is diseased and unhealthy. This is one such place. But you were always fond of this plot of death, and I remember when, as a child, you used to come to dance among its slates in moonlight."

I chuckled at the memory. "And my mother would discover me and scold and snatch me away. She was always so nervous."

My companion shrugged. "Your parents were problematic. Little wonder they escaped the valley once your sister reached womanhood. How they *fled!* How defiantly their offspring insisted on staying put." His voice altered in tone, and his expression became sardonically playful. "But perhaps it was your sibling's insanity they were fleeing, not the valley itself. How frightfully she shrieked at them when angry, and how the blood would trickle down her unfortunate face from the slashes her nails dug into her visage. How she would call out in darkness, your sister, to a thing she could not name. I found it so intriguing."

"It's amusing," I told him, "to hear one as ugly as you speak of unfortunate faces." A spasm of violent anger began to overwhelm me, and I could sense clouds of emotion gathering inside my eyes.

"Ah—the Hungry Place is beginning to have its effect on your human senses. That is one aspect of the taint it wears, you see—how it inspires a kind of maniacal emotion that aches to break out in violence. Does your blood begin to boil in its veins? Do coiling clouds of gloom begin to seethe inside your brain?" He laughed as mockery twisted the shape of his repugnant mouth, and then he walked away and vanished into the woodland.

I loathed the beast, and yet I knew he was right; for as I knelt and clawed my fingers into the ground, a part of me wanted to sink beneath the sod and smell its varied elements of human rot, to blink specks of dirt from my eyes as my tongue paid tribute to the flesh of worms. I spat at earth, stood, and vacated the Hungry Place, then followed the road that led me to our family home, where I had spent many happy years of childhood. I wondered if I could be content, living there again. The one aspect of the valley that I really missed, on those few occasions when the valley came to mind, was the fantastic grove of gigantic ancient oaks not far behind our house, where Catherine and I often played when young. It was strange that the memory of that grove was indeed the only recollection I had of Sesqua Valley after I had moved to another part of the country. All other memories had been wiped from reminiscence, as if some mental veil had been erected that kept the valley far from mind.

I reached my destination, but rather than go inside my home I walked toward the oak trees and their outspread limbs. Someone, long ago, had encircled the thick trunks with large rocks on which mystifying sigils had been etched, although most of the symbols were now so weathered as to be beyond deciphering. I approached the small shrine that our parents had helped us to erect out of blocks of stone and large bricks, a construction that resembled some religious shrines of Father's Roman Catholic faith. Our place of pilgrimage contained a small altar on which we would burn offerings to the gods of the woods; and as I approached that altar I was surprised to see the small pale object that rested on its long-abandoned platform. Strangely cautious, I went to the object and then, seeing clearly what it was, felt my blood grow cold; for it was my sister's favorite toy, an antique French doll attired in what had once been a lovely gown of white silk and lace. Now the gown and portions of the thing's face had been blackened by fire.

From some far-off place within the woodland I heard a melancholy playing of pipes, and I knew that Simon Gregory Williams was at his diabolic play. A chill wind began to whisper through the dendroidal stems above me, a noise that reminded me of the thing my sister and I had tried to evoke audibly as we chanted to imagined music. I began to hum the music that floated from the woodland, and as I peered into that distant expanse of trees I thought I saw two points of alabaster illumination that seemed to observe me. I thought again of the "children" of the valley, they who were called the valley's "shadow-spawn," of whom Simon was the eldest. Indeed, I remembered him from my childhood, as someone my kindred taught me to distrust and shun. There were only a handful of such beings in the valley at a given time—they came and then they disappeared, mysteriously; except for Simon, who seemed always to have been around, unchanging and aloof. We knew their race by their faces, a grotesque combination of frog-like and wolfish features, and by the almost magical quality of their silver eyes, the surface of which shone like pale and polished nickel. These beings were rooted absolutely to the valley in which they lingered, and if anyone could connect with the spirit of the valley that my sister and I had tried to induce with childish ritual, it was this shadow-spawn.

Thus I listened attentively to the music from Simon's flute and imagined that the breeze that brushed my face grew cooler as it carried the remote music to my ears. From underneath the ground on which I stood came a subtle pounding, which I felt deep inside my bones. The dappled light that slipped to me through the limbs of trees darkened, as if it had turned to particles of ash; and as I gazed at that fuliginous curtain I seemed to sense the darker shadow that coiled behind it. Something in my brain snapped violently, and I rushed from the place and sped homeward, where I busied myself in the kitchen brewing water and preparing tea and toast.

How strange that I did not dream that night; for one would imagine that my brain would dwell on hinted horrors and infest my slumber with horrid vision, but instead I fell into a vacuum, sans imagined sight or sound. Having neglected to draw the bedroom curtains before going to bed, I was awakened by sunlight on my eyelids and found that I had slept in the clothing I had worn the previous day. Not bothering to change into fresh attire, I stumbled to the kitchen and made myself a cup of coffee, which I took to the porch and drank as I sat on Mother's old rocking chair. It did not surprise me when Simon Gregory Williams sauntered down the road before my home, pretending to read the book held in one hand.

"Are you haunting me?" I queried.

"I beg your pardon, sirrah."

"They were very clever, your tricks last night. What was it, exactly, that you summoned? Has it a name?"

He knitted his brow and frowned. "Sorry, I don't follow you. Do you think I have nothing better to do than oppress you with playful alchemy?"

"Oh, but I heard your damn flute performance while visiting the grove of oaks. And I sensed—"

"My dear fellow, if you're going to go dreaming at your childhood altar, it has nothing to do with me. Do you imagine that you can return to the valley and not be infected by your past? Do you think that children can call to Outer Darkness in ritual and not be answered? A thing evoked in infanthood does not die merely because you flee the valley and linger in some far-off city for many years. That which is summoned with esoteric language does not dissipate; it links to the soul of whoever has called it, and however far that soul may journey, it always returns to the place of ceremony. As you have now returned."

"And what do you imagine I have summoned?"

His laughter was a cruel sound, and his expression suggested that he thought himself speaking to one who was still a child. "You knew it in childhood, although it remained unnamable. It is the occult essence of Sesqua Valley, the core of which can be sensed in certain tainted places in the valley, such as the Hungry Place. Actually, William Davis Manly has written some few lines that sing of it splendidly, here in his book of verse. Mark his words, Stanton:

> "It whispers to me in the midnight zone.
> The phantom voice, like product of some dream;
> And I converse, although I'm quite alone,
> And push my voice into the moonlight's stream
> Of phantom rays in which I seem to see
> A silhouette, a dark fantastic form,
> A thing that shudders in an ecstasy
> That indicates a kind of mental storm.
> I speak and tell the silhouette my name;
> I listen as it signifies its own.
> I look to where its spark blooms into flame,

A holocaust that will become my home.
I drift like smoke into the firelight,
Where all my fears and fantasies ignite.

"Do not such lines speak to you, intimately, Stanton? Can you deny that they name the thing you and your sister knew in childhood, the thing that has whispered to you yet again? How your lips ache to name it, however much your heart shrinks at the idea of so doing."

Demurely, he tilted his head and grinned at me; and then he shut his little book and continued down the road. Returning to the house, I found my own copy of Manly's poems and read over them, relishing how they suggested the secrets that were especial to my the valley. Leaning back into my recliner, I shut my eyes, intending to rest and think; but soon I sank into slumber, and the dreams that had eluded me the night before found me, although they were nonsensical. I awakened to the storm that rattled window panes; and pushing out of my chair, I walked outside and watched the twisting trees as they danced in the night-wind. My nostrils took in the smells of autumn, and in the moonlight I espied a small cyclone of wind that lifted leaves into the air. The wind was a furious force, and walking into it I raised my arms as if defying the gale to topple me onto the ground. I heard, then, a subtle moaning beneath the rush of wind, a kind of whimper that reminded me of the sounds my sister would often make as she slept in the room that we had shared as children.

The wind lifted leaves that spun before me in the air, and I stalked through this kaleidoscope of motion and moved toward the grove of oaks. Approaching our altar, I suspected that I was still at home, dreaming; for how could the solid limbs of olden oaks stir so sensuously, as if coaxing me into their embrace? And what was the object that flamed atop the altar stone, that expanded so impossibly as I approached it? How could an antique doll take on the ruined features of my beloved sibling?

She reached out to me with blazing arms, and I found myself wound within her infernal embrace. "Do you remember how we wished to call to the essence of place, my brother?—how we tried to give name to the unnamable? Let us try again."

She pressed her blackening mouth against my own, and our conjoined lips moved together. From some place very near I could hear the sound of flute music, and as I pushed my face from hers I imagined that black particles of ash circled all around us. I wanted *so* to speak the unknown name; but that appellation continued to evade me, and thus I spoke the name that burned inside my brain.

"Catherine!" I cried. She laughed and kissed my mouth again. The inferno of that kiss sizzled on my lips, my tongue. I spoke her name one final time, in that place of unholy ritual, as our burning essence broke apart and joined the particles of ash that coiled around us.

The Ghoul's Dilemma

I.

O, weary with this world of commonplace,
And stifled by this air of mundane time,
I prick my finger with a pin and trace
Your formula with stain of scarlet slime.
The fragrant stains of crimson slime evoke
A fantasy within the depths of dream
In which I shuffle off this mortal yoke
And enter into nightmare's chilly stream.
Ah, nightmare!—in your graceless revelry
I dance beyond the veil of common things,
I move beyond my mortal brevity,
I fly without the aid of clumsy wings.
Sans wings I spill unto the cosmic pond
And sip the sweet elixir of Beyond.

II.

The dark elixir of this nether-realm
Coils like a cosmic madness out of time.
The maelstroms of my measured language whelm
The chemicals of this daemonic clime.
The Outer Ones that lurk within the dark
Repeat the language of my profane tongue.
Within the blackness I espy a spark
That links me to the spawn of thousand-young.

One-thousand young commence to bleat my name
With voices that are laced with mockery.
I know the searing kiss of mortal shame
As once again this husk of normalcy,
This human husk, entraps me in its fit
And I awaken in an earthen pit.

III.

Within this earthen pit I feel my fate
And know what I experienced was dream.
Within this chilly clay I curse and hate
The moonlight that descends as cosmic stream.
I thought I could escape this pit of clay
With language culled from page of antique tome.
I thought I could ascend to dream's array
And so escape embrace of chilly loam.
But, no—this hollow pit is my abode,
This yellow bone my dry and drear repast.
My neighbor is the worm, the owl, the toad.
The canine feasters are my ever-caste.
I'll never swim the splendid cosmic flood.
My name is writ eternal in this mud.

Acknowledgments

"The Barrier Between," first published in *Nightmare's Realm*, ed. S. T. Joshi (Dark Regions Press, 2015).

"Beyond the Realm of Dream," first published in *Carnage Hall* No. 5 (1994).

"Born in Strange Shadow," first published in *Terminal Fright* No. 12 (Summer 1996).

"The Boy with the Bloodstained Mouth," first published in *Nocturne Secundus* (1989).

"Child of Dark Mania," first published in *The Pnakotic Series* (September 1996).

"Dust to Dust," first published in *Midnight Shambler* No. 2 (1988).

"Garden of Shattered Faces," first published in *Sozoryoku* No. 6 (June 1992).

"The Ghoul's Dilemma," first published in *Spectral Realms* No. 5 (Summer 2016).

"The Hands That Reek and Smoke," first published in *Sesqua Valley and Other Haunts* (Delirium Books, 2003).

"Heritage of Hunger," first published in *Sesqua Valley and Other Haunts* (Delirium Books, 2003).

"The Horror on Tempest Hill," first published (as "A Presence of the Past") in *Fungi* No. 21 (Summer 2013).

"The House of Idiot Children" (with Maryanne K. Snyder), first published in *Weird Tales* No. 348 (January–February 2008).

"An Imp of Aether," first published in *Tales of Sesqua Valley* (Necropolitan Press, 1997).

"An Implement of Ice," first published in *Weirdbook* No. 38 (2018).

"In Blackness Etched, My Name," first published in *Black Wings V*, ed. S. T. Joshi (PS Publishing, 2016).

"Old Time Entombed," first published in *That Is Not Dead*, ed. Darrell Schweitzer (PS Publishing, 2015).

"Pale, Trembling Youth" (with Jessica Amanda Salmonson), first published in *Cutting Edge*, ed. Dennis Etchison (Doubleday, 1986).

"Pickman's Lazarus," first published in *The Red Brain: Great Tales of the Cthulhu Mythos*, ed. S. T. Joshi (Dark Regions Press, 2017).

"These Harpies of Carcosa," first published in *In the Court of the Yellow King*, ed. Glynn Owen Barrass (Celaeno Press, 2014).

"This Weave of Witchery" (with Maryanne K. Snyder), previously unpublished.

"To Move Beneath Autumnal Oaks," first published in *Black Wings VI*, ed. S. T. Joshi (PS Publishing, 2017).

"Totem Pole," first published in *Fantasy Macabre* No. 7 (1985).

"Visions of William Davis Manly," first published in *Weird Inhabitants of Sesqua Valley* (Terradan Works, 2009).

"Your Kiss of Filth," previously unpublished.

"Your Seventh Eikon" (with Maryanne K. Snyder), first published in *Weird Fiction Review* No. 3 (Fall 2012).

"The Zanies of Sorrow," first published in *Tales of Love and Death* (Delirium Books, 2001); revised version published in *Apostles of the Weird*, ed. S. T. Joshi (PS Publishing 2019).